THE WALLFLOWER'S SECRET WAR

THE WALLFLOWERS' REVOLT
BOOK TWO

VALERIE BOWMAN

JUNE THIRD ENTERPRISES, LLC

She's got a secret...

Lady Beatrix Winslow is a wallflower by choice—and a revolutionary by necessity. While London sees a beautiful duke's daughter who stubbornly refuses to marry, Bea leads a secret double life as *B. Adroit*, the anonymous political cartoonist skewering Parliament's most powerful men. With reform hanging in the balance and discovery looming, one mistake could cost her everything.

He's got a problem...

That mistake arrives in the form of Nicholas Archer, Marquess of Vanover—brilliant, powerful, infuriatingly handsome, and now her unwanted suitor. Groomed for political greatness and trained to play the long game, Nicholas never loses control...until he finds himself drawn to the one woman determined to ruin his reputation.

In Regency London, love is the most dangerous rebellion of all.

Forced into a courtship, Bea and Nicholas are locked in a battle of secrets, strategy, and irresistible attraction—one that threatens to expose Bea's dangerous double life and shatter everything Nicholas has built. Because when a wallflower goes to war, love may be the most dangerous weapon of all.

CHAPTER ONE

London, June 1820

Lady Beatrix Winslow knew two things for certain.

One: the corner of Cheapside and Gutter Lane was no place for the daughter of a duke. And two: that was precisely why she had come.

Clutching the worn hem of her maid's cloak and hunching her shoulders, Bea darted around the corner and pressed herself against the brick wall of a bakery, ignoring the smell of yeast and desperation wafting from within. Her breath came fast. Not from exertion, but from the delightful, illicit thrill of anonymity. No one recognized her. No one bowed. No one tried to foist a dance card or an eligible Tory suitor upon her.

It was glorious.

Her father's coach would have been instantly identifiable, all gleaming black lacquer and gilt trim, utterly antithetical to stealth. That's why she'd paid for a hack today. That, and because the printshop's apprentice had told her—somewhat nervously, as if fearing divine retribution—that a certain

Bow Street Runner had inquired after *B. Adroit's* latest submission.

They were sniffing.

Well, let them sniff.

Let them comb every ball, every club, every gentleman's study for the elusive cartoonist. Let them scrutinize waistcoats for ink stains and examine gloves for charcoal smudges.

Let them look for a man.

Because everyone knew—positively *knew*—that B. Adroit must be a man. Only a man could have the insider knowledge. Only a man could wield such scathing wit and invent such devastating caricatures. Only a man would dare.

Bea smiled to herself as she slipped through the back door of the printing press. The truth? B. Adroit was two and twenty, tall, blond, decidedly female, and hidden directly under all of their noses. And when she wasn't excoriating half of Parliament, she could be found standing dutifully beside her mama at the latest *ton* ball, nursing watered-down ratafia and refusing every dance with the determination of a nun guarding her virtue.

A wallflower.

By choice.

No one knew exactly why the proclaimed Diamond of every Season refused to take a husband. She was too particular, went the rumor. Outrageously so.

How deliciously wrong they all were.

Bea made her debut five Seasons ago, endured the tedium of required flirtation, and gamely danced with the endless queue of suitors her father paraded in front of her. Then, somewhere between being partnered with the Honorable Harold Twitworth (who belched the entire length of the quadrille) and the Viscount Snodgrass (whose greatest conversational skill involved pheasants), her father, the esteemed Duke of Winston, made it clear that she was to marry his *protégé*, Lord Nicholas Archer, the Marquess of Vanover.

That was when Bea had promptly realized something: she would rather rot on the shelf forever than marry Nicholas Archer. A more pompous, full-of-himself, far-too-certain-he-was-always-right bag of wind did not exist.

Thankfully, Mama was reasonable. She had refused to allow her only daughter to be forced into a marriage she didn't want. And so, Bea had gone all these Seasons without a marriage. She was infinitely proud of it. Oh, it would make any other girl an immediate wallflower. Like her friend, Georgiana Chadwick, who, without a dowry, had been a wallflower all this time, until she quite literally was swept off her feet by the Earl of Pembroke earlier this Season while attempting to flee her own wedding to an entirely different man.

Then there was her other friend, poor Poppy Montford. The only child of the scandal-ridden widow of the Viscount of Montague, the colorful Lady Viva. While Georgie had been a wallflower because her debt-ridden father had spent her dowry, Poppy was a wallflower because of her mother's scandalous reputation.

But Bea? Bea was something different altogether. A wallflower by choice. Practically unheard of in the *ton*. Which only made the rumors more pointed. Particular, they called her. Selective was the word Mama liked to substitute. It was laughable, really. But Bea didn't give a whit. They could call her whatever they wanted as long as she was able to continue to dodge the parson's noose. For if Nicholas Archer was her father's choice, Bea would remain a wallflower indefinitely.

But her outing today was not merely about preserving her anonymity. It was about momentum.

The reform bill would be debated again in a fortnight,

and every Tory in London seemed determined to crush it beneath polished boots and pompous speeches. Restrictions on trade were the only way to protect the laborers whose backs bore the weight of the Empire, but men like her father and Nicholas Archer dismissed such concerns as "idealistic" —Bea's least favorite word in the English language.

So she drew. Relentlessly. Strategically. Every cartoon she delivered was a stone thrown at the great, immovable wall of privilege. If she could make enough peers look foolish, if she could sway even a handful of votes, the bill might pass.

This wasn't rebellion for amusement's sake. This was her contribution to the only war she could fight.

Because she'd already decided long ago…she would write her own rules. If Society refused to hear her voice? She would draw it.

With ink.

With teeth.

And with a signature that made men in Parliament sweat through their cravats.

B. Adroit.

She even had a name for her little adventure. *The Wallflowers' Revolt.* Earlier this Season at the Willoughbys' ball, Bea had encountered Georgie and Poppy in the retiring room, and the three of them had formed the Society For Resourceful Young Ladies Who've Had Quite Enough. During their first official meeting, they'd renamed their little group. The Wallflowers' Revolt had a deliciously nonconforming ring to it.

Georgie's escape from her elderly *fiancé* had been their first order of business. It's true that there had been a bit of trouble when Lord Pembroke had inserted himself into the equation. But all's well that ends well. Georgie and Pembroke were married now and quite madly in love with each other.

Of course, that's not how Bea's part of the revolt would

end. Far from it. She wasn't looking for love. She intended to be the first female politician in her family. The only way she could be at least. With scathing drawings printed in the paper. Only she had to make certain her parents never found out. Or anyone else for that matter. Especially her most-used subjects like the detestable Nicholas Archer.

Focusing once again on the task at hand, Bea slipped the newest cartoon—tucked neatly into the pages of a dog-eared pamphlet—into the printer's slot. Her pulse fluttered with that delicious now-or-never anticipation. Today's piece was her boldest yet: a side-by-side comparison of her father and Lord Nicholas Archer rendered as puffed-up peacocks perched atop bags of gold and empty promises.

She'd given Archer an especially pointy beak. Honestly, *that* had been particularly satisfying.

She shut the slot firmly. The apprentice would find it in less than five minutes. By then, she'd be long gone, lost in the morning crush of Covent Garden. But even as she turned to leave, something pulled her back. A flicker of unease, perhaps. Or...hope. Because a small, triumphant part of her couldn't wait for Nicholas Archer to see it. To read it. To recognize himself.

And possibly even wonder if *she* was the one who'd drawn him.

No. That was impossible. Nicholas Archer was just like her father. A pompous ass. Someone who expected everything he said to be immediately agreed with. Someone who would never guess a *woman* was his fiercest opponent.

She hated him. Of course she did. He was a Tory. Her father's sycophant. And her designated future. Father had never been subtle about his intentions. Archer would be a duke one day. She was the daughter of a duke. It was a logical match. A powerful one.

It was also intolerable.

Because Nicholas bloody Archer might be brilliant and powerful—but he was also the very embodiment of everything she opposed. Which just so happened to be everything her father stood for. She knew Father's speeches by heart. Knew the cadence of his parliamentary voice. Knew how many times he'd voted against social reform, against suffrage, against anything remotely progressive. Knew it—and loathed him for it. And she loathed Nicholas Archer for the same reason.

Oh, fine. The marquess was handsome. Devastatingly so. Tall and broad-shouldered, with dark hair, darker eyes, and the sort of mouth a sensible woman tried very hard *not* to think about. And sometimes, when she caught him watching her—really watching her—she wondered if he might find her attractive too, though she would never admit that aloud.

Sometimes…she wondered if he wanted her. Not as a pre-ordained wife. But as a man wants a woman.

Not that it mattered. She wouldn't touch Nicholas Archer if he were the last man in London.

This was her life. Her choice. Her pencil. Her war.

And no man—no matter how irritatingly attractive—was going to stop her.

CHAPTER TWO

Patience was a virtue.

Nicholas Archer knew this not as a platitude, but as a personal creed. In his twenty-eight years, he had learned that those who rushed lost. Those who waited, watched, maneuvered—they inherited kingdoms.

Or, in his case, a dukedom…and a huge amount of political power.

His father had taught him early that a man who declared himself too boldly was a man offering up a weakness to be exploited. The Duke of VanDeVere was a master of caution, a believer in the art of saying a great deal while committing to absolutely nothing. *"Let the other man reveal himself first,"* he would say. *"Certainty is a weapon. Never hand yours over."*

His father called it caution. Nicholas had learned it was control in a gentleman's coat. He had absorbed the lesson well, too well. Every instinct he possessed warned him to hold the center ground, to never speak with passion where measured reason would suffice. Politics was a game of balance, after all—and the man who stood too firmly on one side made himself far too easy to topple.

Though recently, his caution had begun to cost him. Each week, without fail, an anonymous political cartoonist styling himself *B. Adroit* unleashed another satirical assault that skewered Nicholas personally—his speeches, his positioning, his alliances. The cartoons were clever, far too clever, and they were increasingly aimed at him, painting him as a hard-line Tory.

And damn it all, they were effective.

Several of the more volatile members of the House had pulled him aside to ask—too casually—whether he meant to "clarify his views" soon. As though a drawing done by some ink-stained radical should have the power to shake the Marquess of Vanover.

Nicholas's jaw tightened even now at the thought.

The truth was Nicholas didn't fear reform; he feared careless reform—change thrown like a torch instead of shaped like a tool.

But B. Adroit didn't trade in subtlety. And Nicholas needed to find this man…to put a stop to those cartoons before they undermined everything he had spent years constructing.

Because make no mistake, Nicholas was the heir apparent of the political landscape in the House of Lords. A distinction he'd earned because of his ability to see both sides of the issues.

At the moment, it served his purposes to appear to cast his lot with the *current* leader of the House: the domineering, decidedly Tory Duke of Winston.

Nicholas would not hold as much power as his mentor tomorrow, or next year, or perhaps even in five. That distinction still belonged to the current holder of the title—Reginald, ninth Duke of Winston, statesman, powerbroker, and Nicholas's chosen advisor. But the future? That was already being written. Nicholas was being groomed, polished, and positioned. And when the older man finally relinquished his grip on power—willingly or otherwise—Nicholas would be ready.

In the meantime, he watched. He learned. And he waited.

Both his father and Winston, the true hardline Tories, assumed him safely aligned with them, of course. His father had never questioned it. Nicholas had been raised beneath the steady banner of tradition, duty, and Tory certainty. Silence, in that household, was tantamount to assent. Winston, for his part, took Nicholas's restraint as proof of shared conviction. Nicholas did nothing to disabuse either of the dukes of the notion. He nodded when it cost him nothing. He spoke in careful generalities and allowed others to supply the conclusions. In politics, clarity was a gift best withheld, and Nicholas had learned long ago the power of letting powerful men believe what they wished.

He spent a great deal of time with Winston, for the simple reason that the man had much to teach him. Winston was a master at the game of appearances. He could charm a political opponent into submission with little more than a well-placed compliment and a glass of port. He could shift sentiment on the House floor with a turn of phrase. Nicholas had spent the last four years studying him like scripture. Not because he adored the man—he didn't—but because he respected what Winston represented.

Power. Influence. Legacy.

Nicholas intended to have all three.

He already had the pedigree. As the Marquess of Vanover, he was heir to the Duke of VanDeVere, a title his father still clung to with quiet, suffocating authority. Nicholas might have been the only man in England to be simultaneously mentored by one duke and overshadowed by another. But that, too, required patience.

He wasn't in a hurry.

He was simply…preparing.

That was what set him apart. Other young men of his age squandered their youth on gambling, wenching, and useless pleasure. Nicholas was content to play the long game.

And in the long game, every move mattered.

Including whom he chose to marry.

Winston had made his intentions known long ago. He wanted Nicholas to wed his only daughter. Lady Beatrix. It would be a political alliance. A tidy consolidation of influence. Two great houses entwined, merging their ambition beneath the respectable banner of marriage.

It was all very strategic.

It might have been laughably easy as well, if not for the minor problem that Lady Beatrix Winslow wanted nothing to do with him. Oh, Winston hadn't said so in as many words. But the way he kept putting off the discussion with statements such as, "Her mother wishes Beatrix to experience the full breadth of what it means to be a debutante." Nonsense, of course. The whole *ton* gossiped about Lady Beatrix's lack of marital decisiveness. But for whatever reason, one Nicholas very much suspected revolved around Winston's hesitance to anger his wife, Winston allowed Season after Season to pass without so much as a mention of Nicholas courting Beatrix.

But Nicholas knew the truth. Lady Beatrix hated him without reserve. Inconvenient, perhaps, but undeniable.

He smiled to himself at the thought. *God, but she was exquisite when she glared at him with unveiled disdain.*

Lady Beatrix was not some demure Society flower to be handed off to the highest bidder. She was a firestorm in silks. Tall, willowy, with golden hair that seemed spun from sunlight and eyes the precise green of a storm-churned sea. And that body…

He exhaled slowly through his nose.

Temptation incarnate.

But it wasn't just the surface that intrigued him where Lady Beatrix was concerned. It was what simmered underneath. The fury. The intelligence. The contempt.

She challenged him without speaking a word.

Nicholas, ever the strategist, had no intention of forcing her into anything. No, no. That would be foolish. It would make her bolt, bite, or worse—submit out of duty and then loathe him for it.

Lady Beatrix was not a woman to be commanded. She was a woman to be *convinced*.

And *that* was a far more pleasurable pursuit.

So he was patient. In conversation, he was careful. Mildly flirtatious. Never too eager. Always respectful. He paid her compliments sparingly and watched her reaction to each one as if studying a battlefield. He learned her rhythms. Her tells. The way she stiffened when someone tried to tame her. The way her fingers twitched when she held back a scathing retort, and how her eyes flashed when she let one fly.

She was magnificent…and not easily impressed.

Lately, he had adjusted his tactics accordingly.

He had sent her flowers—an experiment, really. Not the dull, obligatory roses favored by unimaginative men who believed romance could be purchased by the dozen. No. He had chosen peonies. Lush. Unapologetic. The sort of flowers that suggested discernment rather than desperation. The sort that might make a woman pause, tilt her head, and wonder what sort of man had chosen them—and what, precisely, he expected in return.

He had not signed the card with anything more than his name. Let her think. Let her question. Let the seed take root.

Nicholas was a man who knew how to wait for what he wanted.

He didn't want Lady Beatrix as a trophy.

He wanted her as a conquest.

Not in the vulgar sense—he would never lay a hand on a woman who didn't give him leave—but in the true, ruthless sense of seduction. Of unraveling her defenses. Of turning the disdain in her eyes into something far more compelling.

Desire.

He wanted her to want him.

And he would win. Because no one—no one—played the long game better than he did.

CHAPTER THREE

The problem with salons—aside from the armchairs filled with smug gentlemen whose self-importance seeped into the upholstery—was that they always smelled faintly of pomade and wind-baggery.

Bea's father's Thursday night political salon was no exception. Her father collected MPs the way other men collected horses—bred for loyalty, trained for obedience. At least he allowed her to attend. Most debutantes were treated as mindless little violets who would wilt if the slightest bit of political discussion was had in their presence.

Bea had been strategic in her attendance, however. She merely slipped in one evening, years ago, pretending to be more interested in the social aspect than the discussions themselves, and now she was simply a fixture. None of the MPs blinked when they found themselves sitting next to her. Nor did they blink (much) when she inserted her opinion on everything from the Corn Laws to the prisons debate.

Tonight was no exception. Bea perched at the edge of a green-velvet settee and sipped weak tea from a trembling saucer. Across from her, a cluster of powdered, puffed-up gentlemen debated policy as if it were a genteel game of chess—moving pieces, trading victories—never mind that real lives lay in the balance.

She told herself to endure it. To sip her tea. To pretend to be ornamental. To remember that patience was the price of admission in rooms like this.

But her patience, she was discovering, had limits.

"Of course, the reform bill will fail," declared Lord Hargrave, an arrogant backbencher who always sounded as if his cravat had strangled his brain. "One cannot simply give the vote to every Tom, Dick, and chimney sweep. It's unseemly."

Something inside her snapped—clean and final.

Bea set her cup down with a distinct clink. "Unseemly," she repeated, lifting a brow. "I daresay breathing is unseemly in certain circles, my lord. But the masses persist."

The surrounding gentlemen fell into stunned silence.

Colonel Smythe choked on his brandy. Lord Peabody coughed into his hand. Lord Hargrave blinked, his mouth puckering like a dried currant.

Bea nearly winced. *Oof.* Too far. She'd gone too far.

Blast it.

She saw it happen in real time, the shift in Lord Hargrave's expression from confusion to offense. He opened his mouth, presumably to scold her for speaking like a man, or daring to engage in political discourse without the necessary appendage beneath her clothing, or worse, accusing her of sympathy with *that* cartoonist.

Bea braced herself.

And then, like some perfectly tailored conjurer, Nicholas Archer appeared.

"Ah, Lady Beatrix," he said smoothly, stepping into the circle with a glass of wine in hand. "You must forgive Hargrave. He forgets we're no longer in the last century.

Why, just last week, he tried to hang his coat on the footman at White's."

A ripple of laughter broke the tension like a needle slipping cleanly through cloth.

Nicholas turned to Hargrave and lifted his glass in mock apology. "To your credit, the lad was rather stiff."

The older men chuckled. Hargrave harrumphed but didn't argue. He reached for his port with the surly air of a man defeated by humor. And of course, all of them adored the heir apparent to the political throne. Archer was everyone's favorite. He could get away with saying nearly anything. Bea curled her lip.

Archer turned to her then, his expression unreadable. "And to Lady Beatrix," he said, raising his glass again, "for reminding us that the sharpest wit often belongs to those the law would exclude. A tragedy, that."

Another round of laughter. Less robust this time. More...considering.

He held her gaze as he drank.

Bea blinked. Once. Slowly. Her skin prickled. He didn't mean that. Of course he didn't. He was merely being gallant. Or trying to be at least.

She should have thanked him. It would have been the polite thing to do. The expected thing. But all she could do was narrow her eyes.

Why had he done it? He was mocking her, wasn't he? He certainly didn't believe the law shouldn't exclude women. Her father said as much night and day. And Archer was her father's toadeater.

But why had Archer defused that particular moment, in that particular way, at that precise instant?

It had been too smooth. Too practiced.

She didn't trust him. Not even a little.

She needed some air. The stifling nonsense circulating in

this room at the moment was suddenly too much for her. She stood, and as she brushed past Archer toward the door, she paused.

"Your rescue is noted," she whispered between clenched teeth. "Though thoroughly unrequested."

Archer's mouth curved. "Forgive me. I thought I was rescuing Hargrave."

Bea tilted her head. "Ah, and here I was rather looking forward to his combustion."

Archer chuckled under his breath and leaned in slightly, just enough for her to feel the whisper of heat from his body. "Perhaps next time I'll let him burn."

Her stomach flipped. And not in an unpleasant way. More like in a way that it should not in Archer's presence. She hated that feeling. And more importantly, she hated that it wasn't the first time it had happened.

She forced a tight smile. "I'll hold you to it." And with that, Bea excused herself from the group.

As she slipped into the adjoining chamber, her pulse still drumming in her ears, she realized something deeply unpleasant.

Nicholas Archer had just saved her.

And worse than the rescue itself was the certainty that he would consider it a debt. Archer was not a man who believed in charity…only leverage.

CHAPTER FOUR

Nicholas let her go.

For the moment.

The clip of her slippers echoed in his ears long after she disappeared into the next room. He sipped his wine slowly, watching the gap in the doorway with the focused stillness of a man who knew waiting could be as decisive as action. The House rewarded certainty in public and punished it in private—precisely the trap his father had taught him to set for other men. And women, as the case may be tonight.

Lady Beatrix hadn't thanked him.

Not aloud at least.

She'd looked at him like he was a match held too close to the wick of her temper. But she had spoken to him.

Interesting. It was more than he'd garnered from her in the last four years, save the occasional polite greeting or formal dismissal.

He waited half a minute more—just long enough to avoid suspicion—and then handed his glass to a passing footman.

Without a word, he left the salon. Not through the parlor though. Too crowded.

He moved through the corridor, stepped into the darker, quieter side hall, and slipped out onto the veranda that lined the back of Winston's grand town house.

Cool air met him.

And there she was.

Framed by moonlight and radiating anger. She gripped the stone banister with both hands, the tendons in her arms tight, her back straight, her hair pinned far too neatly for the fire he knew lived beneath it.

Of course he'd guessed she'd be here. She was predictable in some things. He'd discovered that when he'd begun watching her more closely probably two years ago. After all, when one wanted the upper hand, one had to learn all the secrets of one's opponent. So, he'd made a study of her.

He even knew she had a secret.

Nicholas let the door click softly shut behind him.

She didn't turn.

"I assume," she said, voice low and even, "you've followed me to collect your debt."

He raised a brow, though she couldn't see it. "My debt?"

"For rescuing me from the consequences of my own mouth."

"I'd call it intervention," he said mildly. "You were seconds from making Hargrave apoplectic. I rather enjoy watching him breathe. I need his vote on the next bill."

She turned then, slowly. And God help him, the fire in her eyes made his blood stir.

"Don't play coy with me," she said. "You made me a jest... Wrapped me in wit and defused me before I could finish making my point."

"I saved you from social ruin," he replied calmly, walking toward her. "You're welcome."

"I didn't ask to be saved."

"No," he said, stopping just short of her. "You asked to be heard. But you were about to be dismissed instead."

Her jaw tightened. "And what? You thought a glass of claret and a clever quip would fix that?"

"No," he said softly. "But I thought it might afford you a little more time before they hang you from the chandelier. Or worse…kick you out of the salon. I suspect you wouldn't care for that outcome."

She studied him then. Eyes searching. Sharp as broken glass.

He let her look. Let her measure him. Let her find only what he gave.

"You don't do anything without motive," she said. "Not one thing."

He narrowed his eyes at her. "And yet you're still speaking to me."

She blinked. "You think I'm charmed?"

He chuckled then. He couldn't help himself. "No. I think you're suspicious," he said. "And I find that vastly preferable to indifference."

Her eyes narrowed, too. "Why, Vanover?" she asked, voice suddenly quieter. "Why did you step in?"

Nicholas considered his answer. Truth. Half-truth. Lie.

He chose the only one that wouldn't cost him ground. "Because," he said, "for all your ferocity, you're still vulnerable in rooms like that. And you shouldn't have to be."

A very long pause ensued.

The night wind brushed the hem of her gown. Her fingers twitched on the banister.

He didn't move.

She tilted her head. "You can't possibly be trying to earn my favor."

"Would it work?"

"No." Her reply was sharp, immediate.

He smiled, slow and deliberate. "Then no. Of course not."

She stared at him for a beat longer. Then turned back toward the garden, her profile distinct against the candlelight spilling through the windows behind them.

He let the silence stretch. Let her have the illusion of space. Then, quietly, "You should be careful, Lady Beatrix."

Her eyes narrowed. "Of what?"

"Of drawing too much attention to your words," he said. "Some of us might start to wonder how you know so much about the inner workings of Parliament."

Her breath hitched. Barely. But he caught it.

He watched her shoulders rise.

"I read the *Times*," she replied, lifting her chin. "Like any well-educated wallflower."

His lips twitched. "You're no wallflower."

"I'm twenty-two and unmarried," she shot back. "Society's decided. I'm on the shelf."

He chuckled. "Then I pity the shelf."

She turned sharply at that, lips parted in surprise.

He gave her the smallest bow, turned on his heel, and walked back inside.

Let her chase that quip in circles for a while.

He would wait.

CHAPTER FIVE

Golden puddles of light scattered across the patterned rug and glinted off the crystal decanters on a small mahogany table beneath the window. Bea sat alone on the settee in her second-floor sitting room, her slippered feet crossed at the ankles, a small fire crackling in the grate. The silence felt indulgent, like an hour stolen from expectations.

The guests were long gone. They'd left over an hour ago. She'd kept to her suite. Hoping her father hadn't gotten word about her little war of words with Lord Hargrave. Father didn't like it when she angered his friends. No matter how correct she was.

Winston didn't fear scandal. He feared losing control of the story—and in Parliament, story was power.

She tried to focus on that familiar dread…the predictable consequences, the inevitable lecture.

Instead, her thoughts strayed to Nicholas Archer.

What had he been about earlier? First rushing to her aid in the conversation with Hargrave and then following her out onto the veranda? Not to mention he'd looked quite unfair in his evening coat. The fit had been indecently perfect, the charcoal gray emphasizing the breadth of his shoulders, the taper of his waist. And that expression—half amusement, half challenge—when he'd parried her every verbal thrust with maddening ease. A gentleman had no business being that clever while also looking as if he'd just strode off the cover of a gothic novel, all dark eyes and restrained power.

And it wasn't merely tonight. Lately, he'd developed an irritating habit of…hovering. Not overtly—Nicholas Archer never did anything so gauche—but in little ways that suggested a man intent on garnering her good opinion. As if she were the sort of woman whose favor could be courted with a few well-placed rescues and an exquisitely tailored coat. Then there had been the flowers a fortnight ago. *Peonies*, of all things. Not roses or lilies or anything with a sensible message attached. Peonies…riotous, blousy, impossible-to-read blooms. As if anything meaningful could be divined from peonies. As if she were meant to search for significance in petals when the man himself remained the most confounding puzzle of all.

Bea let out a low groan and pressed the heels of her hands to her eyes. Why was it that the man most in need of being taken down a peg was also the one with an impossibly sculpted mouth and a voice like warm brandy?

She was still scowling at the fire when the door swung open and her mother swept into the room, all elegance and pale green silk. In her forties, the duchess was the picture of refined beauty—tall, fair-haired, and radiant in that effortless way that had once made her the diamond of her debut Season. Her golden hair, braided and loosely knotted for the night, gleamed in the firelight as she glided to the nearest chair with the grace of a woman born to command a room simply by entering it.

Her father followed, just as striking in his own right. The duke's dark hair, touched handsomely with silver at the temples, was immaculate—as was the deep navy of his coat. He too possessed that long, aristocratic frame, all straight lines and crisp precision, as though he had been carved from a single block of dignity. The fact that he chose to remain standing—broad shoulders squared, expression unreadable—was never a good sign.

"There you are, Beatrix," Mother began delicately. Mother was usually delicate.

"We heard about the incident with Lord Hargrave," Father interjected, his voice booming.

"Oh?" Bea tilted her head, playing at innocence. It was usually best this way.

"He said you were...dismissive," Father barked. "Rude even."

"I was not rude," Bea countered, nostrils flaring. "I simply believed that if he insisted on speaking foolishly, he ought to experience the consequence of doing so."

Her mother's mouth flattened. "Oh, Beatrix—"

"Bea," she corrected automatically.

"Enough." Father stepped forward, his face a mask of stone. "We've indulged your...whimsical tendencies for long enough. It's long past time you began thinking seriously about your prospects. I won't have the daughter of the Duke of Winston dismissed as a wallflower—"

"That's what Lord Hargrave called you, Bea," Mama said, an unmistakable thread of worry in her voice. "A *wallflower*."

"I *am* a wallflower," Bea agreed with a wide smile.

Mama gasped.

"Enough," Father thundered again. "The fact that you're calling yourself a wallflower tells me I've made the right decision."

Her mother winced, while panic spread through Bea's

stomach, rising, choking, threatening to spill over into something dangerously close to fear.

"What do you mean?" she forced out, even as her pulse hammered its own warning. She glanced back and forth between her parents' tight faces.

"It is high time we took action," Father continued, his voice filling the room. "You shall be courted. Formally."

Bea's stomach dipped. She pressed a hand against it. Oh, God. She'd really done it this time. Hadn't she? She'd gone too far in front of the wrong man. Everyone knew Hargrave was a complete horse's ass.

"Courted?" she echoed. "Formally?" But she already knew what her father would say next.

Her mother looked away, her brows pinched with a deep, quiet distress she was trying—and failing—to hide.

Father didn't hesitate. "Yes. Courted. By Lord Vanover. This Season."

The air in the room thinned. A cold, sinking dread slid down Bea's spine. "You cannot be serious."

"He is serious," Mother said softly, almost sadly. "And so am I. I fear I've been far too indulgent with you, Beatrix."

"But Lord Vanover and I do not suit." Bea stood as if movement alone could steady the quiver beneath her ribs. Her heart climbed into her throat. "He's smug and vexing and—" Her voice cracked despite her best efforts. "Surely, you must see that we are ill-matched."

"Nonsense." Father sliced the air with a decisive wave, as though her objections were no more than a child's tantrum. "Archer is an *ideal* match. He has wealth, lineage, influence— everything a young woman in your position could want. And he agreed to the courtship long ago. Frankly, he's shown an extraordinary degree of patience. He's been more than reasonable."

"Reasonable?" Bea echoed, the word tasting so bitter she

nearly choked on it. "Reasonable would have been speaking to *me* before arranging my future like I'm a parcel to be posted. Was this his idea?"

"No," Father replied, tugging sharply at the front of his waistcoat. "But I expect he'll be pleased to hear I've finally come to my senses. The man needs an heir someday, after all."

Something jolted inside of Bea, sudden as a snapped harp string. *My* senses. As though her future were a lever to be pulled at his discretion, rather than a life she intended to direct herself. And mentioning Archer's heir so flippantly, as though *she* were nothing more than a breeding horse.

Her father continued, voice hardening. "Let me be perfectly clear. I do not require your agreement. You are *my* daughter, and this is the wisest course."

Bea's throat tightened until it ached. "You speak as though I'm not even in the room," she said, voice simmering. "As though my life is some strategy to be plotted."

"Your mother and I have discussed it," Father said. "You will have time to grow accustomed to the idea of the marriage, but the courtship will begin. *Immediately.*"

Her mother reached out as if to offer comfort, but Bea turned away.

She could still picture Archer in his coat, that slow, knowing smirk when he'd parried every one of her remarks with effortless precision. The maddening, magnetic pull of him. The way his gaze had lingered, as if he understood something about her she hadn't meant for anyone to see.

And he was going to be formally courting her?

Truly?

A cold sweep of dread washed over her, sharp enough to make her shudder. Nicholas Archer—handsome, infuriating, arrogant man—would soon be parading around her life with her father's blessing, invading her routines, her peace, her sanctuary. And he would do it with that insufferable confidence of his, as if the entire arrangement were merely a puzzle waiting for him to solve.

Oh, they had gravely—*spectacularly*—miscalculated.

Because if her father thought she would simply accept this…

And if Archer thought he could waltz through her defenses as neatly as he wielded that wicked tongue of his…

They were both about to learn precisely how formidable Beatrix Winslow could be.

War—quiet, strategic, and devastating—was already taking shape in her mind.

CHAPTER SIX

Nicholas was not, by nature, an impulsive man. He liked a good plan. A solid strategy. A worthy opponent. And Lady Beatrix, in all her vexing, sharp-tongued glory, was a battlefield unto herself.

He leaned against the wooden casing of his bedchamber's open window, coat unbuttoned, the breeze licking at his shirt collar, and thought again of the way she'd looked tonight in the veranda's moonlight—her eyes flaring when she challenged him, her lips parted on a breath of shock when he'd countered with ease. Every bit of her had radiated defiance, intellect, allure.

And her mouth.

Hell.

He closed his eyes and let his head tip against the pane. Patience, Vanover. He hadn't come this far to be undone by a pair of clever lips and a spine made of steel. But it was proving to be...tempting.

He'd always known Lady Beatrix was different. But this Season—this particular evening—had confirmed what he hadn't yet admitted to himself: he wanted her. Wanted her wit and will and impossible fire. Wanted her in his bed, yes, but more dangerously…wanted her everywhere else too. Inconvenient, perhaps…but undeniable.

Of course, he suspected she had a secret. She was far too interested in the workings of politics. Personally, he believed she might well have been the one who'd leaked a few of the Tory secrets to the Whigs of late. He couldn't prove it, of course, but he wouldn't put it past her. The other men thought she attended her father's political salons for the social diversion. But Nicholas knew better. Lady Beatrix didn't give a toss about social calls. She was there to listen. To catalogue. To understand what was being planned.

And that, perhaps more than anything, made her more desirable.

She would make an excellent wife for a man with political ambition—steady at his side, sharp of mind, capable of speaking with authority on matters most women were expected merely to smile through. She would understand his interests, challenge his thinking, and never require him to simplify the world for her comfort.

That was the first reason he wanted her.

The second was far less respectable.

He harbored no illusion that Lady Beatrix would be won without a battle. The catch, of course, was that Nicholas had no intention of playing the fool. He had been a lover. A seducer. And perhaps too many things in between…but never, never a romantic. Not even when the lady in question hurled exquisitely barbed insults that made his blood hum. And he already knew she would do everything in her considerable power to thwart him.

He grinned to himself. Why did he like the thought of that even more?

A rap at the door pulled him from his untoward thoughts.

"Enter," he called, still staring out at the starlit darkness.

Godwin, his ever-efficient butler, stepped inside. "Pardon the interruption, my lord, but the Duke of Winston awaits you in the study."

Nicholas blinked. "The duke?"

"Yes, my lord. He said it was a matter of some importance."

This was odd. Winston rarely sought him out directly—certainly not at Archer House. Their dealings were almost always conducted on the duke's terms. In the duke's study, no less. Nicholas pushed away from the window, tugged his coat straight, and nodded.

"Tell His Grace I shall be down directly."

Godwin bowed and vanished.

Nicholas took one last breath of cool night air, rolled his shoulders once, and strode from the room.

THE STUDY WAS all dark walnut paneling and subdued lamplight. Winston stood near the hearth, a tumbler of brandy in one hand, his other resting lightly on the mantel. He'd obviously helped himself to the drink. He was not a man who liked to be kept waiting.

Nicholas stepped inside and shut the door behind him. "Your Grace."

Winston turned. "Vanover."

Nicholas eyed him carefully. He didn't smile. Something told him this wasn't about politics. He crossed to the sideboard, poured himself a modest splash of brandy, and gestured lightly with the glass. "Unexpected call. Everything well?"

Winston's mouth twitched, almost a smile. "Everything's about to be."

Nicholas took a sip and waited.

The duke straightened and faced him fully. "I won't waste your time. I've spoken to my daughter this evening."

Ah.

Nicholas said nothing, but one brow might have lifted slightly.

Winston went on. "I informed Beatrix that it is high time she married."

A pause. No fanfare. No request. Simply a fact presented with the sort of confidence only dukes and madmen managed.

Nicholas set down his glass with deliberate care. "Indeed."

"She's of an age. And because she's proven must stubborn, I must step in. She'll marry. You, if you'll still have her."

This time Nicholas's brow definitely lifted. "May I ask why you've suddenly decided this is urgent?"

Winston tugged at his lapel. He always did so when he was uncomfortable. Which was extremely rare. "It's come to our attention that she is becoming the object of gossip."

Nicholas refrained from pointing out Lady Beatrix's marital plans had been the subject of gossip for years. Was it possible her parents hadn't heard the rumors until now? Perhaps, but unlikely.

"I see," he replied simply.

Winston gave Nicholas a dry once-over. "My wife assures me Beatrix tolerates you."

Nicholas's mouth quirked. "High praise."

"Don't let it go to your head." The duke moved to the nearest chair and sat, the casual assumption of authority wafting off him like cigar smoke. The man truly thought he was in charge of everything. He had no clue that Nicholas would never marry his daughter or anyone else's daughter unless *he* wanted to. It was only convenient that what Nicholas wanted and what Winston wanted just happened to be the same thing.

Nicholas leaned one hip against the desk. "And how did Lady Beatrix receive this…news?"

Winston waved a hand dismissively. "She has no choice in the matter. Her time of frolic is over."

Nicholas exhaled once through his nose, slow and controlled. "She's not a woman easily cornered."

"She is a girl whose father has run out of patience." Winston leveled him with a stare. "You *are* still interested, I assume?"

Nicholas held the older man's gaze. "I am."

The duke inclined his head. "Good. I've already told her to expect you tomorrow afternoon. Take her riding in the park. Be seen. Do your part."

With that, Winston rose, tugged once at the hem of his coat, and made for the door.

"Your Grace," Nicholas said before the duke could exit. "If I may ask—what did Lady Beatrix say when you told her?"

Winston's expression didn't shift, but something in his eyes sharpened. "I'd be lying if I told you she was pleased with the arrangement. She has been given her freedom for far too long. But if there's anyone I trust to bring her around to the idea of marriage, it's you, Vanover."

Then he was gone, the thud of the door behind him a final, absolute sound.

Nicholas stood still for a long moment after the duke departed, the silence folding around him like a closing fist. He lifted his glass, watching the brandy catch the lamplight, his mind spinning, not with doubt…but with the inevitable chaos to come.

Lady Beatrix was not a woman who accepted commands. Certainly not from her father. And most definitely not from him.

If Winston believed she would simply acquiesce, he was mad. And if Nicholas believed she would accompany him to the park tomorrow with docile agreement, *he* was madder still.

He tipped the glass to his lips and let the burn settle. Then he exhaled a low, rueful laugh.

"Hell," he muttered, rubbing a hand across his jaw. "She's going to have her back up."

Lady Beatrix would not meet this undefended. No—she would arm herself. She would gather allies. She would assemble her inner circle, sharpen her intellect, and construct a plan as intricate and devastating as a military campaign. By the time she was done, he'd be lucky to survive the opening volley.

He set down the glass, straightened, and squared his shoulders.

If Lady Beatrix Winslow was preparing for war…

He had best be ready to meet her on the battlefield.

And God help him. He was looking forward to it.

CHAPTER SEVEN

Nicholas did not go to bed.

He told himself it was because he had correspondence to address—letters from two peers in Cornwall, a memorandum from the committee, the small stack of pamphlets Winston insisted he read, even though Winston's idea of "reading" involved underlining anything that sounded like a threat.

In truth, he didn't go to bed because his skin still carried the faint, phantom weight of Winston's presence in his study.

Winston had walked in as though Archer House belonged to him. As though Nicholas belonged to him.

And the worst of it—the part that sat like a pebble beneath Nicholas's tongue—was that Winston hadn't even needed to raise his voice.

He'd simply *assumed* obedience.

Nicholas had built an entire life on the art of letting men assume what they wanted.

Tonight, it felt less like strategy and more like a collar. It rankled. In fact, the strategy had begun to rankle more and more of late.

Godwin appeared at the study door. "Your carriage is prepared, my lord."

Nicholas looked up sharply. "I did not request my carriage."

"No, my lord." Godwin's expression was faultless. "But His Grace did."

Nicholas stared.

Godwin, with the solemnity of a man delivering an execution order, added, "The Duke of VanDeVere requests your presence this evening."

Of course he does.

Speaking of rankling…Nicholas's father did not ask. He did not invite. He did not *request* in any way that implied a second option existed.

Obedience was the price of being VanDeVere's son—and Nicholas had been paying it since boyhood. Winston could ruin his future. VanDeVere could ruin his sense of self—and Nicholas had always feared the second more than the first.

Nicholas rose slowly, buttoning his coat with methodical care. He could feel his own body trying to do what it had been trained to do—settle, smooth, comply. It was always the best strategy when it came to dealing with his father.

He marched out to the foyer, took his hat from the sideboard, his cloak from Godwin's hands, and paused only long enough to say, "Don't wait up."

Godwin bowed.

Nicholas walked out into the night.

VanDeVere House sat on the finest square in Mayfair. The front steps were spotless. The windows were dark, save for one warm glow on the first floor—his father's study. The lanterns along the walk were lit with careful symmetry, as though even the flames had been arranged to remind a visitor that order reigned here.

Nicholas handed off his coat and hat to his father's butler and was shown to the study without ceremony.

No announcement. No lingering. No greeting from his stepmother or any well-meaning relation or servant.

Just the quiet, inexorable funneling of a son toward a father.

The door to the study was open.

His father stood with his back to the room, hands clasped behind him, gazing out at the square below as if he owned the street, the city, and every living thing that dared walk through it.

Nicholas stopped on the threshold.

"The Marquess of Vanover," VanDeVere said, without turning. His voice was mild. Almost pleasant. Which was always how it began.

Nicholas stepped inside. "Father."

A pause—measured, deliberate.

Then VanDeVere turned.

He was immaculate, as always. Not merely well-dressed, but *precise*—cravat tied with mathematical perfection, coat cut to emphasize the authority in his frame, silver-tinged hair brushed back as though not even a single strand would dare rebel.

His eyes, however, were what had made grown men go silent in committee rooms for decades.

Dark. Assessing. Unflinching.

Nicholas had been trained under that gaze the way a dog was trained under a whistle.

"You're late," VanDeVere observed.

"I came as soon as I received your message."

VanDeVere's mouth twitched, the nearest thing to a smile

he ever allowed when he thought he was about to win. "So you did."

Nicholas waited.

VanDeVere crossed to the sideboard, lifted the decanter, and poured two glasses of brandy. He handed one to Nicholas as if bestowing a prize.

Nicholas accepted, because refusing would make a point. And points were dangerous in his father's company.

VanDeVere gestured toward the chair opposite the desk.

Nicholas sat.

VanDeVere remained standing. Always. As though sitting were an indulgence meant for lesser men.

"I had a visit tonight," VanDeVere said.

Nicholas kept his expression still. "From Winston?"

"Yes."

So Winston had gone from Archer House to VanDeVere House, like a man checking on a transaction. Nicholas's jaw tightened, but he took a slow sip of brandy to hide his irritation.

VanDeVere studied him over the rim of his glass. "You're surprised?"

Nicholas shrugged. "I didn't anticipate Winston moving so quickly," he replied carefully.

VanDeVere's eyes sharpened. "You didn't anticipate it because you've grown complacent with Winston. That ends now."

Nicholas's fingers tightened around the glass. "I see." Vague words were most effective with his father.

"Do you?" VanDeVere's tone stayed mild, but the air changed—pressure increasing by degrees. "Winston has been losing patience. With his daughter. With the cartoons. With the threat of appearing"—his lip curled faintly—"indecisive."

Nicholas did not react at the mention of B. Adroit.

He did not react because reacting would reveal he cared.

And Nicholas Archer did not reveal what he cared about. Not here.

VanDeVere paced once behind the desk, slow as a cat stalking a rat. "Winston believes the reform bill will be pushed forward sooner than expected."

Nicholas's stomach gave the faintest twist.

"It's scheduled—" Nicholas began.

"It will be scheduled whenever the Crown decides it will be scheduled," VanDeVere cut in smoothly. "And the Crown has begun to notice that the House is…restless."

Nicholas's throat tightened. That, at least, was true.

VanDeVere stopped behind his chair—close enough that Nicholas could feel him, like a shadow leaning over his shoulder. "Which is another reason why I sent for you."

Nicholas's pulse ticked once, hard.

Here it comes.

"You will vote as instructed, of course," VanDeVere said.

"Of course." Nicholas kept his gaze forward. Obedience would cost him some pride—and invite a few whispers. Defiance would cost him the machinery that made votes possible. So he let his father hear what he wanted to hear, and he tucked the larger play safely out of sight.

VanDeVere's hand rested briefly on the back of Nicholas's chair, a touch light enough to be mistaken for affection if one did not know better.

It was not affection.

It was ownership.

"The reform bill is a contagion," VanDeVere continued, voice still calm. "It begins with trade restrictions and ends with men who smell of coal demanding a seat in Parliament."

Nicholas said nothing.

VanDeVere moved away again, circling, the way he always did when he wanted a man to feel hunted without ever being chased.

"You have been playing the center," VanDeVere said. "Useful. Clever. But in this case, it has made some people uncertain of you."

Nicholas's spine went rigid.

"There are times," his father's eyes narrowed, "when uncertainty can be mistaken for weakness, Nicholas."

Nicholas forced his voice to remain even. "You *want* me to tip my hand?"

"Not entirely." His father's smile was tight as always. "But it will not hurt to let your peers know how you intend to vote. In this instance, it's not helpful to be vague."

Nicholas nodded once. A single, obedient movement. Inside, something in him pressed back—small, resentful, dangerously alive. But he had never been foolish enough to let that part of himself speak in this room. Such an irony that his father didn't even realize how well he'd taught him to be vague. "I understand."

VanDeVere leaned a hip against the desk. "Winston also made it clear that your marriage to his daughter is no longer optional."

Nicholas's fingers tightened around the brandy glass again. He remained silent. He did not relish talking about Lady Beatrix with his father. She was no more than a political chess piece to him.

VanDeVere's voice lowered, turning almost conversational. "Do you want her?"

Nicholas held his father's gaze and chose the safest answer. "Yes."

It was not a lie. It was simply…incomplete.

VanDeVere nodded, as if they were discussing the purchase of a horse. "Then you will have her. But you will have her correctly."

Nicholas's jaw clenched. What the bloody hell did that mean? "Correctly?"

"You will court her publicly," VanDeVere said. "You will be seen. You will be admired. You will look like Winston's heir in all but title. You're fortunate Winston has changed his mind on the matter."

Nicholas forced his breathing to stay steady. "I'm fairly certain Lady Beatrix isn't eager for the match."

VanDeVere's eyes flicked, quick as a blade. He scoffed. "Women don't refuse. Not when their fathers stop indulging them."

Nicholas's mouth tightened. His father was as predictable as he was awful.

VanDeVere continued as if Nicholas hadn't spoken. "Winston has permitted her freedom because his duchess insisted. That's ended. And if the duchess objects"—he lifted one shoulder in a careless shrug—"she will be reminded what happens when a woman challenges a duke."

Nicholas's stomach turned, but he kept his jaw clenched tight.

He thought of Lady Beatrix's sharp mouth. Her fire. Her refusal to bow. She would not be ordered about…not even by two dukes.

VanDeVere set his glass down with a distinct click. "There is another matter."

Nicholas lifted his gaze again, bracing himself for whatever came next.

VanDeVere's eyes gleamed faintly. "These cartoons."

Nicholas kept his face still. "Yes."

"They've made both you and Winston look ridiculous."

Nicholas's throat tightened despite himself.

VanDeVere noticed, of course.

His father's smile returned, thin and knowing. "They must bother you."

Nicholas didn't deny it. Denial would be a weakness, and VanDeVere fed on weaknesses.

Instead, he said, "I agree. They are an attack on our credibility."

VanDeVere nodded as if Nicholas had recited a lesson properly. "Precisely. Credibility is currency. And you are being robbed in public."

Nicholas's fingers curled around the arm of the chair.

VanDeVere's gaze pinned him. "You will find the cartoonist."

Nicholas's voice stayed even. "I intend to—"

"You will not intend," VanDeVere corrected softly. "You will act. Quietly. Efficiently. Immediately. No mistakes. No excuses."

Nicholas's jaw clenched. "Yes, Father." It was a waste of breath to tell the man he'd already hired a Bow Street Runner.

VanDeVere moved closer, and Nicholas felt, as he always did, that invisible tightening—like a noose being adjusted, not yet pulled.

"Remember who you are," VanDeVere murmured. "You shall not be made a laughingstock by some guttersnipe with a pencil."

Nicholas's pulse ticked again, hard.

VanDeVere's eyes bored into him. His gaze sharpened, as if he sensed something—some future fracture, the hint of rebellion—before it happened. "Do you understand me?"

Nicholas stared up at him.

He could, if he wanted, say something clever. Something barbed. Something that would give him a fleeting sense of power.

But Nicholas had survived his father by never needing the fleeting kind of power.

So he lowered his gaze. And he nodded. "I understand."

VanDeVere's hand rested on his shoulder—brief, firm, a benediction that felt like a brand.

"Good," his father said. "Then we are finished."

Nicholas rose.

He placed his untouched brandy on the desk with careful precision.

VanDeVere watched him like a man watching a chess piece return to its proper square.

Nicholas bowed his head. "Goodnight, Father."

VanDeVere gave a small, satisfied nod. "Goodnight, Vanover."

Nicholas turned and walked out.

He did not breathe properly until he was halfway down the outside steps.

Even then, the air felt thick.

The night was cool and quiet, London unaware that two dukes had just decided the fates of two people as if it was nothing more than a whim.

Nicholas stepped into his carriage and shut the door.

As the wheels began to roll, he stared at his reflection in the darkened glass.

Steady. Controlled. Obedient.

The man his father expected.

And yet—

In the deepest part of him, something small and furious pressed against the inside of his ribs.

Not rebellion.

Not yet.

But the first, dangerous sensation of wanting to speak with his own voice. Much like Lady Beatrix did.

CHAPTER EIGHT

Bea sat primly on the rose-colored settee in her sitting room, though "primly" was a generous interpretation. Her foot tapped and her fingers worried the ivory buttons at her wrist. Her sitting room—normally her sanctuary—felt unusually alive today. Sunlight filtered weakly through the drawn damask curtains, softening the floral patterns that climbed the pale blue wallpaper. The fire crackling behind the gilded screen cast pools of warm gold over the room: the velvet settee, the walnut escritoire littered with sketching pencils, the delicate porcelain figurines on the mantel. It was cozy, feminine, and—this morning—buzzing with the energy of conspiracy. Or, namely, a meeting of *The Wallflowers' Revolt*.

Bea wore a soft cream gown, the hem sweeping over the embroidered carpet. Her sleeves finished with tiny pearl buttons that refused to lie flat unless she fussed with them. Georgie lounged in the low slipper chair opposite, dressed in a lavender muslin that set off her dark-brown hair, which kept slipping from her pins no matter how many times she patted at them. Poppy, in a sunflower-yellow walking dress with sleeves pushed inelegantly to the elbow, leaned against the pianoforte with her arms folded, looking as if she were posing for a portrait.

The three of them, gathered close around the warmth of the fire, looked less like polite young ladies and more like a clutch of conspirators.

Which, given the topic of conversation, was precisely what they were.

"I nearly dropped my toast when I saw it in the paper," Georgie declared, waving her teacup as if dismissing imaginary footmen. "That caricature of Lord Vanover. He truly looked like a peacock in a waistcoat."

Poppy clapped a hand over her mouth to contain a laugh. "And the caption! 'This cock prefers preening over Reform.' Bea, I choked on my tea, I tell you."

Bea flushed—part mortification, part pride—and lowered her voice. "You mustn't say my name anywhere near that cartoon. If anyone overhears—"

"Don't worry. Your parents are out, and your maid is below stairs," Georgie reminded her, waving her teacup once more. "No one's listening."

"Well," Poppy added, "no one except the three of us. And we are better than a vault." She tucked a bright red curl behind her ear.

Bea exhaled and sank deeper into the settee cushions. Her friends *were* a vault, and she needed their discretion now more than ever. She'd shared everything with them. They even knew about her secret advantage.

Her gaze flicked toward the far corner of the room, where a small decorative grate sat flush with the floorboards. "Yes, well, the peacocks may have been well received, but the momentum is always short-lived. If I'm to influence the vote, I must begin my next sketch tonight. I'll require details...and Papa is always generous with those, even when he doesn't mean to be." She tapped her foot toward the grate.

Both Georgie and Poppy grinned wickedly.

The grate was connected to the flue that ran directly above her father's study. From a young age, Bea had discovered that sounds from the study carried straight upward into her room. All she had to do was lie flat on her stomach and press her ear to it, and she could hear everything—every political scheme, every planned vote, every discussion her father had, including those involving one Lord Nicholas Archer.

It was her most valuable tool in the game she hadn't meant to play but now couldn't imagine abandoning. Namely, thwarting the Tories at every turn. It wasn't her fault they were on the wrong side of things. Men dedicated to keeping the status quo at all costs, while the Whigs worked for reform, the expansion of political power to the commoners, and sought to modernize church and state. If women were ever going to become empowered, the Whigs were the party that would help. At least they were far more likely to than the Tories, who wanted absolutely nothing to change.

But at the moment, Bea's biggest problem was no longer political. She'd been rehearsing the words since breakfast, waiting until she could say them without flinching. She smoothed a hand down her sleeve. "I have some distressing news."

Both of her friends snapped upright, their faces edged with concern.

"Papa has demanded that I begin accepting the attentions of Nicholas Archer," Bea breathed. Ugh. It sounded even more awful when she said it aloud.

"What?" Georgie sputtered. "Since when?" She plunked a fist on her hip.

"Why *now*?" Poppy asked, brows drawn tightly together. "Your father hasn't said a word about marriage in all these years."

Her friends were glorious…indignant, loyal, and entirely on her side.

Bea straightened, drawing strength from their outrage as if it were armor. "Apparently," she said with a miserable sigh, "Lord Hargrave called me a wallflower, and Papa took it as a personal insult. So now I must be made 'marriageable.' Immediately."

Georgie exhaled hard, her breath edged with disgust. "That Hargrave truly is a blister."

"What a pompous donkey," Poppy muttered. "And I do *not* use either word lightly." She paused, eyes narrowing thoughtfully. "But Bea…this might actually be perfect."

Bea blinked. "Pardon?"

"Think of it," Poppy said, leaning forward. "If Nicholas Archer is courting you, you'll be welcomed into every Tory salon in London. You'll hear *everything*. And no one will suspect a thing. Not when you're strolling about with him."

"I'd rather keep company with a goat," Bea muttered. "Goats, at least, are honest about their intentions."

"Poppy's right!" Georgie said, brightening. "You can use the courtship to gather information. Imagine the details you'll overhear…conversations between political allies, private remarks, quiet quips. Perfect for your drawings."

Bea stared at them. "But I hear so much of it now," she argued.

"Of course, you do, but what if you heard even more?" Georgie's voice dipped lower, the corners of her mouth curling with implication.

Bea considered this for a few moments. Then, slowly, she allowed her expression to tip into something wickedly amused.

"Hiding in plain sight," she whispered. "Even plainer sight than before."

"Exactly," Poppy said. "And didn't you tell us the Bow Street Runners are sniffing around for B. Adroit's identity?"

"They are," Bea admitted, the thud of excitement rising in her chest. This was the advantage of friends. They noticed the possibilities while you were still composing your despair. A quarter hour ago, she'd been certain her life was ruined. Now? Now she saw an opportunity.

"And what's better," Bea added, tapping a finger against her cheek, "is that when it's just the two of us, I won't have to pretend. I don't give a fig what Archer thinks of me."

Georgie nodded sagely. "Be as rude as you like. As cutting as you dare."

Another grin—sharp as a blade—spread slowly across Bea's face. Espionage disguised as courtship. A perfect mission for a member of The Wallflowers' Revolt. "Very well then," she said, lifting her chin. "Let the *supposed* courtship begin."

CHAPTER NINE

Nicholas was rather proud of his curricle. The pair of matched bays moved with the simple grace of long-practiced partners, the polished brass gleamed in the sun, and the wheels had been reinforced last summer with a bit of ingenuity that made the whole rig feel smoother than silk on cobblestones. Even so, the true triumph of the afternoon wasn't the vehicle. It was the presence of the woman seated beside him.

Lady Beatrix.

Stiff as a frostbitten fencepost.

Nicholas could charm a crowd, sway a committee, and appease a difficult duke. It should not be this difficult to survive a look from Lady Beatrix.

She sat with perfect posture, her gloved hands folded neatly in her lap, her eyes trained somewhere in the middle distance, not quite watching the other carriages in Hyde Park and certainly not looking at him.

She was dressed perfectly, as always. Her pelisse was a soft green, trimmed in ivory silk piping that caught the morning light and played up the gold in her hair. Beneath it, a sprigged muslin gown hinted at pale green, the fabric light enough to shift with the breeze and tempt the imagination. Her bonnet, a wide-brimmed confection of cream straw and palest rose ribbon, shielded her face just enough to give her an air of genteel aloofness—but not enough to hide the delicate curve of her jaw or the flash of sea-green eyes when she deigned to glance his way. Every detail about her had been assembled with intention. Immaculate. Untouchable. And seated beside him, ankles crossed, as if she could not wait for the drive to end.

Nicholas flicked the reins with an idle hand, guiding the team through a winding track near the Serpentine. The pretty summer afternoon had drawn out the usual parade of Society—new gowns fluttering, hats nodding, gentlemen posturing.

Lady Beatrix didn't flinch or preen or even attempt to acknowledge a single one of them.

He allowed himself a slow smile.

The Duke of Winston had taken him off guard when he'd announced the courtship, to be certain, but once Nicholas had recovered from the initial surprise and his father's edicts, he'd recognized the opportunity for what it was.

A formal attachment to Lady Beatrix played directly into his plans, after all. It was the future he'd been angling toward, albeit more swiftly than scheduled. He'd intended to let her come around on her own, to draw her toward him with the slow-burn of innuendo and pointed provocations.

Now, he'd simply do all that…with her father's blessing.

Not a bad hand to play.

Still.

She was not speaking to him.

Which was somewhat inconvenient, as he found her conversation preferable to most of London's, even when it was laced with barbs. Especially when it was laced with barbs.

"I believe that old codger in the blue coat just attempted to bow while seated," he said, with the sort of thoughtful air one might use when spotting a rare bird. "Remarkable flexibility for a man in his dotage."

Silence.

Nicholas turned his head slowly, as if trying to confirm her presence. "Lady Beatrix?"

Nothing.

"I say, have you been replaced by a wax replica? Blink once if not."

She exhaled sharply through her nose.

Ah, progress.

"I did wonder whether you might choose to leap from the carriage at the first curve," he continued mildly. "I'm gratified that you resisted the urge. Though if you're simply waiting for a more dramatic drop—say, near the bridge—I'd appreciate fair warning. I'll need to tighten the reins."

Her gaze slid toward him at last, though her mouth remained resolutely shut.

Nicholas smiled. "There she is."

"I am here against my will," she said finally.

"A fact that wounds me deeply," he returned. "But I must say, you hide it beautifully. Only a hint of murderous tension in your jaw."

She gave him a look that might've set his coat alight. "Do not mistake my silence for submission."

"Never," he said with absolute sincerity. "I only hoped to hear your opinion on the parade of coxcombs ahead. Do you prefer lavender jackets or the puce monstrosity Lord Kerrigan wore last night?"

"I prefer not to discuss Lord Kerrigan's monstrosity with you."

Nicholas clicked his tongue softly. "Now that's uncharitable. I was offering you a rare chance to eviscerate Society's worst offenders."

Her lips twitched…barely. But enough.

He leaned back slightly, giving her space. "In truth, I asked only because I value your judgment."

She lifted her chin. "You're mocking me."

"Only a little. And never when it matters. I wonder at the last time you had a good laugh."

Her brow knitted, but she said nothing.

They rode in silence for a bit longer, the noise of the park filtering around them…the clip of hooves, the trill of laughter, the call of a flower vendor hawking daisies near the corner.

Then Nicholas tried another angle. A more serious subject. Something he was *certain* would pique her interest.

"I read something curious in the papers yesterday," he said casually. "The East India Company's latest trade bill. There's been debate in the Lords about restricting new holdings in the South Pacific."

Still no response. But she was listening. He could see the way her fingers had stilled, her head tilted by a fraction.

"Of course," he continued, as if he hadn't noticed, "there's the argument that limiting expansion protects native interests. Others argue it hampers national progress. I can't decide which argument I find more disingenuous."

A long pause.

Then she cleared her throat. "It's not about native interests. Not truly. It's about optics. Appearing benevolent."

He smiled slowly. "Indeed?"

She turned to him fully now, eyes sharp. "The Company never hesitates when it comes to seizing control of foreign assets, nor do the Crown's ministers. But the moment there's criticism abroad, suddenly it becomes a matter of ethics. It's hypocrisy."

Nicholas let out a quiet breath of satisfaction. "And here I was afraid you'd remain silent the entire ride."

Her head snapped to face forward again. "I *should* remain silent. You've manipulated the situation. You do not care about my opinion."

"On the contrary, yes, I do. Not to mention that I invited you for a pleasant turn in the park."

"After conspiring with my father."

"Who cornered me as thoroughly as he did you."

"Hardly." She rolled her eyes.

Nicholas gave her a sidelong glance. "You think I enjoy being summoned by dukes like an errand boy?"

She snorted—actually snorted—and he considered that a victory of the highest order.

"Don't misunderstand," he added more softly. "I meant what I told him. I am interested."

That caught her attention. She blinked once, eyes narrowing. "Interested. In marrying me?"

"In courting you," he said, voice light. "One should never skip the middle steps. That's where all the best bits are."

"Courtship implies an eventual end."

"Does it?" He smiled again, and this time it wasn't teasing. "Then I suppose I'd best make the middle last. And the last, perhaps the middle?"

For the first time since she'd stepped into the curricle, she seemed at a loss. She turned away, her gaze tracking a family on foot with two small children tossing bread to ducks.

Nicholas didn't press. He kept the horses steady, allowing the quiet to bloom again.

After a long moment, Lady Beatrix spoke. "What do you mean by that?"

"I respectfully decline to answer."

She eyed him warily. "Fine then. Answer this. Why do you want to court me? Knowing I am opposed to it."

Ah. Now they were getting somewhere.

He considered the question carefully. She would never accept a pat answer. No, this called for truth. It was a dangerous moment, to be honest, but anything less would insult her. "Because you're the most exceptional young woman in all of England."

She turned her head toward him again, her gaze sharpening as if she found his words both fascinating and deeply suspect.

He quickly realized…waiting had served him well in Parliament. Here, it would ruin him.

"You don't flatter," he swiftly continued. "You don't dissemble. You don't perform for Society the way the others do. When you speak, I know it's real. And very few things in my life are. I am a politician, after all."

She stared at him, something uncertain flickering in her eyes.

He offered her a small smile. "Also, I find you maddeningly beautiful. But I assumed it was too soon to say so."

Lady Beatrix looked away again, with a slight jerk of her head. She lifted her chin, but her scowl had not faded.

This time he remained silent. Pressing now would tip her from consideration into retreat.

They turned the corner near the lake, the wind lifting the edge of her bonnet ribbon, stirring a few stray strands of golden hair.

She smoothed her gloves but didn't speak.

Nicholas didn't mind.

He had all the time in the world. That had merely been his opening volley.

CHAPTER TEN

The curricle slowed.

Bea felt it before she registered it. Archer was easing the bays into a graceful, measured trot as he turned them off the fashionable path and down a narrower lane running beside the water. Taller willows shaded this part of the park, their branches trailing like whispered secrets along the water. The main carriages were several lengths behind them now, and the noisy crowd thinned to only a handful of strollers.

A more private stretch.

He was up to something.

Archer drew the horses to a stop with practiced ease. The bays tossed their heads once before settling.

He hopped down lightly—far more nimbly than a man of his height had any right to—and came around to her side.

"Allow me," he said.

No doubt it was the same agreeable tone he used when arguing in the House of Lords, right before presenting a devastating counterpoint.

Before Bea could object, his hands went to her waist.

Warm, steady, scandalously confident hands.

She inhaled sharply. Not because of the impropriety—though there was that—but because of *him*, his scent. Clean starch, warm skin, and something crisp and masculine beneath it all, like cedarwood warmed by sunlight. It tightened something low in her stomach.

He lifted her down as though she weighed no more than a pocket handkerchief.

Her feet touched the ground, and she stepped back at once, though it did nothing to steady her pulse. "You ought not to touch me without warning."

Archer's eyes—dark, knowing—danced. "My apologies. Next time I'll call out a full set of instructions."

She recognized the jest for what it was—an olive branch —and declined to take it. "See that you do."

His smile was slow and devastating. Then he offered his arm.

She accepted because refusing would have looked petulant. And because the ground was uneven. And because she was absolutely *not* rattled by the width of his shoulders or the strength beneath his coat.

Not in the least.

They began walking along the edge of the lake, the water glinting pale silver where sunlight met ripples.

She cleared her throat. "I hope you don't think that you can ruin me in order to force me to marry you."

Archer blinked, his surprise convincing enough to give her pause. "Ruin you? Whyever would I do that? Your father would call me out at first light."

"Then why are we here…alone?"

Archer slowed but did not stop walking. "Because I was curious."

She shot him a look. "About what?"

"About why you argue the way you do."

That made her pause. "I argue perfectly well."

"You do," he agreed easily. "But you don't repeat what others say. You build from first principles. It's uncommon."

She narrowed her eyes. "You're fishing."

"I'm listening," he corrected. "Tell me, when others insist the shipping reform bill will harm small ports, are you disputing the point...or the assumptions behind the argument?"

The question landed like a thrown gauntlet.

Bea stared at him. No man had ever asked her that—not as a challenge, not as a trap, but as though her reasoning might actually matter.

"The assumptions," she said at once. "The bill is sound. It's careful. It's necessary. What will hurt small ports is Parliament dismissing it without grasping what it's meant to fix."

Archer's expression changed—not smug, not dismissive, but intent.

"So the danger isn't the legislation."

"It's ignorance," she said flatly. "And indifference."

His mouth curved, slow and genuine. "Then the bill isn't the problem."

"It's the solution," she finished. "If they'd only bother to read it."

"I see."

She narrowed her eyes to absolute slits. "Why did we need to be alone for you to ask me that?"

He smiled faintly. "Because I want to hear what you actually think, not the version you might perform in public."

She opened her mouth—intent upon telling him that she didn't *perform* for anyone—but he didn't allow her the chance. "No need to say it." He lifted a hand. "Shall we begin to get to know each other with something simple? Perhaps my understanding of what you do not like about me?"

Bea flicked her gaze toward him, her wariness intact, but

now threaded with curiosity. She simply couldn't resist. "Oh? Do tell."

"It is no secret to me, my lady," he replied, "that you are not a Tory."

Her brows shot up, suspicion and amusement no doubt warring on her face. "I was not aware that ladies were *allowed* to have political affiliations."

"Allowed?" His low laugh curled warm along her spine. "We both know you've never given a toss about what you're allowed to do."

Bea felt the words settle somewhere they had no right to reach, loosening something she had kept carefully bound. No one had ever said it before, this thing about her, this part she normally kept tightly tucked behind wit and sarcasm and careful propriety, albeit with the occasional outburst toward men as idiotic as Lord Hargrave.

To have Nicholas Archer see it, name it, as though it were the most obvious truth in the world...

Well. It was...unsettling. Off-putting. And entirely too perceptive of him.

She lifted her chin. "If you insist on ascribing rebellious motives to me—"

"I am merely observing," he said smoothly. "You are not governed by fashion or flattery. You form your own conclusions. You speak them. Loudly. And often to someone who is paying attention."

She wasn't certain whether to be insulted or flattered.

"You think I'm a Tory," he continued. "And that is an unpardonable offense."

She whipped her head toward him. "Are you not a Tory?"

He did not answer at once. Instead, his gaze drifted to the water beside them, where the Serpentine lay smooth and bright, sunlight skating across its surface.

"I am," he said at last, "a man who has learned that some truths are best revealed selectively."

Her lips curved, unimpressed. "That was not an answer."

"No," he agreed mildly. "It was caution."

She gave a quiet, derisive huff. "How very political of you."

"Practical," he corrected. "Your father is a formidable man with formidable convictions. I admire him greatly." A pause —carefully placed. "I also prefer that he continue to admire me."

That earned him a sharp look. "So, you *are* a Tory."

"I am…often found in their company," he said lightly.

"That is not the same thing."

A corner of his mouth lifted. "You're right."

She folded her arms. "You're evasive."

They slowed without quite stopping, the gravel path crunching beneath their steps. He turned toward her fully then, close enough that the sleeve of his coat brushed her shoulder…so lightly it might have been an accident.

She noticed the contact. Of course she did. But she did not step away. He would not intimidate her.

He inclined his head. "Evasive? Ah. Another thing you don't like about me. Very well. Let us continue to list my sins since we've begun so neatly." One finger lifted. "I choose nuance where you admire certainty." Another. "I associate with men whose politics offend you…even though your own father is one of them." Then his hand fell, still not quite touching her arm but close enough that she could feel the warmth of him through the thin wool of her pelisse. "And perhaps my greatest sin of all…"

He paused. Deliberately. The space between them felt suddenly charged, taut as a drawn bow.

"I possess influence in Parliament," he said quietly. "Power." His eyes did not leave hers. "Power you—by virtue of your sex—are barred from wielding, no matter how capable you might be."

Her breath stuttered, traitorous and unwelcome.

Then she laughed once, sharply. "You think *that* is why I dislike you?"

"I think," he said, his voice low and intimate despite the open park around them, "it would be reason enough to make you resent me."

She stepped closer, just enough that her skirts brushed his boots, just enough that his knuckles hovered beside her sleeve, so near she was acutely aware of his restraint.

"You mistake me, my lord," she said coolly. "I do not resent power." Her smile was thin. "I resent men who presume I am unable to wield it."

Something flickered across his face then—approval, unmistakable and decidedly not safe.

"Ah," he murmured. "Then I stand corrected."

For a moment, neither of them moved. The water glinted. A breeze tugged at her bonnet ribbon. His hand remained at her side, close enough to feel, not close enough to claim.

Bea had the unsettling sense that he was no longer sparring for advantage but testing how much distance she would allow him to close.

He had relented, even admitted to being incorrect. That was something. But was this only more calculation on his part? More political maneuvering?

Before she could choose her next words, he continued more gently, "Which brings me to a second point. Perhaps we should continue to further our acquaintance with what we have in common."

"Ha." She arched a brow. "*Do* we have anything in common?"

"Well." He waited a beat, clearly savoring her silence before continuing. "We are both devoted to our beliefs. We both admire honesty. And we both have a healthy aversion to Lord Hargrave."

"Most of Society does," Bea replied, flicking an imaginary speck from her glove.

"Then we are practically unified," he said solemnly. "A foundation upon which countless agreements may be built."

"Doubtful," she muttered.

"*Hm*. Very well. Another approach then." He cleared his throat with exaggerated importance. "A most serious question."

Bea rolled her eyes. "Must you?"

"Yes. It is essential." He paused, straightened his back, and grabbed his lapel with his free hand. "Do you find me appealing? Physically, I mean."

She tripped. Actually tripped—only a fraction, but it was enough. His arm tightened, steadying her.

"Lord Vanover," she nearly choked.

"First, we've known each other for years. I think it would be appropriate for us to call one another by our Christian names."

She narrowed her eyes at him again. "And second?"

"I'm still waiting for an answer. Am I physically attractive to you?"

She huffed a breath. "Arrogant," she murmured.

"What?" he said, his tone far too innocent. "A man likes to know."

She blinked at him. "Fishing for compliments?"

"Not at all." His tone dropped, just slightly. "We've established you dislike the *situation*. Perhaps my beliefs. But me?" He tilted his head. "The man?" He waited a beat. "Am I truly so objectionable?"

She nearly snorted. Then she lifted her chin again. "Oh, come now. You must know you're terribly handsome." Her eyes flared wide and then, "I mean—"

His grin was unrepentant. "No. No. You already said it. You cannot take it back."

She nearly growled at him. What in the world had made her say such a thing? She'd given him precisely the sort of praise a man like him should never be trusted with. A grave mistake.

Archer stopped walking. Slowly, very slowly, he turned toward her. For a moment, he said nothing. Then softly, sincerely, "Terribly handsome, eh?"

Warmth rose traitorously along Bea's cheeks. If only one could recall spoken words as neatly as one recorked a wine bottle.

He flicked the brim of his hat, a cocky smile lighting his features. "I have been called many things in my life, Lady Beatrix. Handsome, upon occasion. But I do not think I have ever been quite so glad to hear it as I am when it comes from your lips."

Her breath stilled.

Oh no. She'd handed him a weapon to use against her.

Not to mention he was standing too close—far too close—and she became acutely aware of the way his coat fit across his broad chest, the subtle movement of his throat when he swallowed, the faint warmth radiating from him in the cool breeze. And worse—his mouth.

She should not be staring at his mouth.

His lips curved, not in a smirk, but something quieter. Warmer. Much more dangerous.

"Bea," he murmured.

Her name in his voice—not clipped, not sparring, but almost tender—sent a jolt through her. And he'd used the name she preferred. Beatrix was far too formal, too pompous, too… Wait. How did he know she preferred that name? Was it another thing he'd observed about her, just like her political bent?

Archer reached as though to brush a loose strand of hair at her temple. His fingers grazed her cheek, featherlight. Without thought, she leaned infinitesimally closer.

His gaze dropped to her mouth.

For one dizzying heartbeat, she wondered whether he would kiss her…and whether she *wanted* him to.

Which was absurd.

Completely, utterly absurd.

She drew back so quickly she nearly stumbled. "We… should continue walking."

"Should we?" he asked, clearly amused but not pressing.

"Yes," she said coolly, gathering the remains of her dignity. "We absolutely should."

They resumed their slow pace, though her pulse had not resumed anything resembling normalcy.

She stared ahead with forced interest at a cluster of swans drifting near the far bank.

Anything to keep from thinking about Nicholas's mouth. Or the warmth of his hands. Or the spark low in her belly that she refused outright to acknowledge. Or the fact that she was now thinking of him as Nicholas in her head.

Focus, she told herself sternly. There were political gains to be made. Secrets to overhear. Foes to confuse. And Nicholas—with his maddening charm and dangerously appealing shoulders—might very well be the key to all of it.

But heavens, she needed to stop thinking about how his coat fit or how his eyes softened when he looked at her.

She needed to think about strategy.

Not his lips. Not his hands. Not his voice saying her name.

Strategy.

She drew a steadying breath. *Say something, Bea. Anything!*

"What exactly," she blurted, "is the meaning of peonies?"

His brows drew together. "Peonies?"

"Yes," she said crisply. "A fortnight ago…you sent me a

bouquet of peonies. What sort of message are peonies meant to convey?"

A beat. Then, very quietly but with that maddening confidence, he said, "I thought it would be obvious. Unexpected. Beautiful. Riotous. Unconventional." His gaze slid to hers. "Much like their intended recipient."

Her breath caught—an unforgivable reaction—and she looked ahead, schooling her expression. "Oh," was all she could mutter.

CHAPTER ELEVEN

Bea was trying very hard *not* to think about what Nicholas had said to her in the park yesterday.

He had meant to provoke her. That much was certain.

Maddeningly beautiful?

Ridiculous.

Though it was equally ridiculous that she had called him terribly handsome. Out loud!

She adjusted her gloves for the third time in as many minutes and ignored the fact that her palms were the slightest bit damp.

The Countess of Everly's ballroom sparkled with candle-light, music, and the scent of far too many roses. The Season was well underway, the crowd glossy and chattering, the air thick with perfume and ambition.

She had a revolt to plan. And yet all she could think about was *him*.

Nicholas stood beside the refreshment table, speaking to someone's great-aunt, of all things, with that amiable smile and those unreasonably broad shoulders.

Maddeningly beautiful. Unexpected. Beautiful. Riotous. Unconventional.

Why had he said all those words? It didn't make sense. Men like him didn't court women like her and say *that*. They said predictable, flowery things and recited poetry and a bunch of nonsense. Things that would get on her very last nerve.

And yet, when she'd finally met his eyes across the room earlier, his expression hadn't wavered. It had warmed.

It had *lingered*.

"Lady Beatrix."

The voice, deep and amused, came from just behind her.

It was him. Of course it was. He was obliged to use her title in public.

She turned slowly, chin tilted at a deliberate angle. "Lord Vanover." She would call him that (to his face at least) until the day she died. Anything else was far too intimate.

He inclined his head. "May I claim this dance?"

"Are you in danger of running out of willing partners?" she asked with faint amusement.

"Not at all," he said, offering his arm. "But I find I've no interest in the willing ones."

She glanced over to see her father glaring at her from across the room. Under his watchful eye, she had no choice but to place her hand on Nicholas's sleeve. The touch was scandalously warm through her gloves.

The music began anew—something slow, sweeping—and Nicholas guided her onto the floor with practiced ease. They fit together too well. She hated that she noticed it, which just made her even more annoyed.

"You're scowling," he murmured as they turned.

"I'm concentrating."

His smile was serene. "On how not to enjoy yourself?"

"On how to keep my slippers from sliding. This floor is far too polished."

"Then allow me to distract you properly," he murmured. "You mentioned Manchester once. You think unrest there will spread?"

She blinked. "When did I mention Manchester?"

He narrowed his eyes. "I suppose it's been a few months ago now. At dinner. At Lord Henson's house."

Her brow furrowed. "You remember that?"

"I remember everything you say," he replied, unembarrassed. "Do you believe Parliament is underestimating the unrest?"

She hesitated, then exhaled. "They aren't underestimating it. They're dismissing it. That's far worse."

"Why?"

The single word—quiet, intent—undid her.

Bea forgot the room. Forgot the music. "Because dismissal breeds desperation. And desperation always finds a voice."

Nicholas watched her with undisguised fascination. "You should be in the House," he said.

Her laugh came sharp and humorless. "I would be invisible there."

"No," he said firmly now. "You would be impossible to ignore."

The thought hit her harder than his earlier compliments.

He wasn't flattering her.

He was *evaluating* her.

It was too much. She didn't trust it. "What are you aiming at?"

His brows shot up. "Am I that obvious?"

Her brows drew together. "Yes."

"Then I confess I'm hoping you'll agree to accompany me

to the veranda," he replied with a sly smile. "Though that has nothing to do with my interest in your thoughts on Manchester. But I'd happily agree to continue the conversation on the veranda, seeing as how this dance is about to end."

She didn't want to smile. She *refused* to smile. But her mouth betrayed her. "You hope in vain."

Another slow grin spread across his face. "So quick with the refusals."

She lifted her nose in the air. "You're not the only man who's asked me to meet him on the veranda tonight."

"Perhaps," he replied. "But I may be the only one who asks *twice*."

She arched a brow. "Then consider this my second refusal."

His grin deepened. They danced without speaking for a few moments, and Bea became acutely aware of the way his hand settled at her waist—confident, careful. The way his gaze didn't stray. The way he watched her expectantly, as if he couldn't wait to hear what she would say next.

She glanced over at her parents once more. They were both nodding and smiling at her. It was enough to make her want to cast up her accounts.

When the music ended, Nicholas released her hand and bowed. "Thank you for the dance, Lady Beatrix."

She curtsied, her spine so straight it could have sliced glass. "Lord Vanover."

BEA HAD no earthly idea what she was doing outside.

The moon was far too smug tonight.

She leaned against the stone balustrade, breathing in the night air, half-convinced she'd lost her mind. She should have gone home. She should have danced with Viscount

Merton twice to start rumors, accepted that glass of champagne from Lady Alderidge to settle her nerves, and left without a second thought to Nicholas Archer.

Instead, she had excused herself to the retiring room, walked in the wrong direction on purpose, and now found herself in the shadows of the east-facing veranda like a ninny waiting to be compromised.

Brilliant.

To make matters worse, Georgie and Poppy weren't here. Georgie was traveling with her new husband, and Poppy probably hadn't been invited. With her mother's reputation, Poppy was often left off a guest list.

Bea turned toward the rose bushes, willing her cheeks to cool. She told herself she was here as a test. Did Nicholas truly care about her thoughts on politics, or was he merely asking her about Manchester to get her to agree to meet him? She supposed she'd soon find out.

"There you are."

She spun around.

Nicholas stepped out of the doorway, his emerald-green coat open, hair just slightly tousled by the breeze. He was smiling.

"I confess," he said, "I half thought you wouldn't come."

Her chin lifted. "And yet here you are. Why?"

"Hope," he said simply, "is a powerful thing."

That earned him a reluctant, entirely unwilling smile.

Nicholas approached slowly, hands behind his back like a man with no particular agenda, which was surely untrue.

"I must admit," he said lightly, "I'm flattered."

"By what?"

"That I am, apparently, impossible to resist."

"Oh, I *am* resisting you," she said crisply.

His smile was smug. "You're doing it from a moonlit veranda, alone, with me."

Bea glared at him. "You really are insufferable."

"So I've been told." He took another step closer, not touching her but near enough that her pulse did something deeply unhelpful. It jumped. "So...about Manchester. You said—"

"Wait. I don't want to talk about politics. I have a question for you this time."

He arched a brow. "By all means."

She turned to face the garden again. "You said something yesterday. In the curricle."

"Only one thing?" he drawled.

She spared him a quick look. "You said the middle should come last. And the last should come in the middle."

"I did." He nodded.

"What did you mean?"

He was suddenly very near, his voice a dark, amused murmur. "I fear I'd scandalize you if I told you."

She turned her head, one brow arching. "You vastly over-estimate my fragility."

He exhaled a slow, pleased breath.

Then his voice dropped into something wicked and velvet-smooth. "Very well. What if I told you I have every intention of seducing you?"

CHAPTER TWELVE

For one heartbeat—two—Nicholas waited.

He was prepared for the slap. Half expected it.

Not because she was hysterical—Beatrix Winslow would sooner die than be accused of hysteria—but because she was fire. All flint and spark and blistering wit, and not for the first time, he had just laid a match directly beside the fuse.

But she didn't slap him.

She didn't flinch. She didn't gasp. She didn't retreat like a maiden whose sensibilities had been offended.

No...she fixed him with a slow, assessing stare. A warrior's stare. A tactician's. It sent a curl of heat through his blood.

"If I told my father what you just said," she replied at last, cool as winter glass, "he'd never speak to you again."

Nicholas kept every line of his face smooth. "Would he? Or would he decide you were embellishing?"

Her eyes narrowed at that.

She looked him up and down with deliberate irritation, which amused him far more than it should have.

"Is threatening to accuse me of exaggeration your idea of seduction?" she demanded.

"No," he said calmly. "But I'm not worried."

"Why's that?"

"Because I'm entirely certain you won't tell your father what I said."

Her chin lifted, proud and defiant. "How can you be so sure?"

Because you're not repelled, he thought. *Because your pulse just leapt. Because you're fighting your own curiosity harder than you're fighting me.*

He didn't say that, of course. Instead, he stepped closer. Just enough to test her. Not touching. Not yet. A whisper of distance, barely there, yet unmistakable.

He saw the way her breath hitched. Saw the faint tremor at her throat. Saw the way she did *not* retreat.

"Because," he murmured, "you're not a telltale."

She blinked. And then she laughed.

A real laugh. Warm, bright, unguarded. Honest in a way Society would never coax from her.

He let himself enjoy it. Just for a moment.

"No," she said, recovering with that wicked spark in her eye that he was beginning to crave. "No, I'm not."

Nicholas allowed himself a small smile. Not triumphant —he didn't dare that yet, not with her—but appreciative. Admiring. Because God, she was magnificent when she laughed instead of slicing him apart.

"And," he added, his voice dipping lower, smoother, "because you can handle yourself."

She sobered, though her eyes still gleamed. "You think I wouldn't tell my father when a man says something I don't like?"

"I think," he replied, "you're perfectly capable of deciding when it's worth telling. And when it's not."

Truth. Absolute truth. He'd known it for years. He'd watched her—quietly, from the edges of rooms, the backs of ballrooms, the shadowed corners where one could observe without being observed in turn.

And it struck him again with sudden clarity. She had no idea how well he knew her.

What he'd noticed. What he'd remembered.

There was a beat of silence. A soft breeze tugged at a loose curl near her cheek. She looked...unsettled. Not panicked. Not offended. Just pulled inward, as though weighing his words more heavily than she meant to.

A good sign.

"You're right," she said finally, her voice low and even.

Nicholas's pulse kicked. It was time to press...just a bit further. "And..." He paused for effect. "I don't believe that you didn't like it." He stepped even closer. Still not touching, but close enough that he felt her breath hitch. It was faint, but he caught it. She tried to mask it, but he'd been watching her reactions too long not to notice.

"Oh," she murmured, her voice dropping to a low purr.

That landed. God, it landed beautifully.

Her posture changed.

Not much, a shift of her shoulders, a tightening of her fingers at her side, but he saw it. Felt it.

He leaned in. Slowly. Deliberately. He angled his mouth toward her ear with all the care of a man navigating a minefield. "And I guarantee you *will* like it."

Her pulse fluttered at her throat. A tremor—small, exquisite—ran through her. She thought he wouldn't notice. She was wrong.

She smelled faintly of rosewater and the salt of warm skin, hinting at a heat that had nothing to do with the evening.

She was trying so very hard not to be affected.

He smiled inwardly.

He was winning.

And he knew the exact moment she realized it—her breath caught, her lashes lowered, and for a brief, devastating moment, she swayed imperceptibly toward him. And the fact that he'd apparently rendered her speechless was quite a feat, considering.

He exhaled a barely there breath along the curve of her jaw and felt her shiver.

A thrill went through him—raw, intoxicating.

He'd never been more grateful for his height, his shoulders, his looks, his voice—the tools he normally wielded with political precision. But here, with her, they mattered differently. Dangerously. Deliciously.

"Indeed, I'm counting on the fact," he whispered, velvet-dark, "that you're going to like every single second of it."

She exhaled, shallow, shaky, betraying far more than she intended.

Nicholas went still.

He'd been playing a dangerous game since the moment he decided to pursue her. A woman who claimed to dislike him. A woman who hid her true nature behind barbs and wit and stubborn walls.

But she wasn't pushing him away. She wasn't protesting. She wasn't running.

And in her eyes—in the flicker she tried so hard to suppress—he saw something he'd never expected. Not this soon, at least.

Want.

Real, unmistakable want.

He was winning.

And God help him, he'd never wanted victory more.

CHAPTER THIRTEEN

Bea's heart pounded so loudly she could hardly think. Nicholas Archer stood close enough to disrupt her breathing.

Every breath felt too shallow. Every flutter beneath her ribs far too noticeable. And every nerve she possessed seemed suddenly alive in his presence.

"Now you're being rude," she informed him, lifting her chin in what she prayed resembled dignity.

"Oh?" he said, leaning just the slightest bit closer, in a way that made her tilt her head back to keep his gaze in view. "How so?"

Her mouth flattened into a razor-thin line. "If you think for even one moment that I am some sort of harlot who will—"

He raised both hands, palms out, stopping her mid-sentence with an ease that made her want to bite him.

"On the contrary," he said softly. "I think nothing of the sort."

And his voice—devil take the man—lost its teasing edge

and warmed into something unexpectedly sincere. "In fact, I have the utmost respect for you."

She crossed her arms tightly to hide the faint, mortifying tremor in her fingers. Her body felt too warm, too aware, too everything.

"If you respected me," she said sharply, "you wouldn't think I could be so easily seduced."

His brow arched, slow, amused, wicked. "I never said I thought it would be easy."

Her breath hitched traitorously. Which his keen eyes caught instantly. Of course they did. He noticed everything. Every twitch. Every swallow. Every unguarded reaction she prayed he had missed.

He looked entirely too pleased by all of it, moonlight catching in his dark hair, his lips curving in that maddening half-smile that made her stomach misbehave like an unruly child.

"And here I thought you wanted to marry me," she managed.

"I do," he drawled, rich and smooth as melted chocolate poured over an ice.

A shiver trailed down her spine at the sound. Her knees wobbled. Absolutely wobbled. *Good heavens. Pull yourself together, Bea.*

"You are not making any sense," she said, though her voice came out thinner than she meant. "One does not seduce one's future wife."

Nicholas's smile deepened, slow and devastating, the sort designed to make a woman's knees consider additional wobbliness. "According to whom?"

Her mind produced an entire chorus of scandalized authorities: *My mother. All mothers. Every etiquette book ever written. Society. The Archbishop—*

But what came out instead was an embarrassingly strangled, "Why…why would one try to seduce one's future wife?"

He took one more deliberate step closer.

Just one.

But it was enough for her to feel the heat of his body. Enough to make her lips part in a breath she could not disguise. Enough to make her wonder—furiously—why her pulse responded to him so readily.

"One does what one must…" he said quietly. "Especially when one's future wife seems determined to resist her own inclinations."

Her chest tightened.

Because there it was again, that quiet, unnerving truth he wielded as though he'd been reading her for years. Perhaps he had.

That terrifying thought struck her with more force than his nearness.

How was it that a man she had barely spared polite attention to all these years could now look at her and see…everything? Her bravado. Her defiance. Her hunger for something more than the life laid out for her. Her unanswered wants.

Her breath trembled. She prayed he hadn't noticed.

He did.

Of course he did.

"I believe I've had quite enough fresh air," she said too quickly, stepping back just enough to reclaim the space his body had warmed. Her voice held a steadiness her pulse violently contradicted.

Nicholas only nodded, maddeningly composed. "Of course. Shall I see you back inside?"

"No," she blurted, wincing internally at how shaken she sounded. "I can manage."

He inclined his head with maddening calm, neither smug nor apologetic. "As you wish."

She turned, but the motion felt clumsy, rushed, as though the ground beneath her had become unnervingly unreliable.

He remained where he was—silent, shadowed, far too handsome in the moonlight—as she strode back toward the house.

Don't look back. *Do not look back.*

She did not look.

But she felt him. Oh, she felt him, his gaze, steady and sure, trailing her with unnerving awareness, as though he knew precisely how rattled she was. As though he knew he had unmoored her.

She slipped through the open doors into a corridor, heat rushing to her cheeks despite the cool air inside. Her breath came quicker than decorum allowed. She pressed a hand to her stomach, willing her wildly disobedient body to calm down.

She was just about to step into the ballroom once again when her mother found her just outside the doors.

"There you are," the duchess said, frowning. "The carriage is ready."

Bea nodded, dazed, and let herself be guided toward the foyer like a woman walking through a dream she was not entirely certain she wanted to wake from.

Because as she moved toward the exit, she could still feel Nicholas's nearness clinging to her skin—warm, intense, knowing.

And the most alarming part of all was that he seemed to understand her—truly understand her—more than anyone ever had. More than her mother. Certainly more than her father.

And that, she thought, as she stepped into the night air once again, was far more dangerous than seduction.

Far more dangerous indeed.

~

THE INSIDE of the coach was quiet, too quiet, her mother humming a tuneless little melody beside her, her father riffling through papers by the faint lamplight as though nothing in the world were amiss.

Bea sat between them, rigid as a pressed leaf, her gloves clenched in her lap so tightly her fingers ached.

She should say something. She should tell them. Tell her father that Nicholas had whispered a promise no gentleman should ever speak to a lady of her standing. That he'd leaned in as though she were a secret he meant to taste. That he'd said it with confidence, dangerous, deliberate confidence. Father would call off their courtship immediately. He would have to.

But another thought quickly followed on the heels of the first. *Would* he call it off? Or was Nicholas correct? Would Father accuse Bea of lying to escape the courtship she hadn't wanted to begin with?

It was a sobering thought. But she couldn't bring herself to be angry about it.

All she could think about was how Nicholas looked at her…and asked her questions…and waited for her answers. As if he truly cared.

Her throat tightened.

She should never speak to Nicholas again. She should despise him. She should have slapped him—should have *wanted* to slap him at least.

And yet.

The memory of his breath against her jaw still lingered, impossible to shake. The sound of his voice—dark, wicked, and scandalously certain—still echoed through her mind.

She stared out the coach's window as the moonlit buildings marched past, jaw locked in a futile attempt at composure.

Nicholas had been right about her.

She wasn't the sort to run to her father when something unsettled her. She never had been. She did not flinch, or swoon, or call for assistance. She did not retreat behind her mother's skirts or seek protection like a frightened hare.

She handled things herself. She made her own decisions. She fought her own battles.

Nicholas knew that.

He had named it—named *her*—in a way that made her ribcage feel too small.

And that, she realized grimly, was exactly what he was counting on.

Her mouth twisted, though her pulse thudded traitorously on.

He thought she'd melt. Thought her curiosity, her breath hitching, her utterly treacherous reaction would mean something as foolish as surrender.

He thought he could seduce her.

Her. Beatrix Winslow. The one debutante in London who prided herself on seeing through men like him.

She squeezed her hands into fists. Her fingers ached under the pressure of her grip.

Well. Nicholas had better think again.

Because, yes, he had rattled her. Yes, her body had reacted to his words. Yes, his nearness had made her dizzy, and his certainty had shaken something at her core she didn't want to name.

But that did not mean he had won.

She dragged her gaze away from the window, forcing her breath into something resembling normalcy.

Across the coach, her father turned a page, oblivious. Her mother hummed on, equally oblivious.

They had not noticed a thing. Not her trembling hands. Not her flushed cheeks. Not the storm still roaring in her chest.

Perhaps that was the most peculiar part of all. Nicholas Archer, with his wicked mouth and knowing eyes, had seen more of her in ten minutes of moonlight than her parents had noticed in her entire life.

Bea closed her eyes for one steadying, infuriated moment.

It didn't matter. She would not be seduced. She would not be undone. She would be ready next time.

Nicholas thought he understood her? Thought he could seduce her? Well, let him try again. She would make certain he regretted it.

CHAPTER FOURTEEN

Bea found the entire thing supremely ironic.

Her father, who would have been struck speech-less with outrage had he heard even half of what Nicholas had murmured into her ear last night, had insisted she accompany the man on a walk.

Alone. Through the gardens behind their town house.

Because according to her father, Nicholas was a *respectable suitor.*

If only Father knew how thoroughly *unrespectable* Nicholas's imagination had proven itself to be. She'd thought long and hard about it last night as she tossed and turned in her bed, unable to sleep. Nicholas had been trying to rattle her. That was all. He wanted to see how prudish she was. How easily he could affect her. And she'd played right into his hands. Today, she had every intention of giving him no quarter.

In fact, she had a new strategy. A man like Nicholas desired power...and control. And what was the opposite of wielding power? Being mocked, of course. Which was precisely how she intended to handle him today.

Bea stepped through the garden gate, letting it fall shut behind her with a faint clink, and found Nicholas already waiting near the trellised archway at the path's edge. The morning sunlight caught on his dark hair, but his powder-blue coat was cut as perfectly as ever.

He bowed slightly. "Lady Beatrix."

"My lord," she returned, sweeping past him. "Shall we walk and pretend my father didn't just order me to be alone with a man he'd hang by his neck if he had the faintest idea what that man whispered last night?"

Nicholas chuckled as he fell into step beside her. "I already know you didn't tell him."

"Oh, do you?" she asked sweetly.

"Yes," he replied with a grin. "Or he'd already have called me out. Seems I was right about you all along."

"Right about what, precisely? My intelligence? My restraint? Or my exceedingly poor judgment in allowing you within ten paces of me last night?"

They walked along the pebbled path between neatly clipped hedges, their steps silent but for the gentle crunch of gravel and the occasional chirp of a bird overhead. The scent of lilies lingered in the air.

"You're quiet this morning," he said after a moment.

"I'm reflecting on how not to be seduced."

"Ah. A worthy intellectual pursuit."

"Indeed. So far, I'm finding it remarkably easy." She gave him a tight smile.

He pressed a hand to his heart. "Cruel."

She shrugged.

They reached a moss-covered bench, but she ignored it, veering down the side path that led toward the stone garden wall and the slightly overgrown area her mother and the gardener never quite managed to care about.

Nicholas followed, naturally.

"Perhaps," she said, casting a glance over her shoulder, "you're not very good at this seduction business."

His smile didn't slip. "Is that so?"

"Well." She stopped by the low wall, turning toward him with one brow raised. "Would you prefer I simply leaned back here...like this"—she pressed herself lightly against the cool stone—"and waited for you to kiss me?"

He stopped short. His eyes locked on hers. "That's not funny," he said softly.

"Isn't it?" she asked, voice bright and teasing.

"No," he said. "Because if you keep doing that, I *will* kiss you."

She laughed lightly, brushing her fingers along the edge of the wall. "You're not terribly convincing. I still don't feel seduced."

"Ah," he said, straightening. "Now that hurts."

"Perhaps you should try harder."

He tilted his head, his smile sly. "Or perhaps I'll try something else."

With no warning, he stepped closer, close enough that his body blocked the sun.

But just as quickly, he turned away.

"Do you know," he said lightly, "I think your mother replanted that hydrangea bed near the hedge. The blue variety. They do best in shade."

Bea blinked. "What are you—?"

But he kept walking, gesturing casually at the greenery like a man far more interested in horticulture than she guessed him to be.

She frowned and followed. "You changed the subject."

"Did I?"

"Quite obviously."

"Ah." He glanced back over his shoulder. "Seduction is all in the timing."

She snorted. "That's convenient."

But the path curved, and before she realized it, they'd reached the back corner of the garden—the part screened by tall hedges, shaded by an ancient oak, and bordered by that same weather-worn stone wall.

Nicholas stopped, turned, and in a single unhurried motion, backed her against the wall.

The air changed.

He braced one hand beside her head, the other settling lightly at her waist, and leaned in so slowly she could feel her heartbeat stutter before he even touched her.

His mouth hovered near her ear, his voice deep and smooth. "How is this?"

Her breath caught.

He hadn't touched her skin.

Not yet.

But she felt the promise of it like a tremor.

"How do you do that?" she asked, her voice barely audible. "How do you make everything feel so...?"

"Effortless?" he offered.

"Disorienting."

He smiled. "It's a gift."

She met his gaze, refusing to acknowledge the flutter in her chest.

Because she had reached another conclusion sometime near dawn. He was bluffing. Nicholas might enjoy proximity and implication, but he would not risk his relationship with her father by doing anything truly scandalous.

Which meant this—whatever *this* was—had limits.

And she was about to find them.

She forced herself to meet his gaze. "If I were to allow you to seduce me. What," she said, her voice lower, rougher, "would you do next?"

Nicholas didn't move, just looked down at her with slow-burning intent.

"Oh," he said, mischief dancing in his dark eyes, "I would begin with your neck."

He raised his hand, one fingertip tracing the curve of her neck in an impossibly soft, maddening line.

"Right here," he murmured. "Where the skin is softest. Where your pulse flutters."

Bea's breath caught. She swallowed hard. Hmm. His touch felt quite real…for a bluff.

"And then?" she asked, her voice barely audible. It was a stand-off now. Only a matter of time to see who would blink first.

"Then," he said, "I would touch your bottom lip." His hand moved, slow and deliberate, until his thumb brushed the soft swell of her lip. "Ever so gently. To be certain it's ready for my kiss."

Her lips parted. Her pulse thundered.

Oh, he was good. She'd give him that.

"And then?" she whispered.

Nicholas smiled, no longer teasing, but heated and intense.

"And then," he said, "I'd stop talking."

The pause stretched, and in it, she understood her mistake. Bluffing men hesitated. Nicholas Archer did not.

He kissed her.

Hard.

Hot.

Hungry.

For one traitorous heartbeat, she kissed him back—because her body was not loyal, because his mouth was not fair, because the world narrowed to heat and pressure and the sharp, intoxicating shock of being wanted.

And then she remembered herself.

Bea made a sound that was half gasp, half curse, and shoved a hand flat against his chest.

Nicholas froze—actually froze—as if the boundary in her palm had weight.

"Don't," she said, voice low and shaking with fury she refused to name.

His mouth hovered a breath from hers, his eyes dark. "Bea—"

"I said don't." She pushed again, harder this time, forcing space between them. She could still feel the imprint of his kiss on her lips, like a brand. Like proof.

Like a victory he didn't deserve.

"You do not get to do that," she snapped, chin lifting. "Not because I teased you. Not because you *wanted* to. Not because you think you can turn my resolve into a parlor trick."

His jaw flexed. "You asked me what I would do next."

"I asked," she said, breath catching, "as a test."

"And?" His voice went rough. "Did I pass?"

Heat flashed—shameful, unwanted, undeniable. She hated him for it.

Bea stepped out from under his arm, smoothing her skirts with hands that were only slightly unsteady. "You're insufferable."

His mouth curved. "You kissed me back."

"I did not." The lie came out too quickly.

Nicholas's gaze dropped—just once—to her mouth. "Bea."

Her pulse skittered, but she turned sharply toward the path. "This walk is over."

She made it three steps before she heard him behind her, unhurried.

"Running away?" he drawled.

Bea didn't look back. "Absolutely not. I am *withdrawing*," she said through her teeth. "Strategically."

"Looks quite similar to running if you ask me," he drawled.

Bea swung around to face him. She could feel the fire in her eyes. "Why are you doing this?"

"Doing what?" he asked, blinking at her innocently.

"Trying to seduce me," she said in a low, harsh whisper.

Nicholas slowly grinned. "Why, so you'll *want* to marry me, of course."

CHAPTER FIFTEEN

"Nicholas Archer is trying to seduce me," Bea announced.

She and her friends were gathered once more in her sitting room—the unofficial headquarters of The Wallflower's Revolt—sunlight slanting through the tall windows and catching motes of dust above the tea table. Bea stood near the hearth, still flushed, her pale blue muslin gown creased where she'd twisted her fingers into the fabric. Georgie lounged on the settee in a pink-striped walking dress, bonnet abandoned on the chair beside her, teacup poised in one hand. Poppy sat cross-legged on the rug at their feet, embroidery hoop balanced against her knee, her soft yellow day dress already speckled with stray threads. It was meant to be a meeting. It had become a confession.

Georgie choked violently on her tea. Poppy dropped her embroidery hoop on the rug.

"What?" they both screeched simultaneously.

Bea turned to face her friends, fingertips pressed to her temples. "He told me. Directly. That he intends to seduce me. And then—and then—he somehow managed to kiss me."

Georgie stared, the look on her face half-horrified, half-impressed. "Did you slap him?"

"No," Bea muttered. She was still wondering at herself about that. Why *hadn't* she slapped him? If anything deserved a slap in response, it was that kiss.

"Did you bite him?" Poppy asked, far too hopefully.

"No," Bea groaned. Honestly, she hadn't thought of it at the time. Not a half-bad idea. Something to consider for next time. *Not* that there would be a next time. Because while she might have to pretend to allow him to *court* her, she certainly didn't have to allow him to *kiss* her again…ever.

"What did you do?" Georgie asked, blinking in confusion.

"I kissed him back," Bea admitted, expelling a long sigh.

"Oh," Georgie breathed, eyes widening.

"Oh?" Poppy echoed, obviously scandalized.

"Yes," Bea admitted. "But only briefly. *Quite* briefly."

Georgie leaned forward, pursing her lips. "So let me ensure I understand this correctly. Nicholas Archer kissed you and you enjoyed it enough to kiss him back?"

"Briefly!" Bea repeated.

"Too briefly to know whether you enjoyed it?" Georgie pressed, a sly smile on her lips.

"He infuriates me," Bea insisted. "His politics are wrong, his humor is uncivilized, he's smug and glories in it—and yet—"

"He's an excellent kisser," Georgie supplied, another wicked grin on her face.

Bea scowled. "You're not helping."

"Very well," Georgie said, setting her teacup aside and smoothing her skirts. "If you're determined to be a spinster—"

"Wallflower," Bea corrected.

"Then why not kiss him?" Georgie shrugged. "I mean it. If it's enjoyable. Be discreet. Have fun."

Poppy gasped so hard she nearly inhaled a needle. "Georgiana! You cannot possibly mean that."

"I mean exactly that," Georgie replied. "Why shouldn't Bea enjoy herself a bit? You don't have to marry the man to enjoy him."

Bea opened her mouth, then she closed it and scowled again. "I cannot possibly enjoy myself with Nicholas Archer."

"I believe you," Georgie hummed, giving her a slow wink.

Bea groaned again. "Stop looking at me like that. This is not about kissing. Or seduction. Or...his ridiculous mouth." She rubbed her forehead vigorously. "We have more important concerns."

Poppy perked up. "Such as?"

"Such as *everything*." Bea drew a breath, straightened her back, and fixed both her friends with a determined stare. "Our revolt," she continued. "Have you two forgotten? Parliament convenes again next week. There are rumors the shipping reform bill will be voted on earlier than expected. If the Tories block the bill, everything I've worked for will be undone. I need to influence public sentiment...hard. And swiftly."

Georgie nodded. "Which means—"

"Which means," Bea interrupted, "my caricatures must be sharper than ever. Devastating. Unignorable. And as usual"—she grimaced—"my best material comes from my father and Nicholas themselves."

Only things had changed. The vent had gone quiet since the courtship began—Nicholas came to visit her now, more often than Father. Her movements were too managed. If she wanted information, she'd have to take it the dangerous way: from Nicholas himself.

Poppy snorted. "Well. At least Lord Vanover is giving you...fresh inspiration."

"You're calling him *Nicholas* now?" Georgie asked, fluttering her eyelashes.

Bea glowered at both of them. "I have no time to be distracted by seductive whispers and fingertips trailing down my neck and—" She clamped her mouth shut, then added, "And other nonsense."

Georgie exchanged a knowing look with Poppy.

Bea ignored it. She stalked over to her escritoire, grabbed her sketchbook, and held it like a shield. "We need a plan. We need strategy. We need outrage distilled into ink. And if Nicholas thinks one stolen kiss is going to convince me to marry him, he is very much mistaken."

Georgie tilted her head. "Out of curiosity, have you attended any new Tory gatherings? Since Lord Vanover began courting you, I mean."

Bea waved a dismissive hand in the air. "Of course, I—" She stopped.

Poppy frowned. "Any dinners? Salons? Political suppers?"

Bea opened her mouth again. And closed it again. "Well," she said slowly, irritation creeping in, "not formal ones. We've…spoken."

"Spoken," Georgie repeated. "Where?"

"In the park. On a walk. Once on a veranda. At night." Bea's brow furrowed. "Privately."

Poppy's eyes widened a fraction. "So not a single drawing room? Not one room full of overheard conversations and indiscreet opinions?"

The silence stretched for several seconds.

Bea felt it then. The shape of it. The truth she had somehow missed.

"He's kept me alone," she said quietly. Not accusing, but realizing.

Georgie leaned back, lips pursed. "That does seem… convenient. For Lord Vanover, at least."

Heat flared in Bea's chest—annoyance, sudden and unsettling, but not at Nicholas alone. At herself.

"I allowed it," she said. "I let him distract me." Her jaw tightened. "By God…that stops. Immediately."

Georgie picked up her teacup again and tilted her head, eyes dancing. "So, no more kissing?"

Bea hesitated for only a fraction of a second. "Absolutely not."

Poppy arched a brow. "You're certain?"

"Positive," Bea said firmly. "I will not be swayed by flirtation. Or charm. Or the width of his"—her cheeks warmed treacherously—"shoulders."

"Oh dear," Poppy murmured. "You've mentioned his shoulders more than once."

"Enough about Nicholas," Bea declared. "I have work to do. Caricatures to draw. A nation to sway." She clutched her sketchbook tighter, her jaw setting like iron.

Nicholas Archer could promise seduction until he turned blue, she vowed silently. *He could whisper wicked things until her bones melted. He could even kiss her senseless.*

But she would not—*would not*—allow any of it to pull her from her mission.

This was not a romance.

It was a revolution.

CHAPTER SIXTEEN

Nicholas arrived at the Duke of Winston's residence at precisely eleven o'clock the next morning.

Not with his curricle this time, but with his coach.

A closed carriage—with a coachman—was the only intelligent choice today. If he was going to coax Bea into wanting another kiss (and he very much hoped to), he needed her beside him, present—without wind to blame for the trembling in her breath, without a crowd to hide behind, without any confusion about what she was choosing.

She may have pushed him away and gotten angry at him two days ago, but he'd felt the heat in her response at first. He hadn't imagined it. She *had* kissed him back.

Of course, if she wished to leave, she would. He would make certain of it. It would be her choice at all times.

But if she stayed, it would be because she wanted to.

She had fled the gardens. Right after he'd told her he wanted her to *want* to marry him. She'd picked up her skirts, and all but ran from him back into the house. He hadn't followed her. Instead, he'd sent round a note asking her to accompany him for another ride in the park this afternoon.

She hadn't answered.

Which he had chosen to interpret as a possibility rather than a refusal.

He would accept an actual refusal the moment she gave it, of course. But silence was merely uncertainty…and uncertainty deserved patience.

So here he was.

The butler took one look at him and nodded him inside without comment.

Nicholas waited in the foyer, glancing once at the wide, sweeping staircase. He expected Bea to descend in an impatient flurry of skirts, her temper leading the way.

She did not disappoint.

She came down the steps dressed for purpose rather than pleasure, wearing a tailored walking gown in a cool, unobtrusive shade of blue, white kid gloves fitted tight to her hands, and bonnet ribbons tied with more determination than grace. Everything about her said she expected a battle and had dressed accordingly.

Her expression indicated she was already suspicious. Good. Suspicion kept her alert. Alertness made her reactive. And he needed her reactions—every one of them. Especially the breathy, reckless ones.

"Lord Vanover," she said coolly, her nostrils flaring.

He allowed himself the smallest smile. "Lady Beatrix."

"Your parents?" he asked politely.

"In the morning room," she replied. "Busy."

Of course they were. The duke and duchess were always busy, too busy to notice their daughter's increasing agitation as she crossed the foyer toward the open door, where his closed coach waited, an invitation she was free to refuse.

He offered his arm. Not stepping closer. Not crowding her. Giving her the space to decide.

She stared at his sleeve long enough that a lesser man might have felt the sting.

But she took it…eventually.

Her fingers brushed his sleeve, light, reluctant, her touch sparking through him like a flare.

"Well then," she said, resigned but trying hard not to look flustered, "let us get this over with."

Perfect. Exactly the tone he wanted, controlled disdain masking something considerably warmer.

The butler opened the door, and they stepped outside.

They descended the front steps together, Nicholas unhurried, utterly decisive. The vehicle waited at the curb. She faltered for the barest fraction of a step. She'd expected the curricle.

He noticed, of course. The flare of irritation she tried to smother. The faint tightening at the corner of her mouth.

Still, he said nothing.

At the street, one of the footmen sprang down and opened the door. Nicholas gestured her inside, his hand firm at her elbow, as if the matter were already settled.

She hesitated. Just a beat. Long enough to imagine the interior. Long enough to imagine the two of them inside it. Alone.

Nicholas didn't speak. He didn't reach for her.

He let the silence hold, allowing her time to choose.

After a moment, Beatrix lifted her chin and climbed in.

He followed, closing the door behind him with a soft, definitive click. If she asked to stop, he would stop. If she asked to leave, the door would open again just as easily.

He was many things, but never a man who took what was not freely offered.

Bea sat opposite him, spine straight, arms folded as if she were about to question him before a jury.

"You didn't bring the curricle," she said at last.

"No."

"Astonishing," she muttered. "I could have sworn you enjoyed showing it off."

"Oh, I do." He relaxed back into the seat, allowing himself to appear unhurried. "But today's excursion required something…different."

She arched a brow. "What an ominous choice of words."

He flashed her a smile. "I prefer to think of it as promising."

She narrowed her eyes—there it was, that spark of suspicion—and Nicholas had to bite back a wider smile. The woman was a battlefield, all tactical positioning and sharp defenses, but God, she was exhilarating to spar with.

The coach lurched into motion.

Bea braced herself with a gloved hand at her side, her expression betraying a very faint awareness that she was in an enclosed space with a man who had whispered seduction into her ear quite recently.

She wasn't comfortable. Not because she mistrusted him, he realized. Because she mistrusted herself.

Good.

"About our destination," she said, brisk and overly composed, "I've decided a ride through the park would be… unproductive. I think we should go…elsewhere."

Nicholas lifted a brow. He should have known she'd been planning something. "Decided, have you?"

"Yes." Her chin tipped up. "Hillary House. Lord Hillary is hosting a political salon this afternoon."

Ah. Of course he was.

Nicholas let his gaze linger on her a moment before answering. "He is indeed. Though I'm not certain it's customary to escort a lady one is courting directly into a room full of political observers."

She met his gaze without blinking. "Then let us dispense with the notion that you are courting me."

A corner of his mouth curved. "That seems premature."

Her eyes flashed. "So does another visit to the park."

Well played.

"Very well," he said easily. "Let us be practical. A brief turn through the park—long enough to satisfy convention—and then I shall deliver you straight into Lord Hillary's salon."

"I would prefer to go directly—"

"—to the salon," he finished, unfazed. "Yes, I know." His smile turned knowing. "But even the most determined plans benefit from a touch of diplomacy."

She narrowed her eyes. "You are enjoying this, aren't you?"

"Immensely."

She waited a beat. Then, tight-lipped, she said, "Fine. But make it brief."

"As brief as you like," he said, already settling back against the seat. "You are, after all, the one in a hurry."

She shot him a glare that promised future retribution.

Nicholas grinned at her again.

And then they were off. Park chosen. Coach enclosed. Bea alert, irritated…and entirely too aware of him.

Excellent.

Not a quarter hour later, Nicholas's coach had made it through the London traffic and rolled through the gates of Hyde Park.

As the wheels crunched over gravel, Nicholas watched

Bea in the shifting morning light—her posture rigid, her gloves twisting in her lap. She appeared to be full of arguments she refused to voice.

She was fighting herself. He could practically see it.

Good. Let her fight. Let her resist. The trick, after all, was simple. If Bea was to kiss him again, it must be her idea.

He didn't need to press. He didn't need to chase. He simply needed to make her want him.

So Nicholas turned his head, looked out toward the bright sweep of the Row, and said nothing at all.

He could feel her looking at him.

Perfect.

Nicholas glanced at her. Then he turned to look out the window again, a man settling comfortably into mischief. "Don't worry. I have no intention of kissing you again."

"I don't believe you." Her voice was sharp.

"You needn't fault yourself, you know. I think it was all too much for you...too soon."

Her eyes narrowed. "What do you mean?"

He leaned back on an elbow and shrugged one shoulder in the most nonchalant way he could muster. "I realized something. I was perhaps...too quick to praise our kiss."

Beatrix blinked, utterly nonplussed. "What?"

"Well." He adopted a thoughtful tone. "It wasn't entirely your fault, of course. First attempts are rarely exemplary."

Her jaw dropped. "First attempts?"

"Kissing is a skill like any other," he continued helpfully. "One must practice to truly excel. So, you oughtn't feel discouraged if your first time was...well. Adequate."

"Adequate?" she echoed, voice strangling itself.

"Yes. Perfectly serviceable. Pleasant enough. But—" He gave a sympathetic shrug. "One can hardly expect brilliance out of the gate."

Bea stared at him, her eyes shooting daggers. No doubt she was deciding whether to throttle him or set him aflame.

"I'll forgive you, naturally," he added. "Inexperience is nothing to be ashamed o—"

He didn't finish.

Because she launched at him.

Not delicately. Not ladylike. She seized him by the lapels of his coat, hauled him forward with startling strength, and crushed her mouth to his in a kiss that had *nothing* of innocence in it.

Nicholas made a low, unguarded sound—half surprise, half delight—before his instincts surged, hot and unquestioning. He kissed her back with immediate intensity, hands sliding to her waist as he pulled her across the space between them.

She tasted furious…and delicious.

Her fingers tightened in his coat, tugging him closer still, and Nicholas responded with a deep, possessive groan. He shifted, guided her, and in one fluid motion drew her onto the velvet seat beneath him, bracing his weight above her without crushing her.

She gasped, and he took advantage of the opportunity, sliding his tongue against hers—slow, coaxing. Her back arched. Her hands moved up to clutch his shoulders. Heat curled low in his groin.

Hell. She was magnificent.

He dragged his mouth from hers only long enough to kiss along her jaw, then lower—his breath warm against the delicate skin of her throat. "Is this *adequate?*" she demanded, breathless.

He smiled against her throat. "It's a start."

"Oh, I'll show you a start—"

But Nicholas didn't let her finish. He caught her mouth again—slower this time, as if he meant to make her *feel* the difference between "serviceable" and ruin. His lips moved over hers in a measured glide, then deepened, coaxing a sound from her that went straight to his cock.

Bea answered with a rough little noise of her own, fingers fisting in his coat as she tilted her chin and met him without flinching—no hesitation, no doubt, only the fierce insistence of a woman who refused to be outdone.

He tasted her on his tongue—sweet and sharp and furious—until his control frayed at the edges. His hand slid up her side, thumb stroking along her ribs beneath the line of her stays, and her breath hitched hard against his mouth.

"There," he murmured against her lips, voice wrecked. "That's better."

She kissed him again as if to shut him up properly.

Nicholas smiled against her mouth—aching, thrilled, undone by her—and kissed her harder.

She gasped, and he followed that sound, tracing the new line of her throat with his lips, letting his breath whisper heat against her skin.

"Adequate?" she demanded again, voice trembling with both anger and desire.

"A tragic miscalculation," he murmured.

"You are impossible," she whispered. Her breath caught. He felt it—everything—every tremor, every small intake of breath.

"And you," he breathed at her ear, a shudder racking his body, "are astonishing."

And then, just as quickly as it had begun, she pushed him away, rolled out from under him, and moved back to the opposite seat. "Oh, you are a complete rogue!"

"What? What do you mean?" He blinked at her, still quite undone by the kiss and the alacrity with which she had ended it.

Her eyes narrowed. "You did that on purpose…baiting me into kissing you."

A sly smile touched the corner of his lips. "Oh, come now. You wanted to…a little…you're far too intelligent to have been fooled."

Bea sat there contemplating his words for a beat. Then she took a deep breath, the intense scowl back on her face. "Blast. You're right. I am far too astute to blame all of this on you."

He couldn't help his laugh. God. She was refreshingly honest. It was not a trait he encountered much as a politician.

"You stay over there," she insisted, pointing at where he sat, across from her. "There will be no more kissing."

He bit his lip but remained on the opposite seat, where he adjusted his clothing.

Bea did the same, righting her coiffure and smoothing her skirts. "Now, I'd like to go to Lord Hillary's salon," she informed him as if they had not just been passionately kissing moments earlier.

"If you insist." Nicholas knocked on the top of the coach, signaling to the coachman to change course.

"I do insist." She folded her arms across her chest and didn't speak another word until they reached their destination.

CHAPTER SEVENTEEN

Bea had attended a hundred drawing rooms in her life. This was not a drawing room. This was Parliament with better upholstery.

Hillary House glittered with polished mahogany and smug men. The air smelled of beeswax and brandy and the faintest trace of cigar smoke—an invisible border meant to keep women politely to the edges. Conversation hummed like a hive, all sharp opinions and sharper laughter, the sort that carried the unspoken message: *We are the ones who decide things.*

Bea's spine straightened the moment she entered the drawing room.

She had come here for a reason. Not to be dazzled. Not to be charmed. Not to be—she glanced sideways at the man beside her—*seduced.*

Nicholas offered his arm without looking at her, the gesture so effortless it was almost irksome. As if escorting her into enemy territory was as ordinary as escorting her through Hyde Park.

Bea took his arm. Not because she needed it. But because she refused to give him the satisfaction of a refusal.

A footman announced them. Heads turned—some curious, some assessing, some already bored. A few women looked up from their embroidery circle across the room with the expression of people watching a carriage crash in slow motion.

Lord Hillary swept forward to greet them, radiating the kind of genial smugness that made Bea instantly want to draw him as a plump cat with a powdered wig. His moustache looked very much like whiskers.

"Lady Beatrix," he boomed, taking her hand as if she were a visiting dignitary. "How good of you to come. And Vanover—" His grin widened. "I hope you've brought your famous wit with you. Our guests have been dreadfully civil."

Nicholas's mouth curved. "If incivility is what you require, Hillary, you ought to have invited my father."

Bea felt the slightest jolt of surprise.

Had that been a dig at his father? The powerful Tory Duke of VanDeVere? *Interesting.* She'd never really heard him discuss his father before. The man was older, yet still wielded great power in the House of Lords. He rarely attended her father's salons, preferring instead to allow his son to do so in his stead.

Lord Hillary laughed. "You'll do, Vanover. I have no desire to be flayed alive before luncheon."

Nicholas's gaze flicked to Bea. "A wise man."

Bea continued to watch Nicholas as they moved into the heart of the salon: a broad, elegant chamber with chairs arranged in loose clusters, a tea table at one end, and a low marble hearth at the other. Men stood in groups of two and three—peers, MPs, younger sons eager to sound clever, older men quick to sound pompous. Every surface held crystal glasses and small plates of pastries that no one seemed to actually eat.

It was a room built for talking.

And for being heard.

Which made it absolutely perfect.

Bea's fingers tightened around her reticule.

She had made herself heard in ink—sharp lines, sharper truths, delivered anonymously under cover of night. In person, in rooms like this…she was meant to smile. To nod. To exist prettily in the background like wallpaper. That's what her father wanted.

But Father wasn't here today.

She watched Nicholas greet his friends. He was as charming, friendly, and yes, witty as always. But it wasn't his wit that caught her attention. It was the ease with which he deployed it. A relaxed confidence, not performative—an assuredness that did not need to dominate the room to own it.

She hadn't noticed that about him before. She'd been far too preoccupied with hating him.

She was contemplating what else about Nicholas she hadn't noticed before when a familiar voice rose near the hearth. "—if you reward the lower orders with political power, you will spend the next decade cleaning up after their appetites."

Bea's stomach turned.

Sir Edwin Langford stood before the fire, flushed with righteousness, his hands clasped behind his back as though he were delivering a sermon. Several men nodded approvingly.

Bea had met Langford before. At Father's salons. The man was even more odious than Hargrave, if that was possible. At least Hargrave was older and set in his ways. Langford had no excuse. He spoke of "the people" as if they were livestock.

Nicholas angled his head, listening. His expression was neutral, unreadable.

Bea leaned in and murmured, "If I'd known Langford would be here, I'd have brought a bucket."

Nicholas's brows lifted. "A bucket?"

"For the nonsense," she said. "It's spilling everywhere."

Nicholas's mouth twitched. "I'm afraid a bucket wouldn't be nearly big enough. You'd need the whole Thames."

Bea bit back the laugh that threatened to escape her. Curse him. Curse him for being...*this*. Clever, and witty, and...supportive.

Langford's voice rose again. "The reform bill is a fever. Once you give them a vote, they will demand everything. They will demand land. They will demand titles. They will demand—"

"They will demand to be treated as citizens," Bea said, too softly to be heard by anyone but Nicholas.

She hadn't meant to speak aloud.

Nicholas glanced at her. "Do you truly believe that?"

Bea lifted her chin. "I believe men who work twelve hours a day and still cannot feed their children are not the ones threatening the stability of the country."

Nicholas's gaze held hers, intent. "And who is?"

Bea's breath caught at the question—not because it was difficult, but because no man ever asked her such things as if the answer mattered.

"Men like him," she said, nodding toward Langford. "Men who speak of people as if they are a nuisance rather than the nation itself."

Nicholas was quiet for a moment.

Then he did something Bea did not expect.

He guided her forward.

Not by pulling—Nicholas never pulled. He simply placed

his hand at the small of her back, light, steady, and moved as if the room would part for them.

And it did.

The men turned. The women looked up. Conversations shifted, the way the sea shifts when something large swims beneath it.

Nicholas Archer, Marquess of Vanover, was taking the Duke of Winston's daughter directly toward the center of the salon.

Bea's pulse skittered. "Nicholas—"

"If you intend to stab someone, do it where witnesses can appreciate it," he murmured, giving her a wink.

She huffed a laugh. "I will not stab anyone."

His voice dropped. "A pity. I daresay it would enliven Hillary's afternoon."

Bea shot him a look, but she couldn't quite summon genuine indignation because her nerves were too alive. Because the room was watching. Because she had never been *invited* into the middle of such a space.

Nicholas stopped a polite distance from Langford and waited until a pause opened in the man's monologue—then stepped neatly into it.

"Sir Edwin," Nicholas said, smooth as silk, "you make it sound as though the English people are a pack of hounds waiting to be loosed."

Langford's eyes narrowed, recognition dawning. "Vanover."

Nicholas dipped his head, all manners. "If you'll forgive me, I should like to test your argument."

"Oh?" Langford's gaze flicked to Bea and dismissed her instantly, as though she were a decorative vase. "And how do you propose to do that?"

Nicholas turned slightly—enough to include Bea. Enough to make it impossible to pretend she was not there.

He did not place her behind him. He did not place her beside him like a possession. He placed her *with* him.

"Lady Beatrix has been following the Reform question with rather more attention than most men in this room," Nicholas said mildly. "And she has a habit of spotting the holes in an argument."

Bea went utterly still.

Langford blinked, then let out a short, humorless laugh. "Surely you do not mean to tell me—"

"I do," Nicholas said pleasantly.

A ripple went through the room. A few men shifted as if uncertain whether to be amused or offended. A few women straightened, suddenly alert.

Bea could feel heat climbing her throat.

Nicholas looked at her, and there was something in his gaze that made her lungs fill as though she'd been given permission to breathe.

He was not laughing at her.

He was not using her as a prop.

He was—damn him—*offering her the floor.*

"Tell them," he murmured.

Bea's mouth went dry. She didn't relish being watched. Didn't particularly enjoy being examined. But the fury that lived in her chest—the one she poured into ink—rose to meet the moment like a pencil finding her palm.

Bea lifted her chin. "Sir Edwin speaks as though the people are infants who must be managed," she said clearly. "But the people are the ones who build the wealth this country spends. They work in mills and mines and fields and shipyards. They serve as footmen in the homes of men who would deny them a voice."

All eyes momentarily turned to the footman, who cleared his throat and glanced away.

"And you would have them vote because they labor?" Langford's voice dripped with condescension.

"I would have them vote because they are governed," Bea replied. "Because they pay taxes. Because they fight in wars. Because they are punished by laws they have no hand in shaping."

"Sentimental nonsense," Langford snapped. "A vote does not feed a child."

"No," Bea said, voice steady. "But laws can. And wages can. And the ability to hold a person accountable can."

Someone near the hearth made a small sound of interest.

Langford's face reddened. "It is easy for a duke's daughter to preach about accountability."

Bea's jaw tightened. She would not be shamed into silence. "It is easy for a man with a seat in Parliament to mock hunger."

A murmur, sharper this time. A few men exchanged glances.

Langford's eyes flashed. "Women are not meant to meddle in these matters."

Bea felt the room tilt. The old, familiar pressure. She could hear her father's voice in her head. *Smile, retreat, don't make a scene.*

She opened her mouth—

And Nicholas spoke first.

"How fascinating," he said, with a calm that made several heads turn. "I wasn't aware Parliament's legitimacy depended on what women are 'meant' to do."

Langford stiffened. "Vanover—"

Nicholas's gaze was cool now, his voice still mild. "If your position is strong, it can survive being questioned. If it cannot survive a question, then perhaps it deserves to be replaced."

A beat of silence.

Then one of the younger MPs—Lord Ashby, Bea thought —let out a short laugh. "Well said."

Another voice chimed in, "Hear, hear."

Langford's lips compressed into a tight line. "This is absurd."

"No," Bea said softly, and when she spoke, she realized she was no longer shaking. "This is debate. And despite my status as a female, I do indeed have opinions."

Langford looked as though he might explode. Instead, he snapped a stiff bow and stalked away.

The room exhaled.

Bea stared after him, adrenaline blazing in her veins, half expecting someone to scold her for speaking too loudly. For stepping out of line. For daring.

No one did.

Nicholas turned toward her, and for the first time since she'd known him, his expression in a room filled with Tories wasn't teasing. It wasn't smug.

It was…quietly approving.

"You're perfectly right," he said.

Bea's throat tightened in a ridiculous, unexpected way.

Because she had spoken before—in private, in secret, in ink.

But she had never spoken aloud like this, in a room that mattered.

And she had never expected Nicholas, of all people, to agree with her.

Bea drew a breath, forcing herself to recover. "I wasn't prepared."

"I know. My apologies. I wanted them to hear you."

Bea's heart gave an absurd little lurch.

She frowned at him, searching his face for the trick. The strategy. The angle.

There wasn't one.

Not that she could see.

Nicholas had just used his influence—his name, his place in that room—to give her the one thing she had never been handed by a man like him.

A platform.

Bea swallowed. "Why?"

Nicholas didn't answer right away. His gaze drifted over the room—over the men who were now speaking a bit more carefully, the women who were suddenly watching her with additional interest.

Then he looked back at Bea.

"Because I'm tired," he said quietly, "of watching the cleverest person in the room be treated like furniture."

Bea's breath caught. She stared at him, abruptly disarmed. Not because he was handsome. Not because he had kissed her.

But because he had seen her.

And in that moment, Bea realized something she did not like at all.

Nicholas Archer could be dangerous in more ways than one.

Soon, Lord Hillary bustled over, delight shining in his eyes. "Magnificent, Lady Beatrix," he whispered, as if she were an actor who'd just nailed her cue. "Absolutely magnificent. Langford has been insufferable for weeks. I'm tempted to invite you every week. You certainly provide some much-needed interest."

Bea managed a tight smile. "How generous. I should like that, my lord."

Nicholas's hand brushed her elbow—guiding, careful. They stepped away before Nicholas whispered, "We should go before Hillary tries to put you on a dais."

Bea's pulse flickered again. "Are you trying to rescue me again?"

Nicholas leaned in, his mouth near her ear. "Never," he murmured.

Her stomach flipped traitorously.

Bea straightened, regaining her composure with effort. "Very well. Let's go."

Nicholas's eyes warmed, and for the briefest second she saw something in him she hadn't expected to find.

Not a rake's triumph.

Not a politician's calculation.

Something steadier. Something…kind.

He offered his arm again.

Bea took it.

And as they walked out of Hillary House—past the watching faces, the whispering mouths, the little sparks of curiosity her words had ignited—she realized she was seeing Nicholas in a way she hadn't allowed herself to see him before.

Not as an opponent.

Not as a seducer.

But as a man who, when it mattered, had stood beside her. Who had been an ally.

The coach waited at the curb.

Nicholas helped her in, his hand warm at her waist— brief, proper, maddeningly decent.

Bea settled onto the seat, trying to gather her thoughts, trying to pull herself back into the armor she wore so well.

Nicholas climbed in after her and shut the door.

For a beat, the enclosed space felt different than it had earlier. Not only charged. Not only dangerous. Intimate in a new way.

Nicholas watched her as the carriage lurched forward. His gaze dropped to her mouth, then lifted again. "You were brilliant in there."

The simple sincerity of it hit her harder than any compliment had the right to.

Bea looked away quickly, as if the window might save her. "Don't."

"Don't what?"

"Don't..." She gestured vaguely, frustrated by the flutter in her chest. "Say things that sound like you mean them."

Nicholas's voice turned softer. "What if I do mean them?"

Bea's breath caught.

The coach rolled on, wheels humming over cobblestone, the world outside oblivious.

And Bea realized—with sudden, treacherous clarity—that the most dangerous thing Nicholas had done today was not kissing her.

It was making her feel as if she mattered.

"If you should care to try your skill at kissing again, do let me know," Nicholas drawled, his smile pure cunning.

Bea rolled her eyes. "Don't you wish." Despite the heat rising in her chest, she forced a laugh.

"You've *no* idea." But this time...the wink he gave her made her toes curl.

CHAPTER EIGHTEEN

Bea sharpened her pencil until the point was fine enough to do damage. Not to anyone in particular, of course. Merely…to reputations.

The household had settled into the quiet rhythm of late evening—footsteps softened, lamps lowered, voices tucked away behind closed doors. From her little sanctuary of a sitting room, Bea could hear the faint tick of the clock and the distant sigh of London beyond the windows, as if the city were finally exhaling.

Bea, however, could not seem to breathe properly at all.

She stared down at the blank paper in front of her and found her mind stubbornly refusing to land on the subject at hand.

Langford.

Sir Edwin Langford, if one wished to be respectful, which Bea most certainly did not.

She straightened her shoulders, set the page squarely, and began with the thing she always began with: the shape of his head.

It was astonishingly satisfying to reduce a man's sense of importance into a few cruel lines.

First, the jaw—too square, too self-satisfied. Then the cheeks—fattened with complacency. Then the nose, which Bea elongated just enough to make him look perpetually offended by the scent of other people's existence.

She darkened the eyebrows until they became two furious caterpillars.

Much better.

Still, her pencil paused as she considered what to do with his mouth.

Langford had the sort of mouth that never smiled without condescension. A man who believed laughter was an instrument: something to wield, not share. She drew it thin and pinched, a line of disdain.

Then she added the smallest suggestion of spit at the corner.

Bea sat back, pleased.

There were some men in this world who deserved to be immortalized.

Not in marble.

In mockery.

She angled the paper toward the lamplight, assessing. The resemblance was excellent—if Langford were ever to see it, he would erupt like a kettle left too long to boil.

Bea's lips curved faintly.

She could already imagine the caption.

THE GREAT PROTECTOR OF ENGLISH STABILITY, it would read, *TERRIFIED OF VOTES FOR THE COMMON MAN.*

She raised her pencil to add a ridiculous little crown atop his head—something pompous and absurd—when her hand stalled again.

Because the moment she thought of that salon—of Langford near the hearth, red with self-importance, preaching about "contagion" and "hounds"—she could not help thinking of the other man who had stood there.

Nicholas.

She scowled at the paper as if it were responsible.

She had not meant to think of him.

She had meant to think of Langford's smug face and the delicious satisfaction of skewering it.

But Nicholas had been there in the middle of it, hadn't he? Not lurking at the edges like most men did when a woman's temper threatened to embarrass them. Not tugging her backward with a whispered, *Beatrix, do hush.* Not glancing around as if to say, *Please don't make this awkward for me.*

He had done the exact opposite.

He had stepped forward.

And, damn him, he had taken her with him.

Bea's pencil hovered.

She closed her eyes for a beat and saw it again: the shift of bodies in the room as Nicholas guided her through, the way conversations had faltered, the way men who had not noticed her at all suddenly had no choice but to.

And then his voice, maddeningly calm, as if he were announcing a change in the weather.

Lady Beatrix has been following the Reform question...

He had said it as though it were natural. As though she belonged in that discussion. As though her mind were not an ornament but a weapon worth unsheathing.

Bea's throat tightened—an irritating, inexplicable thing—as if she were moved.

She was not *moved.*

She was...annoyed.

Because she had not expected to be seen that way.

And she had certainly not expected to be seen that way by

Nicholas Archer, who was supposed to be a snake, a menace, a smirk in human form.

Yet he had looked at her in that salon with something that had felt dangerously close to respect.

"You were brilliant," he had said afterward.

Not *you were pretty.* Not *you were spirited.* Not *you were entertaining.*

You were brilliant.

Bea's fingers curled around the pencil. He didn't agree with her of course. He was as loyal a Tory as the rest of them. But he hadn't tried to silence her. He'd listened to her thoughts. And he'd complimented her.

She was not accustomed to compliments. They made her feel as though she'd been handed something she didn't know she'd been missing.

She bent over the page again and began shading Langford's cheeks with vigorous displeasure.

Harder. Darker. More ridiculous.

That ought to fix it.

It did not.

Her mind kept slipping back to Hillary House like a toe finding the same worn path inside a slipper.

Nicholas's quiet interjection. His cool dismantling of Langford's pompous certainty. The way he'd said, with vexatious ease, that if a man's argument could not survive being questioned, perhaps it deserved to be replaced.

Bea had nearly choked on the urge to grin.

And then—worse—she had felt a flicker of something warm inside her chest.

Something that was not anger. Something that was not triumph. Something dangerously like…gratitude.

Bea drew Langford's ears larger. Enormous, in fact. The better to hear the "lower orders" he so feared.

There.

She pressed her lips together, determined to focus.

But the end of the evening insisted on replaying itself.

The coach. The enclosed space. The wheels humming over cobblestone, the city oblivious. Nicholas watching her as if he were still listening to her speak.

His voice softer than it had any right to be.

What if I do mean them?

Bea's stomach gave a small, traitorous swoop.

She set her pencil down with exaggerated care.

It was appalling. Absolutely appalling.

Not the man. The…*feeling*.

Because she had spent days convincing herself Nicholas was merely a complication to endure. An obstacle in her path. A handsome irritant with far too much confidence and far too much knowledge of how to tilt his mouth just so.

And then tonight he had done something unpardonable.

He had made her feel as if she mattered.

That was the sort of thing that sank its claws into a woman when she wasn't looking.

Bea rubbed at her forehead, as if she could smudge the memory away like graphite.

It did not help.

Because right after making her feel like she mattered, Nicholas had gone and reminded her exactly what he was.

If you should care to try your skill at kissing again, do let me know…

Bea's mouth tightened at the recollection of his drawl, his smile—pure cunning—like a man dangling a sweet in front of a child purely to watch her pretend she didn't want it.

Her eyes narrowed.

Clever devil.

He had done it on purpose, hadn't he?

He had been kind—genuinely kind—in the only way that would get past her armor.

And then, once her defenses were softened, he had slid the flirtation back in like a knife between her ribs.

Not cruelly.

Just…efficiently.

Bea's cheeks warmed.

The worst part was that it had worked.

Not entirely. She had not thrown herself at him in the coach like some heroine in a lurid French novel.

But she had felt it.

That spark again.

That inconvenient, undeniable awareness of him—the warmth of his hand at her elbow, the closeness of his body in the coach, the way his gaze had dipped to her mouth like it belonged to him in some future he'd already decided upon.

Bea stared at the drawing.

Langford looked back at her, ridiculous and smug and crowned like a very stupid king.

Bea sighed. "Well," she muttered to him, "at least you are simple."

Langford did not answer, which was one of his better qualities.

Bea reached for her pencil again and, with sharp little strokes, added a tiny speech bubble above his head: *WOMEN SHOULD NOT MEDDLE.*

Then she drew a tiny teacup in his hand—delicate, trembling—and wrote: *CAUTION: MAY SPILL AT THE FIRST FEMALE ARGUMENT.*

It was satisfying. It was righteous. It was exactly the sort of thing that made her feel like herself again.

Except…Nicholas still lingered in the corner of her mind, like a smudge she couldn't quite erase.

Bea tapped the pencil against her lip, thinking.

Georgie's voice came to her unbidden—practical, amused, maddeningly modern.

You don't have to marry the man to enjoy him.

Bea's mouth twisted.

She had nearly thrown a cushion at Georgie when she'd said it. As if Bea could simply…*enjoy* her sworn enemy.

As if "fun" were something a woman like Bea was allowed without consequences.

But the truth was that Georgie had a point, vile creature.

Bea was being forced to accept Nicholas's courtship. She could protest until her throat went raw; her father would still arrange their walks, their visits, their appearances, and call it propriety.

So if Bea could not control the fact of it…

Could she control the terms?

She stared at the edge of the paper, watching the lamplight catch the graphite.

Nicholas wanted something from her. That much was obvious.

He wanted her kisses. Her attention. Her reactions. He wanted to win.

But today, at Hillary House, he had also wanted something else. He had wanted her voice to be heard.

And that complicated everything. Because it meant he wasn't only taking.

He was giving too.

Bea did not like men who gave her things. They made it difficult to hate them properly.

Her gaze drifted to the window. Outside, London sprawled in darkness and lamplight—carriages passing, distant laughter, lives continuing as if a woman had not just stood in a salon and challenged a man who believed women were furniture.

As if Nicholas had not stood beside her and said, in effect, *Let her speak.*

Bea's throat tightened again, and she hated it.

She bent over the paper and began sketching again—not Langford this time, but a quick little thumbnail in the margin.

A marquess with wicked eyes and a too-knowing smile.

Bea froze, startled, then scowled at herself and immediately scratched it out.

Ridiculous.

She would not sit here drawing Nicholas Archer like a schoolgirl with a fancy.

She would draw Langford, and she would publish it. If she delivered it to the printer at dawn, it would be in tomorrow morning's paper.

And she was going to remind the world that men like him were the problem.

That was her mission.

Nicholas was merely…a distraction.

A dangerous distraction.

Bea stared at her page and, despite herself, felt her lips curve.

Kissing him again wasn't the *worst* idea in the world.

Not because she liked him.

Not because she trusted him.

Not because she had any intention of letting him win.

But because…well.

It might be satisfying.

It might be the sort of fun that felt like rebellion—delicious and defiant in the face of men who thought they owned her choices.

And if she was going to be forced into this courtship, perhaps she could at least steal a bit of pleasure back for herself.

Georgie would approve.

Bea's mind flicked back to the coach. To the way

Nicholas's wink had made her toes curl. To the way his voice had dropped low as if it were meant only for her.

You've no idea.

Bea swallowed.

Her pencil hovered over the page again, and this time, when she worked on Langford's crown, she made it even more ridiculous—crooked, unstable, teetering.

As it should be.

Because stability built on contempt deserved to topple.

Bea sat back, satisfied.

Then, because she was not an idiot, she folded the paper carefully and slid it beneath her blotter—out of sight, safe, waiting for the right moment.

She would wake before dawn. She'd have to move quickly. If she could get the sheet into the right hands—before the city woke and the gossip cooled—Langford would be in print by morning.

Her pulse still felt too lively. Her thoughts still felt too tangled. Nicholas still lingered in her mind like a handprint on skin.

Bea rose, smoothing her skirts as if she could smooth her nerves the same way.

She crossed to the mirror and studied her reflection in the dim lamplight.

Her hair was slightly loose. Her eyes looked brighter than they had a right to.

Her mouth…looked like it remembered something.

Bea narrowed her eyes at herself. "Do not," she said firmly.

Her reflection did not listen.

Bea turned away, extinguished the lamp, and headed for bed with the fierce determination of a woman who would absolutely not be seduced by kindness, or cleverness, or wicked winks in a coach.

Except...as she slipped beneath the covers, her mind offered her one last, traitorous thought.

If Nicholas tried to kiss her again...

She might not stop him. She might not push him away.

Not because she wanted him.

Certainly not.

Only because she was beginning to suspect Georgie was right.

She didn't have to marry the man.

But perhaps—just perhaps—she could have a little fun while she let him try to convince her.

And that, Bea decided as sleep finally began to creep in, might be its own small kind of revolt.

CHAPTER NINETEEN

Nicholas Archer had always prided himself on waking with a clear head. This morning, his head was perfectly clear.

It was his thoughts that were a problem.

They arrived one after another as he sat at his desk with a cup of coffee cooling at his elbow, the window cracked just enough to let in the spring air, and the pale light of London slanting across the polished wood.

He told himself he was thinking about Parliament.

He told himself he was thinking about Winston's demands, his father's expectations, the reform bill vote…only days away, the ridiculous dance of alliances that governed the entire country.

He told himself a great many things.

And yet the first image that surfaced—uninvited, vivid— was Lady Beatrix Winslow standing in Lord Hillary's salon with her chin tipped up and her eyes bright with that same dangerous fire she carried like a concealed blade.

Not *in* the room.

In the center of it.

Nicholas took a sip of coffee.

It had been a risk. He'd known that the moment he'd guided her forward, the moment he'd stepped into Langford's sermon with a smile and offered Bea to the room as if she belonged there.

Because she did.

But men like Langford did not care about what was true. They cared about what was permitted. And what was permitted, in their minds, was simple: women listened. Men spoke. Votes were counted by people with the appropriate anatomy.

And yet Bea had spoken regardless.

She'd spoken without hedging, without fluttering her lashes to soften her words, without doing that tiresome female thing where they pretended their opinions were merely decorative.

She had been bold, and sharp, and wholly, spectacularly unmanageable.

It had pleased Nicholas more than it should have.

He set his cup down with unnecessary precision and tried, for the third time, to read the memorandum on his desk.

The words blurred into meaninglessness.

Because whenever he saw ink on paper, his mind supplied a different image.

Bea's mouth.

And what it might taste like the next time she decided—very nobly, very stubbornly—to act as though kissing him was an insult she was forced to endure.

He leaned back in his chair, letting the leather creak.

It had been a peculiar outing.

He hadn't expected her to enjoy the salon, for one thing. Bea disliked being managed with the passion of a woman who had spent her whole life being managed.

And yet—there had been a moment, after Langford stalked off, when Bea's eyes had flashed and her breath had caught, and the satisfaction on her face had been so bright it was…beautiful.

Nicholas had watched her then and thought, quite simply, *There.*

That was what she was meant for. Not meek smiles in drawing rooms. Not polite obedience at the end of a duke's leash. But that fearless, furious truth.

He had wanted the room to hear her. He had wanted her to feel what it was like to be taken seriously. And perhaps—if he was being honest—he had wanted to be the man who gave her that.

An absurd thing to want. And Nicholas did not do absurd.

He did strategy. He did leverage. He did winning.

But when he'd murmured, *I wanted them to hear you,* it hadn't been strategy.

It had been…well. It had been honest.

Nicholas rolled his shoulders, impatient with himself.

In his world, honesty was a liability. Which was why he preferred his honesty dressed up as banter. Like the banter he'd shared with Bea in the coach afterward.

His mouth twitched at the memory.

Bea, bristling with the aftershock of her own courage, trying so hard to pretend she wasn't pleased. Nicholas, doing what he did best: prodding until she snapped, and then smiling as if he hadn't been aiming for that exact reaction.

And then—

What if I do mean them?

He could still hear how softly he'd said it, as if the words had slipped out before he had time to examine them. Bea's breath catching. That brief, unguarded stillness that always came just before she shoved her pride back into place.

Nicholas's gaze drifted to the window, unfocused.

He had enjoyed that stillness far too much.

And then, of course, he'd ruined it the way he always did…with a provocation. With a wicked little invitation, a wink meant to remind her he was not some earnest reformer seeking her approval.

He was Nicholas Archer, after all.

He used words to produce his desired result.

And yet when he'd teased her—when he'd asked her to try her kissing again—Bea had rolled her eyes, yes, but she'd been interested. He'd seen it in her eyes. Felt it in the charge of energy within the coach air. The tiniest, most delicious betrayal of her own self-control.

You've no idea, he'd told her.

And she didn't.

Not yet.

Nicholas dragged his attention back to his desk. He had an entire day ahead of him. Meetings. Letters. A committee session that would likely devolve into men shouting about "order" as if the word itself could solve hunger.

Not to mention he would almost certainly be summoned by his father to explain himself once the duke received word that Nicholas had escorted a young woman who had vociferously argued *for* the reform bill at a political salon. He smiled to himself. How satisfying it would be when he explained to his father that the young lady in question was none other than his soon-to-be betrothed, the Duke of Winston's daughter.

He would bear his father's chastisement as he always did. Because his father had taught him well. The best way to deal with him was to feign agreement. And wouldn't his father have an apoplectic fit when he learned that his own son, the presumed pride of the Tories, had changed his mind on the reform bill…after listening to the arguments made by a woman?

It was true.

Nicholas had given Bea's words considerable thought last night and had decided that far from agreeing with his father and Winston on the topic, Bea was perfectly right. Why shouldn't the men who did all the work be allowed a voice in the decision making? It was only logical.

His father and Winston would hate it, of course. But they wouldn't find out until the vote was taken.

The thought made Nicholas's smile widen.

He reached for the stack of papers Godwin had placed on his desk—correspondence and the morning post.

The newspaper lay on top, folded neatly.

Nicholas hesitated.

It was not unusual for him to delay reading the papers. He rarely found them useful. They were filled with gossip and opinion and the occasional fact disguised as entertainment.

But this morning, his hand paused for a different reason.

Because, somehow, he already knew what he would find.

He opened it regardless.

And there, as bold as a slap, was B. Adroit's latest work.

Nicholas's gaze sharpened.

Sir Edwin Langford, rendered as if God had carved him out of arrogance and left the rest unfinished. His mouth a thin sneer. His eyes bulging with indignation. A ridiculous little crown balanced crookedly on his head as though he'd stolen it from a child.

And beneath it—merciless, elegant, perfect:

WOMEN SHOULD NOT MEDDLE.

Below that, a teetering teacup and a second line, dripping with mockery.

Nicholas stared. Then he smiled.

He couldn't help it. The cartoon was *excellent.*

It was also, in a way Nicholas did not enjoy, terribly… timely.

He lowered the paper, his mind already turning.

He'd never been a betting man. But what were the odds that Bea had a public clash—however controlled—with Langford at Hillary House, and then within hours, B. Adroit skewered Langford in precisely the way Bea would most want?

Nicholas's eyes narrowed.

A coincidence was possible.

After all, the salon had been full of men, and any of them could have carried the exchange into the street. Some might even have taken pleasure in Langford's humiliation. Hillary himself would happily feed a cartoonist a dozen juicy remarks if it meant the next issue was more entertaining and his salon more popular.

But it wasn't only that Langford had been the target—it was that the cartoon echoed his exact phrasing, the same insult he'd aimed at Bea like a blade.

It could have been anyone.

And yet—

Nicholas's gaze returned to the drawing.

There were details here. Not merely Langford's general pompousness, but the particular phrasing. The emphasis. The *tone* of it. That teacup felt personal, like a woman's fury given ink.

Nicholas tapped the paper once with his forefinger, thoughtfully.

Bea.

Bea had been quick with her words, precise with her points, and she'd spoken like someone who had been practicing the argument for weeks. She'd looked around that room not as a guest but as an observer.

As if she were cataloging it.

As if she might later...*report* on it.

Nicholas had suspected for some time that Bea knew the cartoonist. She could easily be the source of information. She moved in those circles by birth. She heard things. She saw things.

And she vehemently disagreed with her father.

A woman who disagreed with the things she knew could do a great deal of damage with the right ear at her disposal.

Nicholas's mouth tightened.

It did not help that Bea had been entirely too composed last night after they left Hillary House—after the shock, after the attention, after she'd tasted what it was like to say what she chose.

She'd seemed...satisfied.

As if she'd gotten something she'd wanted.

Nicholas folded the paper back slowly. Then he leaned forward, resting his forearms on the desk. He looked again at the folded newspaper, as if he could see through the pages to the ink beneath.

If Lady Beatrix was feeding information to B. Adroit, it meant she was even more dangerous than he'd assumed.

Which, of course, made her even more interesting.

Nicholas's mouth curved faintly.

He wasn't a fool. He knew exactly what he was doing with Bea.

Winston wanted a courtship. Society wanted a story. Nicholas's father wanted obedience and power, and a neat alliance tied up with ribbon.

But Nicholas wanted a wife. A wife who would challenge him. One who would make him think. Exactly the way Bea had.

And he didn't want just any wife. He wanted Bea. But he wanted her to want him. Agreeing to the forced courtship merely bought him time. It gave him access. It gave him proximity.

And proximity, with a woman like Bea, was an advantage.

Last night, he'd used that advantage to draw her into the middle of a salon and let her set a man on fire with words.

He'd also used it to convince her to kiss him in a coach.

Both had been satisfying.

Nicholas stood, crossing to the window. Outside, the square was brightening with morning. Carriages rattled past. A pair of boys chased one another with sticks, shouting as if they owned the world.

Nicholas watched them without seeing them.

He was thinking about Bea.

He was thinking about the way she'd looked when she spoke—like someone finally permitted to take up space.

He was thinking about the way she'd looked when he'd teased her—like someone annoyed to discover she enjoyed it.

He was thinking about the way she might look the next time he leaned in close and murmured something improper just to watch her pretend she didn't like it.

He was also thinking—because he was not an idiot— about what she might be hiding.

Nicholas turned back to his desk and rang the bell.

Godwin appeared.

"Have the carriage readied," Nicholas said. "In an hour."

Godwin bowed. "Very good, my lord. Shall I inform the Duke of Winston—"

"No." Nicholas's gaze sharpened. "Not yet. I'm merely going for a ride."

Godwin's brow lifted a fraction, though his face remained appropriately blank. "A ride, my lord."

Nicholas's mouth curved.

"Yes," he said softly, already imagining Bea's scowl. "A simple, innocent ride."

He picked up the folded newspaper again, eyes narrowing as he looked at B. Adroit's handiwork.

A coincidence perhaps.

Or proof.

Nicholas didn't know yet.

But he intended to find out.

He set the paper down, reached for his gloves, and allowed himself one last, private thought—half amusement, half anticipation.

This time, he rather hoped Bea wouldn't suggest attending another political salon.

Nicholas smiled to himself. He had a feeling the coach would be far more interesting than a salon.

And if Bea decided that kissing him wasn't the worst idea in the world—

Well.

Nicholas had never objected to a woman having a bit of fun.

Bea stood in the front hall with her gloves on and her chin lifted, pretending she could not hear her own heartbeat thumping too loudly in her chest.

Outside, Nicholas's carriage waited... The closed one, again. Another deliberate choice, and they both knew it.

When the butler announced him, Nicholas entered as if he belonged there—coat immaculate, posture irritatingly relaxed, eyes bright with that particular brand of arrogance that should have made Bea want to throw something heavy.

Instead, her stomach tightened.

He bowed over her hand with maddening courtesy. "Lady Beatrix."

She did not offer him a smile. She offered him a look. A deliberate one.

Nicholas's mouth twitched as if he enjoyed trying to guess her mood.

Bea dropped her hand before he could linger. "To what do I owe this...call?"

Nicholas straightened, gaze lingering on her mouth for a beat too long to be accidental. "I've come to ask if you'd like to go riding in the park. Unless...there's another political salon you'd like to attend." He blinked at her innocently.

She narrowed her eyes on him, then stepped past him toward the door without waiting to be offered an arm. "Have you come to attempt to seduce me again?" she whispered scandalously as she walked past.

Nicholas fell into step beside her, voice smooth. "I wouldn't dream of it."

"I'm not certain I believe you."

"Don't sound so disappointed." His tone turned conspiratorial. "I must say I'm surprised you don't have another salon picked out. I thought you might miss the thrill of publicly humiliating grown men."

Bea's mouth betrayed her with the smallest twitch. "I do not *humiliate* men."

Nicholas opened the door for her, the morning air rushing in cool and bright. "Of course not. They humiliate themselves. You simply...hold up a mirror."

Bea paused on the threshold, struck by how accurate that was. She regained her composure in half a breath. "Where are we going, then?"

Nicholas's eyes warmed. "Riding."

"In Hyde Park."

It wasn't a question.

Nicholas's grin was pure wickedness. "You read my mind."

Bea held his gaze for one long, steady moment. Because she did read his.

Because they both knew no one went *riding* in a closed carriage with the windows drawn for the sake of fresh air.

They went because the world outside could not see what happened inside.

Bea's pulse stumbled. She turned briskly toward the steps

as if she hadn't felt it. "Very well. If my father asks, I shall tell him you wished to admire the trees."

Nicholas's laughter was low. "The trees. Yes."

Bea marched down the steps like a woman going to battle. Which, she told herself, was essentially what she was doing. She was simply—strategically—allowing Nicholas to take her—*ahem*—riding in the park.

That was all. Nothing to do with the fact that Nicholas had stood beside her at Hillary House. Nothing to do with the way he'd looked at her afterward, as if she were brilliant and dangerous and worth listening to. Nothing to do with the way his wink in the coach had made her toes curl.

You don't have to marry the man to enjoy him.

Bea cleared her throat and proceeded him to the coach. She reached the conveyance first. The door was already open. Nicholas offered his hand.

Bea stared at it for a beat, as if she still hadn't decided whether to accompany him. But one glance back at him and her decision was made. This could be quite a pleasant outing...if she allowed it to be.

Nicholas helped her up with slow, careful deliberation, his touch lingering just long enough at her waist to remind her that his touch was never accidental.

Bea took a seat.

Nicholas climbed in after her and sat across from her. All perfectly proper.

Then the door shut with a soft, decisive thud, and the carriage immediately felt smaller.

Bea fixed her gaze on the opposite window. She could feel him watching her—like sunlight, like pressure, like a hand hovering just above skin.

Nicholas leaned back with the ease of a man entirely too confident in his ability to be charming.

"You're very quiet," he observed after a few minutes of silence passed.

Bea did not turn her head. She stared harder out the window as the carriage began to move, the wheels catching the rhythm of the street. "I could say the same about you."

Nicholas shifted slightly, the leather creaking. "Tell me," he murmured. "Did you see the paper today? There was a political cartoon with Langford as the subject."

Bea's breath caught. She lifted her chin, still refusing to look at him. "Was there?" she asked in the most nonchalant tone she could muster.

"Yes. It mentioned what Langford said to you at Lord Hillary's house." His tone was mild, but she could hear the curiosity underneath it.

"Did it?" Now her gaze was fixed out the window like a condemned woman awaiting her sentence. "How...enterprising of the artist."

Nicholas's voice stayed pleasant. Too pleasant. "Enterprising," he repeated, as if tasting the word. "Is that what we call it when someone repeats a remark that was spoken in a private room?"

Bea's pulse skittered. She forced her shoulders to remain loose. "Lord Hillary's salon wasn't private. It was packed."

"True," Nicholas said, unhurried. "And yet the cartoonist captured Langford's phrasing rather precisely."

Bea lifted one shoulder in what she hoped was an indifferent shrug. "Sir Edwin is predictable. Men like him always are."

Nicholas made a low sound that might have been agreement. Or amusement. Or suspicion. "Or perhaps someone in that room took a particular interest in the exchange."

Bea's fingers tightened around her reticule. "Are you accusing me of something?"

"I'm asking a question." Nicholas's tone remained mild,

but his gaze—she could feel it on her profile like heat—was not. "Did you see the paper?"

Bea allowed herself a small, airy laugh. "I don't make a habit of reading political cartoons, Lord Vanover."

"No?" he murmured.

Bea finally turned her head, meeting his eyes with practiced boredom. "Do you?"

Nicholas's mouth twitched. "Oh, yes. Particularly because the artist in question frequently uses me as his subject."

Bea pressed her lips together. "How terrible for your vanity."

Nicholas shrugged. "I've come to expect it. But I do wonder...where this particular cartoonist gets his information."

Bea let out a loud, long sigh. "I'm sure I've no idea. But as I said, Lord Hillary's salon was packed. It could have been any number of people."

"You're right," Nicholas allowed. "I do hope Langford isn't too greatly affected."

Bea tilted her head and offered a small, indifferent hum. "If the cartoon embarrassed him, he may learn to keep his opinions to himself."

Nicholas leaned back slightly, studying her with the patience of a man who enjoyed puzzles. "You seemed remarkably passionate about his opinions last night."

Bea blinked slowly. "I dislike fools."

"So do I." His voice dropped a fraction. "But this fool was skewered in print before the city finished its breakfast. Seems...fast, doesn't it?"

Bea's heart hammered once—hard enough to hurt. She kept her expression serenely blank. "Not particularly. London moves quickly."

Nicholas's gaze slid to her mouth, then back to her eyes.

"It does," he agreed. "Especially when someone helps it along."

Bea held his gaze, refusing to blink first. "Are you accusing me of something, my lord?"

Nicholas's smile returned—lazy, wicked, and entirely unhelpful. "Oh, I don't know yet. But you have a terrible habit, my lady." He leaned in just enough that she could smell him—clean, warm, dangerous—his voice turning velvet-smooth. "…of looking guilty when you're delighted."

Bea's breath caught.

She recovered quickly, narrowing her eyes. "You are imagining things."

"Am I?"

"Yes."

She turned back to the window with a snap, heart racing, conveying as much loftiness as she could manage, but Bea's stomach did an unhelpful little flip.

She kept her eyes on the window, on the passing blur of London, as if she could stare her way out of trouble. But she could feel him beside her—watching, waiting—like a man who had all the time in the world.

And Bea, for the first time, realized something with a jolt of cold clarity.

If Nicholas truly began to suspect she was connected to B. Adroit… He would not let it go. He would come closer. He would keep coming. Until either she slipped—

Or she decided to stop running.

CHAPTER TWENTY-ONE

The carriage rolled past the first stretch of park walls, the city sounds dimming, the air turning greener, quieter. Somewhere outside, a horse whinnied. Hooves clipped. Distant laughter floated like something harmless.

Inside the carriage, everything felt…not harmless at all. First, Nicholas moved to sit next to her. Then he shifted again—just enough that his knee brushed hers.

Bea went very still.

Nicholas's eyes dropped for a moment to the point of contact, then lifted again, dark, assessing. "You're tense."

"I am not."

"You are," he said softly. "It's rare."

Bea's eyes flashed. "Stop talking."

Nicholas blinked, delighted. "Is that an order?"

"Yes."

He leaned forward slightly, elbows resting on his knees, expression the picture of attentive obedience. "As you wish."

Bea narrowed her eyes. "Don't do that."

"Do what?"

"Pretend you can be obedient."

Nicholas's smile sharpened. "On the contrary, if you wanted obedience, you should have chosen another suitor."

"You are not my suitor. I am not marrying anyone!" Bea snapped.

Nicholas's gaze dipped to her mouth again, slow and deliberate. "Who said anything about marriage today?" he murmured.

Bea's breath stalled.

Because suddenly she understood what he was doing—exactly what he had done in the coach yesterday.

He was taking the thing she refused to say out loud and laying it between them like a dare.

Fun.

Temptation.

A kiss without consequences.

But did she dare? Especially now that he clearly suspected she was connected to B. Adroit?

Bea's fingers curled around her reticule so hard they ached. This wasn't only about Nicholas. It was about draw-ings—and her revolt. She wouldn't trade those things for a few moments of pleasure, no matter how tempting.

But was it possible to have both?

"Take care." Nicholas's voice lowered, velvet-smooth. "If you're going to glare at me like that, you'll set my coat on fire."

Bea tipped her chin. "Then step away before you burn."

Nicholas's mouth curved. "You don't want me to step away."

Bea held his gaze—steady, unblinking. She exhaled once, slowly, and let the decision settle in her bones. "No," she said softly. "I don't."

The carriage hit a small dip in the road, rocking them. Bea's shoulder brushed his—an accident, nothing more.

Except Nicholas didn't move away.

And this time she didn't retreat.

His hand lifted, hovering for a beat near her cheek as if he were asking permission without words.

Bea stared at it.

At him.

At the wicked patience in his eyes, as if he were willing to wait all day for her to admit what they both knew.

Her throat tightened with the sheer maddening pull of it —the way he could be clever and kind one moment, and then unapologetically seductive the next.

First, he had made her feel as if she mattered.

And now he was making her feel as if she was wanted.

Bea swallowed.

Nicholas's thumb brushed her cheek—barely a touch, barely a claim.

Bea's breath shuddered.

"Say it," Nicholas demanded.

Bea glared at him. "Say what?"

"What you want," he replied, voice low, eyes steady. "Just once. I won't have you accusing me of forcing you into anything. You want this as much as I do. I know it."

Bea's entire body felt too hot, too awake, too alive.

She looked away for half a second—toward the curtained window, toward the safe world outside.

Then she looked back at him.

At his mouth.

At the faint curve of his smile, as if he already knew how this would end.

Bea's pulse thudded. "Oh, shut up," she hissed.

Nicholas's eyes gleamed brighter. "Gladly."

Bea leaned in, furious at herself for doing it—and furious that she wanted to do it even more. But if she kissed him, it would be because she decided to—because for once she wanted something without thinking about it endlessly first.

"Shut up," she said again, closer now, a hot whisper, "and kiss me."

Nicholas's smile vanished. Not into softness. Into something sharper. Hungrier. As if she'd finally given him permission to stop pretending this was a game.

"Yes," he murmured.

Nicholas's hand slid slowly along her hip, not fumbling, not presumptuous—asking and guiding all at once. He wanted her to feel every moment, to understand why she was trembling. And he wanted to make her tremble even more.

His lips brushed against hers, softly at first, but not tentatively. Merely playful—an easy, testing touch that stole her breath and then gave it back. He wanted to hear her decide to take more.

Bea's fingers tightened on his coat, not pulling him away, not yielding entirely either—holding him there in that delicious, undefined middle space.

"Still glaring?" he murmured against her mouth.

"Still talking," she whispered—and then she lifted her chin and met him properly.

Nicholas made a low sound that wasn't quite laughter. His mouth slanted over hers again, lingering this time, tasting rather than teasing. He nudged at her lower lip— once, twice—patient, a man with all the time in the world, until Bea parted for him with a moan.

"That's it," he breathed, guessing that praising her would make her furious enough to give him exactly what he wanted.

It did.

Bea kissed him back with sudden heat, a sharp press of mouth to mouth that turned his indulgent control into something ragged. Nicholas's hands slid to her face, steadying her as the carriage rocked, fingers splaying along the curve of her jaw with quiet certainty. He deepened the kiss, slow at first—drawing it out, letting her feel every shift of pressure, every careful drag of his lips over hers, until her breath stuttered.

Bea's palm flattened against his chest. His heartbeat pulsed under her glove—too fast for a man who liked to pretend nothing could touch him.

"Again," she demanded when he broke away just a fraction.

Nicholas's eyes gleamed. "So commanding."

"Do it," she whispered.

He did.

Nicholas kissed her again, mouth opening on hers as if he meant to devour her stubbornness at his own unhurried pace. One hand moved down to her waist, and a thumb stroked there once—an almost absent caress that sent heat curling through her. Bea made a small, traitorous sound and surged closer, closing the space completely. She was done with courtesy and consequences.

Nicholas's breath hitched. The next kiss was not playful at all. It was hungry—still controlled, still deliberate, but edged now with the kind of need that made a man forget to be clever. His fingers slid up her side, catching lightly in the fabric at her ribs, and Bea's hands went up—one to his shoulder, the other slipping into his hair at the nape of his neck before she could stop herself.

It was absurdly soft.

Nicholas went still for half a heartbeat, as if he were startled by the intimacy of it.

Then he groaned, low and helpless, and the kiss turned molten.

His hand slid to the back of her head, not forcing, not

trapping—guiding. His fingers threaded into her hair, loosening pins with a skill that suggested far too much practice, and Bea's pulse skittered at the realization even as she clutched him harder.

"Nicholas," she breathed into his mouth, a warning she didn't quite mean.

He answered by kissing her more deeply.

His tongue traced the seam of her lips in a slow, coaxing stroke—an invitation more dangerous than any command. Bea shivered, then opened for him with a fierce, reckless decision, and Nicholas took it—tongue to tongue, warm and intimate and unpardonably delicious. The kiss became a tangle of breath and heat, his mouth moving with patient certainty as if he meant to teach her exactly how far pleasure could be taken in the space of a few stolen minutes.

Bea's fingers tightened in his hair, tugging just enough to make him curse softly against her mouth. She felt his smile there—wicked, satisfied—and she bit his lower lip in retaliation.

Nicholas made a sound that was pure approval.

The carriage lurched gently over cobblestones, and they rocked together, foreheads nearly touching, mouths still chasing, refusing to let the kiss end. Nicholas's hair was mussed beneath Bea's hands, falling out of its perfect order; Bea felt her own pins giving way, strands slipping loose around her face.

When Nicholas finally pulled back, it wasn't far. Just enough to breathe—just enough to look at what they'd done.

Her lips were swollen. Her breath was uneven. A lock of her hair had fallen across her cheek, and Nicholas—still too close—tucked it back with a thumb that lingered at the corner of her mouth.

Bea glared at him out of habit.

Nicholas's eyes flicked to her lips, then up again, dark with triumph.

"You've ruined my hair," Bea said, voice unsteady.

Nicholas's smile was slow and sinful. "I'm just getting started."

Her only answer was a delighted smile.

His hand moved—slowly, deliberately—to the neckline of her gown. He hesitated only a second, seeking her eyes. She didn't look away. She didn't stop him.

He tugged down the edge of the fabric, revealing the swell of her breast above her chemise.

Her breath stuttered.

He lowered his head.

Her hands flew to his hair…but she didn't push him away. She held him. Urged him.

Nicholas pushed her back down onto the seat, as his lips closed around the hard peak of her nipple through the thin linen. His mouth was warm and teasing at first, then sucked her with deeper intent as she arched into his wet heat. A trembling sigh broke from her throat—quiet, shocked, utterly undone.

He groaned at the sound.

He drew the fabric lower, just enough to bare her fully, and his mouth covered her again—hot, hungry, reverent. His tongue circled the little bud, slow and decadent, and she gasped, her fingers tightening in his hair.

"Nicholas…" she whimpered.

He dragged his mouth along her, tasting, savoring, letting every suppressed desire he'd been carrying pour into each heated stroke of his tongue.

She writhed beneath him.

He felt her legs shift, her body arch, her breath catch in his ear…

And God help him, he wanted her. All of her. Completely.

He lifted his head, chest heaving, his mouth swollen from her skin. She was a beautiful mess—flushed, lips parted, bodice askew, hair tumbling like loosened silk.

Gorgeous.

He kissed her again instantly, deeply, instinctively. She tasted like defiance and an admission she'd never speak aloud.

His mouth angled over hers, teasing, then claiming, slow enough to tempt, deep enough to undo. She arched into him, fingers sinking into his shoulders as though she'd forgotten she ever meant to resist him.

She shivered beneath him.

"Bea," he murmured.

She opened her eyes, dazed, lips parted.

He brought her hand to his chest—right over the frantic beat of his heart—and held it there. "Feel what you do to me," he said softly.

Her fingers curled, unthinking, drawn to the warmth of him. He watched her realization bloom—slow, startled, hungry.

Then, still holding her hand, he guided it lower…enough that she felt his gasp as she touched first along the line of his waistcoat, and then beneath it, where desire and restraint collided in the smallest, sharpest tremor of his abdomen.

Her lips parted in a soft, startled sound as he moved her hand to his throbbing cock, starkly outlined beneath his breeches.

"That," he murmured, "is how you affect me."

Her knee pressed lightly against his thigh, unbidden.

He felt the delicate tremble of her whole body.

She didn't pull away.

He let his hand drift down to the hem of her skirts—slow, deliberate, warm—urging her subtly closer, showing her the rhythm of how bodies leaned, how want drew two people together without force or command.

Her breath broke on a sigh.

"Bea," he said again, voice thickened now, more plea than tease, "do you touch yourself? Do you know how it feels to…"

Her fingers tightened on his shoulders. But he could tell from the hint of confusion between her brows that she didn't know what he meant.

He gently pulled up her skirts. Then he took her hand and carefully led it down between her legs. With all the delicate attention in the world, he showed her exactly where to find the nub of pleasure between her thighs. Her body softened under him, melting into the curve of his arm. He rubbed her in small circles, teaching her, as her head fell back and throaty moans escaped her lips.

He lowered his mouth to her throat—just barely, reverently—letting his lips brush skin in a way that was almost too gentle.

Her back arched instinctively, a soft gasp escaping her. Her eyes flared with surprise as if he'd revealed something entirely unknown.

He smiled, slow, wicked, adoring. Then he moved his hand away and let her continue with the small circles of pleasure. "You see?" he whispered. "You do know how."

She trembled helplessly, biting her lower lip.

His hand slid lower, cupping the back of her thigh, urging her even closer, letting her feel how intimately their bodies aligned when she did. She made a sound…soft and shaken.

Nicholas's breath faltered.

He murmured her name like a vow. Then he drew two fingers into his own mouth, eyes never leaving hers, before leaning down and sliding one inside her—slowly, steadily—until she trembled beneath him.

"Nicholas—" Her mouth fell open, a nearly pained expression on her face. But she wasn't in pain. Far from it. She was panting, and a soft "oh" fell from her lips as he crooked his finger inside her.

He watched her face as she drew closer and closer to her pleasure. Moving his finger on the exact spot he knew she needed, while he whispered encouraging words in her ear. "That's right. Feel it. Enjoy it. Don't stop."

She groaned.

"That's it. Just like that. You learn quickly."

She made a gasping sound that made his cock even harder.

"I knew you would," he continued.

He pressed his mouth to her ear. "Do you know what you are doing to me, watching you touch yourself like this?"

She whimpered, the sound small and helpless, her breath shuddering as the tension inside her drew tighter and tighter.

"You have no idea," he murmured, his voice rough with want. "Every sound you make tells me exactly what you need. Exactly what you want."

"Nicholas—" she breathed, her lip caught between her teeth, eyes squeezed shut as though the feeling were too much to bear and not nearly enough all at once.

"I have you," he whispered against her ear. "Don't stop. Let it happen."

BEA'S BREATH WAS GONE. Her body felt as if were foreign to her. The sensation building between her legs was unbearable. The world narrowed to that sensation...to heat and pressure and the unbearable sweetness of release hovering with something wonderful just out of reach. Her breath fractured, her body tensing as if bracing for impact...and then she broke.

Not quietly. Not gently.

The pleasure swept through her in a rush so powerful it stole the strength from her limbs, a soft, broken cry escaping her as the wave crested and carried her with it. She arched toward Nicholas, caught in the moment, utterly unguarded, the feeling unlike anything she'd felt before.

NICHOLAS WATCHED HER, transfixed. Her face was flushed, radiant, filled with astonishment. Pride surged through him, fierce and humbling all at once—not ownership, not triumph, but the knowledge that she had trusted him with this. That he had been the one to guide her there. That whatever this was between them, it was real.

And he would never forget the look on her face when she let go.

He withdrew his hand from beneath her skirts, slowly and deliberately. She moved both her hands back up to his shoulders.

He stilled instantly.

Her eyes—still hazy with pleasure, still stormy with want —cleared with sudden alarm.

"Nicholas," she whispered. "We—I—what was that?"

The air between them shifted, rushing in where heat had been.

He forced himself to stillness, to patience. "Are you all right?" he asked quietly.

"I think so." She shook her head, a breathless, disbelieving laugh catching in her throat. "No. I just—this—we shouldn't..." Her voice faltered.

"Please don't tell me you regret it," he said gently,

searching her face, preparing himself to hear the answer even if it undid him.

She looked up at him through lashes still damp and dark. "No," she admitted, worrying her lower lip. "It was…astonishing. But—"

He nodded once, slow and measured, and shifted back to sit beside her…just enough to give her space. Her skirts rustled softly as she smoothed them with unsteady hands.

Nicholas braced his arms on the seat beside her, close but no longer touching, aware of her warmth, her presence, the fragile line between what had been and what must not go further.

"It was only meant to be kissing," she whispered, as though trying to restore order by naming it. "Just kissing. That's all."

Nicholas looked at her—truly looked—and something inside him eased and tightened all at once.

"I don't think it ever could be just kissing between us," he said quietly.

Her breath caught, not with fear, but with recognition. With truth.

And she did not tell him he was wrong.

CHAPTER TWENTY-TWO

Bea could not sleep. But not for lack of trying. She had blown out her candle, folded her hands primly atop the coverlet, and willed herself toward peaceful oblivion.

It did not work.

It did not even come close.

Every time she closed her eyes, she felt *him.*

His mouth on hers. His breath against her cheek. His body over hers, solid and warm and so devastatingly certain of itself.

Heat slid through her at the memory, slow, molten, and impossible to ignore.

Bea groaned into her pillow. What had he done to her today? It had been surprising. Entirely unexpected. Pure, base lust. Completely beneath her as a serious political thinker, as the mastermind behind B. Adroit, as a revolutionary.

And yet…

As a woman…

Her fingers curled into the sheets.

He'd asked her if she regretted it. That was the most damning part of all. She didn't regret it. She wanted more.

Oh, at first she'd tried to tell herself he had coaxed her, maneuvered her, tricked her into kissing him again. That he had manipulated the moment, arranged it like a chessboard so her only possible move was to lean in.

But that wasn't true. In fact, it was the opposite.

She'd told him *exactly* what she wanted.

She had *felt* what he was doing. Every gentle prod. Every cleverly placed remark. Every heated glance meant to lure her closer. She had recognized the strategy as it unfolded and still taken hold of his lapels and dragged his mouth to hers.

A shiver ran through her at the memory.

It had not been Nicholas who forced the moment. She had wanted him. She hadn't allowed him to goad her like before. Let him draw her in. Let him kiss her and touch her while she'd done the same to him.

And good heavens, the way he had looked at her before he'd pulled her hand down between her legs. Teaching her something she could never banish from her fantasies.

She shifted restlessly, staring up into the darkness.

Nicholas Archer. Impossibly handsome. Apparently infinitely skilled with his hands.

And—curse him—every bit as tempting as he believed himself to be.

He had kissed her back with something more than triumph. More than tactics. More than smug certainty.

He had kissed her like a starving man.

And then—oh Lord—then he had laid her back against the cushions, braced above her, his weight a sinful, perfect pressure she had never known she needed. She could still feel the solid line of his chest, the way his breath had caught when she touched his shoulders, the way he had murmured her name like a secret.

And his mouth on her breast—

Heat swept through her so quickly she had to squeeze her eyes shut more tightly.

Her nipples tingled at the memory. The slow, deliberate pull of his lips. The shocking, delicious scrape of his teeth. The low sound he'd made—half growl, half groan—when she'd arched helplessly beneath him.

Bea pressed a trembling hand to her sternum as if she could calm the frantic beat of her heart.

No one had ever touched her like that.

No one had ever *wanted* her like that.

Certainly no one had ever listened to her the way he did. No one had cared what she thought about anything, Parliament, the country, the injustices she secretly sketched in ink. Her father dismissed her. Her mother soothed her into silence.

But Nicholas…

He watched her as if she were not merely present, but essential.

The thought made her breath catch painfully.

Bea shifted under the covers, her thighs brushing, and the spark of sensation that followed was almost too much. She exhaled sharply, her breath unsteady.

This was madness. She was a grown woman, not a schoolgirl sighing over a handsome face. She had a mission— an actual mission—to influence Parliament, to undermine dangerous legislation, to expose hypocrisy wherever she could.

Nicholas was not part of that mission.

He was not part of any plan she had ever made.

And yet her mind refused to quiet. Her body refused to forget. Her pulse refused to settle.

Her gaze swept through the darkness above her bed. What would it feel like—if she let herself imagine it—to have him here? In this room? On this bed? His hands braced on either side of her, his voice a low, rough whisper against her ear?

The image struck her with such force she let out a sound, soft, breathless, dangerously close to a whimper.

Her legs drew up beneath the sheets without her conscious permission, thighs pressing together in sudden, helpless need.

He had done this to her. Nicholas and his wicked mouth and his wicked confidence and the wicked things he'd murmured against her skin.

"Future wife," he had called her.

She should find that infuriating.

Instead, she found herself picturing his lips trailing down her body, his breath warm against her chest, his hands spreading heat everywhere they touched—

"Oh…" The whisper escaped her before she could swallow it.

Her body curled inward, the tension coiling low, hot, insistent. Each remembered sensation sharpened the next, the weight of his torso pressing her down, the soft velvet of the seat beneath her back, the warm rasp of his breath as he'd whispered her name like a vow he had no right to make.

Her nipples tightened painfully as she pictured his mouth on them—slow, reverent, unbearably focused—and she arched off the mattress, chasing a memory that felt far too vivid for comfort.

Bea pressed a hand to her mouth, as though she could contain the unspooling ache inside her.

This was madness. It was dangerous and foolish, and entirely improper.

And she wanted it so badly her bones were liquid.

Her breath shuddered out of her as she dropped her knees apart and sought the aching spot between her legs with the tip of her finger, seeking relief she could not allow herself to name.

She touched herself. Slowly at first. And then more quickly. The tension built. Climbed. Twisted through her like a silken thread drawn tighter and tighter.

She tried—for one last, futile second—to banish the image.

But she still saw him.

His dark hair mussed by her fingers. His mouth swollen from kissing her senseless. His eyes heavy-lidded, hungry, focused on her like she was something he'd dreamed of too many nights to count.

Bea let out a shaken, desperate sigh, and the tension snapped. Not gently. Not quietly.

It broke over her like a wave, hot and shivering, stealing her breath and arching her spine as the world went white behind her eyelids. Every muscle tightened, then trembled, and she melted into the mattress in a warm, liquid collapse.

She lay gasping in the soft dark, sheets tangled around her legs, her heartbeat wild and unsteady.

The aftermath washed through her in pulses, sweet, dizzying…overwhelming.

Slowly, her thoughts drifted back into shape.

Good heavens. What had he done to her?

What had she done to herself?

She flung her arm over her eyes as if to block out the implications entirely.

She wanted him. She knew what it meant to lie with a man. Georgie had told her. It had all sounded a bit unbelievable at the time, but now she knew exactly what she'd been missing.

She wanted Nicholas with a force that shook her. And that was dangerous. Because desire made women foolish.

Desire made women reckless. Desire made women do stupid, compromising things.

And Bea could not—would not—allow Nicholas to become her downfall.

Not when she had a vote to influence. Not when she had a cartoonist's war to wage. Not when her entire purpose relied on her remaining perfectly, stubbornly un-swayed.

She exhaled shakily.

No matter how good he felt. No matter how intoxicating he tasted. No matter how thoroughly her body betrayed her when she was in his company. She would not let him win. All men wanted was to control women. She could never forget that fact.

Bea rolled onto her side and hugged her pillow.

But long after the aftershocks faded… Long after her breathing steadied… Long after the flush cooled from her skin…

She could still feel his mouth on hers.

And all of it was dangerous…because just before Nicholas had taken her back home this afternoon, he asked her once again about the cartoon in the morning paper. There was no denying it. He suspected something.

CHAPTER TWENTY-THREE

Bea had successfully delivered another cartoon. Just now, she'd sneaked out, tucked the folded drawing into the usual pamphlet, and dropped it into the slot at the printshop. She *should* have felt triumphant.

Instead, her cheeks warmed at the memory of last night, the stolen moments in her darkened bedchamber when her thoughts had drifted, unwisely, inexcusably, back to Nicholas. To his mouth. His hands. The way he had looked at her as if he could see straight through every layer she presented to the world.

She'd be lying if she didn't admit to herself that she'd created another caricature so quickly in order to draw Nicholas's attention away from the Langford drawing. He'd been far too perceptive when he'd asked her about it. She'd cleared her throat and glanced away, then hurriedly disembarked from the carriage before he'd had a chance to say anything more.

Of course, last night, she'd been far more preoccupied with the memory of Nicholas's mouth on her breast, driving her mad, than the discussion about B. Adroit.

Fine. She was a woman with desires, not a marble statue. There was nothing sinful in wanting what any warm-blooded creature might. And Nicholas was handsome enough to haunt a woman's imagination. Nearly irresistible, if she were honest. But none of that meant they were suited. Nor that they would marry. And it certainly didn't mean she agreed with his politics any more than she ever had. She still had a mission to accomplish.

The drawing she'd just delivered was deliciously sharp—Nicholas drawn as a smug fox in a perfectly tied cravat, whispering sweet nothings into the ear of Britannia with one paw while the other slipped coins into the pocket of another fox dressed like a duke, one who bore a startling resemblance to her father. The caption read: *A pretty mouth and prettier lies. Who profits from the seduction of a nation?*

She'd thought of it after listening to her father read her the riot act after she'd returned home yesterday afternoon. She'd been forced to sit in silence—her hair and clothing still no doubt mussed—while both of her parents told her how disappointed they were in her 'unfortunate outburst' at Lord Hillary's salon. They'd apparently got wind of it from a friend who'd stopped by for tea while she'd been out in the park with Nicholas. How terribly helpful.

First, they'd forbid her to attend another one of Lord Hillary's salons. Then they'd threatened her with a shorter courtship if she 'couldn't control her words.' Of course she'd promised them both she would be more than able to control her words. She would have promised them anything in order to escape their diatribe for the quiet stillness of her sitting room.

She'd sat in silence for a while before deciding that her father would be the perfect target for her next drawing. She'd added Nicholas almost as an afterthought. Perhaps he would believe she had nothing to do with the cartoons if he were the subject of the very next one. A tenuous plan, but in the moment, it was all she had.

Bea straightened, turning away from the printer's shop, and brushing a curl behind her ear.

The cartoon was, objectively, rather brilliant.

Though it did come with a twinge of guilt, now that she'd had longer to consider it.

Because in a matter of hours, the man she had just dismantled in ink would arrive to collect her for another outing. An outing she had agreed to. Worse—one she was looking forward to. The contradiction pressed uncomfortably at her conscience.

Which was a problem…because if she was going to face Nicholas again—if she was going to spend time with him—then she would need to be cool. Careful. Entirely in command of herself.

Of course, she was absolutely not planning to kiss him. Not today. Not again. She'd had enough fun. It had been enjoyable, to be certain. But she didn't particularly care to be a woman who would expose a man's politics to public scrutiny and then lose her composure in his arms.

Not to mention, yesterday their antics had hardly stopped at kissing. And she tended to agree with Nicholas when he'd pointed out that it probably could never just be kissing between them. He was right. And she suspected Nicholas would make that line far more difficult to hold than it had any right to be.

Which meant she needed to be on guard.

Determined.

Unflappable.

Even if the man's mouth was… No, his mouth was irrelevant.

She pulled her borrowed cloak tighter and quickly walked away from the shop.

There would be no seduction today. No kissing. No shoulder touching. No hands anywhere they did not belong.

~

BEA REPEATED all of this sternly to herself when Nicholas arrived that afternoon, punctual as always.

He'd brought the coach again today. Of course he did. No doubt he was eager for them to repeat the scandalous things they'd done yesterday.

"There shall be no kissing today," she informed him in what was probably far too loud a voice the moment the coach door closed behind them.

"Noted," he said, with that same self-satisfied grin she'd seen too often lately. "Actually, kissing wasn't my plan for this afternoon."

"Oh, really," she muttered, knowing full well her voice dripped with skepticism. "What else were you planning?"

"Parliament will be back in session soon. The first vote," he continued, "will be on the trade restrictions for the East Indies. I thought we might discuss it."

Bea tilted her head, studying him. Of all the directions he might have taken the conversation, that was certainly not the one she'd anticipated.

"Discuss it?" she echoed. "You and I?"

"Yes." His tone was so simple, so maddeningly unruffled, that her pulse tripped. "Would you like to?"

She stared at him, searching his face for mockery…but there was none. His eyes were steady, thoughtful, sincere.

Sincere about *her* opinion.

A flutter of something sharp and unfamiliar tightened beneath her ribs. Here he was again, asking her thoughts on a matter of state—not as a novelty, not as flirtation, but as though her opinion belonged naturally in the conversation.

Again. Manchester. The reform bill. And now this. Conversations he had not merely begun but continued. It was becoming a habit of his, asking, listening, remembering.

Caring.

Too often, in her own home, her words were indulged or tolerated. Rarely were they *engaged*. But Nicholas was looking at her again as though every syllable she might speak mattered.

This time, she knew exactly what the feeling was. That was the problem. It was the sensation of being *met*—not humored, but answered. Of being seen not as an inconvenience or an ornament, but as possessing a mind worth engaging.

Nicholas chuckled softly, the warm, intimate sound that always seemed to slip beneath her defenses. "You don't have to pretend with me, Bea. I know your secret."

She sucked in her breath. "Pardon?" Surely, he couldn't possibly mean—

"How much you care about politics." Another chuckle.

She closed her eyes and expelled her breath in relief.

When she opened her eyes again, his face had turned serious. "You don't have another secret...do you?" There was that probing gaze again.

"What? No. I—" She cleared her throat. "Of course not."

"Good. Then"—he spread his arms across the back of his seat—"I would love to hear your thoughts. About *any* of the votes coming up."

Her gaze narrowed once more. She tilted her head. "How? Why?"

Nicholas's mouth curved slowly. "Because when you speak," he said, "I find I want to hear every word you say."

Bea inhaled sharply, her heart slamming so violently she was certain he must hear it. It was absurd—completely absurd—that such a simple admission could undo her. Her fingers curled reflexively into her skirts, as if she needed to hold on to something.

He actually wanted to listen.

To *her*. About politics?

It was dangerously intoxicating.

She forced herself to blink, to breathe, to reclaim her wits. If he wanted to discuss politics…she was game.

"How do you intend to vote on the restrictions?" she asked. If he insisted on discussing it, she might as well ask what she truly wished to know.

Nicholas met her gaze. "I'm voting *for* the reform bill, if that's what you're asking."

Bea frowned. She couldn't possibly have heard him correctly. "What?"

"I'm voting *for* the restrictions," he repeated calmly. "To protect colonial laborers and limit private profiteering. It isn't perfect, but it's something. I completely agree with what you said about indifference being the real problem. I admit I hadn't entirely made up my mind, but you made excellent points to Sir Edwin."

Bea stared at him as though he'd begun speaking ancient Greek. "But that's not how my father is voting. That's not how the Tories are voting."

Nicholas met her gaze. His expression was smooth, unreadable. "Do you believe I always vote the way your father does?"

"Yes," she said bluntly. "Obviously."

"Well," he replied with a slight grin, "you're wrong."

She hated the little swoop in her stomach. The shift in her chest. The uncomfortable flicker of…respect.

"But you work with him," she insisted. "You listen to him."

"I do work with him," Nicholas agreed. "And I listen, but at the moment, I'm trying to persuade him to reconsider."

She snorted. "Parliament's stone steps are more yielding than my father once his mind is settled."

Nicholas only smiled. "I've managed more difficult feats."

Bea opened her mouth to argue, but stopped. This didn't make any sense. She'd listened to them, endlessly, through the grate in her bedchamber, and Nicholas always...*always* agreed with her father. She'd never heard him disagree with him. Not once. Not ever.

But then again... Now that she considered it... She'd never heard him explicitly *agree* with him either.

Oh, God.

She swallowed hard, her heart thumping in her chest. Because suddenly, horribly, she remembered the cartoon she'd dropped off this morning.

The fox.

The bribery.

The insinuation of corruption.

The caption: *A pretty mouth and prettier lies.*

Her stomach sank.

She had drawn Nicholas as precisely the sort of man he had just said he wasn't.

Her fingers tightened in the fabric of her gown, guilt washing over her in a hot, disorienting wave. She had misjudged him. Misrepresented him.

Hadn't she?

The thought snagged, sharp and unwelcome.

Because the alternative was far more unsettling. Was he lying to her now? To court her favor?

Her chest tightened at the thought.

"How do I know you're telling the truth?" she countered.

His frown was immediate. "Why would I lie to you about it? You can see my record. It stands for itself. I'm more moderate than the Tories. In fact, I can prove it to you."

She didn't have time to ask what sort of proof he meant.

Just then, the coach slowed, the rhythm of the wheels changing, the familiar scrape of stone replacing gravel. When it stopped, she looked out and felt her breath catch. They were before the very steps she had just mentioned—directly in front of the Houses of Parliament.

"Would you like to see inside?" he asked quite jovially, as though he were offering her a tour of an art museum, not a political institution.

But seeing Parliament, the inner workings of the place she most often dreamt about, was too much of a temptation even for her. Despite her obvious interest, her father had never offered to show her this place.

All she could do was nod.

CHAPTER TWENTY-FOUR

The great doors to the building rose before them like a fortress of power and possibility, all stern stone and soaring arches. Bea had seen it from the outside countless times, but never like this, never while being ushered through its private entrance by a man who strode as though he belonged to every chamber, every echoing corridor, every whisper of influence that traveled through those walls.

Nicholas offered his arm. She took it, her heart still beating so quickly she thought she might need assistance.

"Try not to look so nervous," he murmured as they crossed the threshold.

"Nervous?" she scoffed. "I'm perfectly— Oh." Her breath caught.

The interior was a cathedral of political history. The scent of ink and old wood. The low murmur of distant voices behind closed doors. The weight of decisions made centuries before her birth.

It was magnificent.

As Nicholas watched her take it all in, his expression softened into something unbearably warm. He knew. He knew exactly what this would do to her.

Blast him.

"You brought me here on purpose," she said under her breath.

"Of course," he replied lightly. "Why else does one bring Lady Beatrix Winslow anywhere?"

"Usually to irritate her," she said with a laugh.

"Irritating you is a privilege, not a purpose," he said with a smile that said *I know precisely what I'm doing.*

"Here," he continued, guiding her to the first gallery. "Members' Entrance. You'll want to remember it for the day you take over Parliament yourself."

She blinked. "Pardon?"

He nodded seriously. "I've no doubt you will run the place someday."

She eyed him carefully.

"You think I haven't noticed the way you watch debates at your father's salon? Or the way you listen, not for rhetoric, but for subtext? The way you analyze who holds which opinion and why?"

Her pulse skipped. She hoped it did not show. "You notice far too much," she muttered.

"I notice precisely enough."

He gestured her through the doorway, his hand hovering politely at the small of her back, close but not touching. It sent a line of heat along her spine, regardless.

"This," he continued, "is the antechamber outside the Lords. Here is where the real arguments occur. Quiet ones, between men who pretend to be on the same side."

She inhaled sharply. This was the heart of the world she'd studied in secret. The place behind all the doors she'd only imagined. The place where the reform bill would be voted upon in only a matter of days.

Nicholas leaned closer, his voice brushing her ear. "Would you like to see the voting records?"

Her breath stilled.

Was he teasing her? Mocking her? She studied him. No, he was looking at her with the same keen, knowing awareness he always did.

"Very much," she said before she could stop herself.

Nicholas smiled—slow and pleased—and led her deeper into Parliament.

Parliament was not in session today, but as they walked, she noticed the way he nodded respectfully to clerks, how some bowed slightly, how others greeted him with quiet deference. He belonged here. He thrived here.

And somehow, impossibly, he had brought *her*.

In a private alcove lined with shelves, Nicholas pulled a ledger free and set it gently on the table before her.

She opened it.

Her breath hitched. There they were. Votes, dates, debates, amendments, exactly as she'd imagined them. Oh, the papers reported on the important stories, but never the details. Never the intricate things she wanted to know. Now, she devoured them.

She combed through every vote Nicholas had cast in the last few years, page after page. And he was right. He *had* voted moderately more often than not, frustratingly principled in all the places she'd assumed he was merely posturing. Which only raised the far more aggravating question. If he were not a blind Tory loyalist, then why exactly was he so close with her father and the other Tories? It made no sense.

Then another thought occurred to her. According to the papers, the reform bill vote was so close that even a whispered rumor could tip the vote. Another reason she'd decided on her fox cartoon. But if Nicholas truly wasn't a hardline Tory, with his influence over the Tories, he might well be able to swing the vote *for* reform.

Bea looked up to find Nicholas watching her, arms folded lightly. Not arrogant. Not triumphant. Just…present. Aware.

Awaiting her reaction.

"It's true. You did vote moderately more often than not," she said, her voice softer than she intended.

"Mm," he murmured. "You sound disappointed."

"I'm not disappointed," she said quickly.

He arched a brow.

"All right, I might be slightly disappointed," she admitted. "I do hate to admit I was wrong."

He laughed, a soft, rich sound that warmed her as thoroughly as a touch.

"But if that's true," she continued, turning a page, "why do you agree with everything my father says?"

Nicholas paused, just long enough for her to notice. "Do I?" he asked mildly.

Bea kept her eyes on the book. Her stomach dropped. Had she revealed too much? Said more than she should have?

She pressed a hand to her throat. "I mean…I presumed…"

"You presumed incorrectly," he informed her with a wink.

Bea swallowed hard. "But if you disagree with them, why are you such friends with Father? Hargrave? Hillary? Any of them?" The question escaped before she could temper it. "Not to mention *your father* can hardly approve."

His expression softened. "Well, for one thing. Arguing with my father is an exercise in futility. I allow him to believe I agree with him because it suits my purposes. And for another…I realized long ago that I can't change men like Hargrave and Hillary by declaring war on them. I have to earn the right to disagree. I've never lied to your father. Or any of the Tories."

The certainty in his voice unsettled her. This was not the

answer she had prepared herself to dismiss. It shifted the ground beneath her feet, rearranging assumptions she had taken for fact.

"Is that why you brought me here?" she whispered at last. "To prove to me that I've been wrong about you?"

He did not answer at once. His gaze dropped briefly to the stone beneath their feet, as though choosing his words with care. "Honestly, yes…partially. But also because you deserve to see the world you care about. Because you care more deeply, more honestly, than any woman—or man—I've ever met. I knew you would appreciate it."

Her breath left her. Just…left, as if it had been stolen from her lungs.

And then it hit her. She'd been wrong about him. This entire time…she'd been wrong about him. The enormity of her mistake settled heavily in her mind.

"Nicholas—" She swallowed.

"And also…" He looked at her—truly looked—and there was no calculation in his expression, no easy charm to soften the moment. "I brought you here because I want you to know me as I truly am. Not as you imagine me to be. And I want"—he hesitated, rare and telling—"the chance to know you as well. All of you."

The silence that followed was heavy, taut with things unsaid. With implications she could no longer pretend not to see. Guilt pressed low and sharp beneath her ribs—the cartoon, the accusation she had inked without certainty, the ease with which she had assumed the worst of him, simply based on the company he kept.

Nicholas extended his arm once more. "Come," he said gently. "There's a gallery above the chamber. It's for observers when we're in session. Would you like to see it?"

She hesitated for only a heartbeat.

Then she took his arm, not because it was easy, and not

because it felt right, but because walking away would not undo what she had done. Because she suspected she would soon have to tell him the truth. And because, guilt or no, she could not deny the pull of standing beside a man who had offered her honesty…and who deserved it in return.

AN HOUR LATER, they were back in Nicholas's coach, headed toward her father's town house. The day had been…well, one of the best of her life. Nearly a dream, if dreams came laced with a sharp, persistent thread of guilt tightening around her ribs.

Bea stared out the window, watching London blur past. Her chest felt too tight. Too full.

Because all she could think about was the cruel precision of her own drawings. The fox's smirk. The coins in the duke's pocket. The sly, insinuating lines she'd drawn as if she *knew* Nicholas.

As if she'd understood anything.

But she couldn't bring herself to tell him. Any of it—why she'd formed such a firm opinion of him, how she'd overheard her father's conversations. Overheard them and apparently misinterpreted them. Or that *she* was B. Adroit. That secret was dangerous, fragile, and more deeply kept than anything else she possessed.

So she sat there in silence, desperately searching for some appropriate, dignified way to thank him for taking her to Parliament. Something that didn't sound inadequate.

Soon, the coach pulled to a stop outside her father's house.

After the footman pulled down the coach steps, Nicholas helped her alight and then walked her slowly to the door.

Just as she gathered her courage to speak, she looked down to see the afternoon's paper sitting on the top step.

And there it was…on the front page.

The latest caricature. The one she'd delivered this very morning. *Her* caricature.

Nicholas looked down at it and then scrubbed his face with a weary groan.

"I can hardly blame you for thinking I was a devout Tory," he said dryly. "Most of London does. Everyone's seen these blasted caricatures in the papers." He nudged the paper with one booted foot. "Whoever this fellow is, he's got me entirely wrong."

Bea forced herself to breathe, shallow, careful.

Nicholas shifted his weight, exhaling through his nose. "But don't worry," he added with a note of irritation, "I have it on the best authority that the Bow Street Runner I hired is about to run the scoundrel down. B. Adroit is about to regret the day he was born."

Her heart hammered against her ribs.

Nicholas had hired the Bow Street Runner? Nicholas was the one hunting her?

He glanced up and met her gaze, his brow furrowing. "Do you know who B. Adroit is?"

Her throat clenched. She swallowed hard, too hard. The guilt punched low in her stomach, thick and sickening. They'd spent the afternoon together. He'd shown her who he truly was, and now he was no longer implying. He was asking her directly. She could not lie.

"Yes," she whispered. "I do."

CHAPTER TWENTY-FIVE

Nicholas had risen this morning with an unusual sense of purpose, and not merely because he would be seeing Bea again tonight. His early meeting with Fletcher, the Bow Street Runner he'd hired, had finally produced a genuine lead.

Bea had admitted she knew B. Adroit's identity. And for now, that truth had to be enough. She had not given him a name. And he did not press her for one. She'd looked terribly distressed. But Nicholas had assured her she needn't betray her friend. Fletcher was close to learning the truth. He already had an address. It was only a matter of time before he had a name. It would be easier this way for both of them.

And Fletcher hadn't disappointed. He'd informed Nicholas this morning that the anonymous caricaturist delivered his drawings with predictable regularity. Fletcher had traced the bloke to a residence in Mayfair. He'd assured Nicholas he had only to conduct a bit more investigating to learn the precise identity of the cartoonist. Apparently, Fletcher suspected the man had used a household servant to deliver the drawings for him.

The thought had simmered in Nicholas's mind all afternoon, the slow burn of impending revelation. At last, he might meet the culprit behind those maddening drawings, might demand an explanation, or a correction, or perhaps a cessation entirely. One way or another, the sketches would end. Nicholas would see to it. He would not allow B. Adroit to ruin everything Nicholas had worked for.

However, like most things in his world, this too took patience. And Nicholas could wait for confirmation. He wanted the cartoonist's identity to be certain, after all. Despite his father's demands for immediacy, certainty took time.

Speaking of his father, the man hadn't even bothered to summon him this time. Instead, he'd merely sent a note. So certain he'd be obeyed by his only son that he didn't even feel a meeting was necessary.

The Winslow chit makes rash statements, the missive had read. *See to it that you marry her soon and teach her to keep her mouth shut. The outburst at Hillary's salon was unforgivable.*

So, Father had heard about the incident at Hillary's salon, just as Nicholas suspected he would. Predictable, but no matter. It was better that Father didn't see him again until *after* the older man learned he'd voted against his wishes.

And he did have every intention of voting for the reform bill. He'd been privately weighing the decision, but after Bea's impassioned speech to Sir Edwin, he'd been convinced. Not just by her words but by her conviction. Bea was right. And her certainty was appealing. His father would be furious, but for the first time in his life, Nicholas no longer cared.

Instead of replying, he'd crumpled his father's note in his fist and tossed it directly into the fire where it belonged.

~

BY THE TIME Nicholas reached Winslow's town house that evening, all thoughts were eclipsed by the sight before him.

Bea stood in the foyer in a gown of pale pink muslin, light, summery, impeccably chosen. The color warmed against her skin, the neckline framed the graceful line of her collarbone, and the bows at her sleeves lent her a softness in direct contrast to the restless tension he sensed beneath it.

Something in her posture—too correct, too contained—made Nicholas's own breath draw tighter.

Her coolness toward him wasn't disdain. He knew that tone well, could recognize it at twenty paces. This was different. This was distance. A retreat. A silent pulling inward that he could not, for the life of him, explain.

Especially after the way she'd looked at him in Parliament yesterday.

"Are you all right?" he whispered as he escorted her outside.

"Did you…m…meet with the Bow Street Runner?" she asked, her voice shaking a little.

Was that what she was worried about? That he would learn the identity of someone she was protecting? He understood her concern, but he would not lie to her. "Yes," he replied. "He's close to getting a name."

Her shoulders dropped a bit as if with relief. But she remained tense.

His words from yesterday echoed through his head…*B. Adroit is about to regret the day he was born.* He hadn't meant it as a physical threat…more as a bit of exaggeration. But he couldn't blame her if she was worried he would do something to harm her friend. "I only intend to speak with him," he assured her. "To ask him to stop. There won't be pistols at dawn or anything brutish."

She gave him a tentative smile, but her mouth remained tight.

The four of them—Bea, her parents, and Nicholas—settled into Winslow's carriage. They were all going to the same dinner party tonight. The duchess fussed with her gloves, while the duke gazed out the window with the air of a man surveying his personal dominion. Bea sat next to Nicholas with her hands folded neatly, fingers giving the tiniest betraying twitch every few seconds.

Why wouldn't she look at him?

Before he could puzzle it out, the carriage rolled to a stop in front of Chelmsford's grand town house, all blazing lamplight and an unavoidable swarm of Tories at their most self-satisfied. Voices drifted out—braying laughter, pompous pontificating, half-baked policy pronouncements.

Nicholas helped Bea down from the coach.

"For the record, my father has threatened me with bodily harm if I say anything untoward this evening," she whispered.

"Where is the fun in that?" Nicholas answered lightly.

A flicker—so quick he might have imagined it—passed through her eyes. Guilt. Yes. But something deeper. Something that had absolutely nothing to do with tonight's dinner.

He almost reached for her hand. He wanted to squeeze it. To assure her he would be at her side this evening…whatever may occur.

Instead, he offered his arm. She accepted with the lightest possible touch, barely there, the kind of contact that implied obligation, nothing more.

But he knew better. This wasn't a distance born of dislike. It was distance born of something she was desperately trying not to say, and she still wouldn't meet his eyes. Nicholas narrowed his eyes at her. How close was she with B. Adroit?

Inside, the foyer was a crush of velvet coats, glittering jewels, and political egos. Footmen darted between callers, and the air buzzed with talk of trade bills, royal health, and Manchester unrest.

Bea murmured under her breath, "I should have feigned illness."

Nicholas smiled faintly. "If you care to feign a swoon, I'll gladly catch you."

She shot him a look, weary in a way she never allowed herself to be. Whatever she was carrying tonight—whether related to B. Adroit or not—it was…different. Which only made Nicholas more determined to stay at her side.

Lord Chelmsford himself waddled forward to greet them, ruddy-faced and beaming. After greeting her parents, he turned toward Bea.

"Lady Beatrix! So delighted you are here," he declared, grasping her hand to kiss it with too much enthusiasm. "And with Lord Vanover, no less. I'd heard you two were courting."

Nicholas watched Bea stiffen almost imperceptibly. But before she could even answer Chelmsford's loaded greeting, the man barreled on cheerfully with, "It's such a pleasure to have you here."

Bea smiled sweetly. He could tell it took effort. "Of course, my lord. It's a pleasure to be here."

The guests drifted toward the dining room, and Nicholas maneuvered himself and Bea to the center of the long table, safely away from her mother but, regrettably, directly across from her father.

Winston's stare clearly warned his daughter: *Behave.*

Bea's lifted chin promised: *We'll see.*

Nicholas took his seat beside her.

The first course passed uneventfully. Watercress soup. Harmless remarks. Compliments on gowns. Talk of horse breeding. Wine poured. Laughter trickled.

Then came the inevitable.

Lord Hargrave.

Of course it was Hargrave.

The same pompous blowhard Bea had verbally slaughtered in Father's salon days ago was now seated across from them, sweating into his cravat as he demolished his pheasant.

"The trouble with reformers," Hargrave announced loudly, "is that they believe every common cobbler deserves a vote. Next, they'll want to put shopkeepers in Parliament and allow women to—" He barked a laugh. "Well. No need to indulge in absurdities, despite what B. Adroit did to Langford."

Several men chuckled obediently.

Bea's fingers tightened around her wineglass. Nicholas sensed the storm gathering next to him like a rising tide.

"What, precisely," Bea asked, voice soft enough to be lethal, "is absurd?"

Hargrave blinked. "Come now, Lady Beatrix. Women have no interest in politics."

"I have an interest," she said.

"Ah," Hargrave replied, patronizing, "but a proper interest? Or the sort that leads to unnecessary opinions? Like what happened between you and Langford at Hillary House?"

Nicholas stopped breathing. *Hell.*

Winston shot his daughter a warning look. She ignored it.

"Is there an unnecessary kind of opinion, Lord Hargrave?" she asked. "I hadn't realized men were filtering them for us."

There was a ripple of murmurs as the tension thickened.

Hargrave sniffed. "Opinions require logic. And logic—"

"Is not exclusive to men," Bea cut in.

More murmurs. Winston stiffened. Bea's mother went pale.

Hargrave sputtered, "Lady Beatrix, you mistake my meaning."

"No," Bea said simply. "I believe I've understood it perfectly."

Her father snapped, sharp as the crack of a whip, "Beatrix. That is enough."

The table fell silent.

Bea lifted her chin, but Nicholas saw past the fire to the flicker beneath it. The tiny wound inflicted when a parent scolds an adult as if she were a child. The sting she tried to hide. The same sting Nicholas knew all too well.

Winston turned toward Hargrave. "You must excuse her, my lord. She has been indulged far too long in—"

"She does not need excusing." Nicholas heard his own voice before he consciously decided to speak.

Every head swiveled toward him—even Bea's.

Winston looked thunderstruck. "Vanover?"

Nicholas set down his wine with deliberate calm. "Lady Beatrix understood Lord Hargrave perfectly. She merely chose to disagree. She is entirely capable of forming her own opinions without any man's permission."

A stunned silence reverberated down the length of the table.

Hargrave gaped.

Winston's face deepened to a violent shade of plum.

But Bea... Bea looked at Nicholas as though he had just done something impossible. Something she hadn't dared to hope for. Something that reached inside her and lit the dark corners.

And Nicholas felt it, felt her attention strike him like a bolt.

For years, he had practiced diplomacy with these men, listening, nodding, placating, pretending neutrality so he could persuade them later. He'd thought it strategy— patience, positioning, playing the long game.

But sitting beside Bea, watching her sit in a room full of

men who wanted her silent, he suddenly saw it for what it was…what it always had been. Indecision.

He had been patient when he should have been principled.

And now—because of her, because of her courage, because her refusal to shrink was the most extraordinary thing he'd ever witnessed—he realized he *did* stand for something.

He stood for her.

And God help him…he was falling for her.

Deeply. Irretrievably. Probably stupidly. Given that she still wouldn't even admit they were courting.

Winston tried again, sounding strangled. "This is hardly—"

Nicholas cut in smoothly, eyes never leaving Bea. "Her place," he said gently, "is wherever she chooses it to be."

Gasps traveled the table.

Bea's lips parted. The faintest flush painted her throat.

And Nicholas knew—without question—that he would face down an entire party of Tories, an entire Parliament, an entire country, if necessary, if it meant defending her again.

"If we might return to the original point," he said, turning back to Hargrave with effortless composure, "the matter of broader voting rights is hardly destabilizing. The lower classes already support the weight of England's labor. Granting them fractional representation would strengthen the nation, not weaken it."

A murmur rose. Some agreement, but mostly disapproval.

Winston stared at Nicholas as if attempting to determine whether to strike him dead or have him arrested.

Bea, however, simply watched him with wonder.

Nicholas's pulse thundered. He'd never felt more certain of himself, or more alive.

The rest of the dinner blurred. Debate, muttering, the

scrape of cutlery. Hargrave sulked. Winston seethed. The duchess fanned herself as though she might swoon at any moment.

But Nicholas barely noticed any of it.

Because each time Bea glanced at him—just small, secret glances—the air between them tightened, pulled, hummed with something he had no business wanting but could no longer deny.

When the ladies rose to withdraw, Bea's fingers brushed Nicholas's sleeve.

Light. Accidental.

Devastating.

Heat rushed through him.

Oh yes. He was falling for her.

And there was absolutely nothing diplomatic about it.

CHAPTER TWENTY-SIX

After dinner, it took Nicholas approximately two minutes before he excused himself from the men drinking port in the dining room to go in search of Bea in the drawing room.

He spotted her immediately. She'd drifted away from her mother and stood near a marble column, pretending to examine a painting. Nicholas approached quietly, his arms folded behind his back.

"Did you intend to start a riot?" she murmured without turning.

"No," he said softly. "I intended to defend you."

She turned to face him slowly.

Her eyes—sea-green, bright with unshed emotion—searched his. "Why?"

He could have given a dozen answers. A hundred. Political advantage. Point-scoring. Courtship strategy.

All lies.

So, he gave her the truth.

"Because you were right."

Her breath hitched.

"And," he added, voice lowering, "because Hargrave deserved his humiliation."

A soft, startled laugh escaped her. It was barely more than a breath, but it undid him.

Nicholas stepped fractionally closer and touched her wrist. "You do not need anyone's permission to think."

"No," she whispered, eyes dropping to his mouth before jerking back up, "but no one has ever said so aloud."

"I am not 'no one.'"

"I know," she said. Too soft.

The air changed.

He felt it as surely as he felt the pulse beneath her skin. A pull. A shift. A surrender neither of them had meant to give.

Bea's lips parted, as if she meant to say something more, something dangerous.

But her mother called from across the room. "Beatrix, dear, Lady Crawford wishes to speak with you."

Bea blinked hard, as if waking from a spell. "Yes, of course." She stepped back, the movement too quick, almost flustered.

Nicholas let her go.

Because he had to. Because if he reached for her, even briefly, even innocently, it would only complicate things.

AN HOUR LATER, when the men rejoined the ladies in the drawing room, Winston wasted no time cornering Nicholas near the mantel.

"That display at dinner was ill-advised," the duke said. He was not snarling, but he said it with the precise tone of a man accustomed to being obeyed.

Nicholas met his gaze steadily. "With respect, Your Grace, your daughter deserved better than to be dismissed."

Winston's expression did not change, but something tightened at the corners of his eyes. "A gentleman may disagree without staging a performance."

The phrase landed with a familiar chill—his father's rule dressed up in another man's mouth: don't perform, don't feel, don't give them you. Nicholas inclined his head, a gesture of courtesy, not concession. "If defending Lady Beatrix appeared theatrical, then I make no apology for the spectacle."

A faint beat of silence.

The duke's jaw flexed slightly.

Across the room, Bea glanced up from a conversation with a pair of older matrons. Her eyes found Nicholas at once. Gratitude flickered there—a soft, unguarded warmth—followed almost instantly by that same shadow he'd noticed in the carriage. Guilt. Again. She masked it quickly, but it was unmistakable.

Winston followed his daughter's gaze, then looked back at Nicholas. His voice remained perfectly even when he spoke again. "We are still in the early stages of arranging a match," he said. "Stability matters. Diplomacy matters."

Nicholas narrowed his eyes. Was that a threat?

Heat surged up his spine. "And integrity matters. Lady Beatrix should never be expected to silence herself for anyone's comfort."

The duke studied him for a long, heavy moment, measuring the man who had just contradicted a dining room full of Tory peers. "Take care, Vanover. Agreements not yet sealed may still be withdrawn."

Oh, that was definitely a threat. Nicholas's jaw tightened, but his voice stayed calm. "If defending her costs me your favor, I will bear it."

Something in Winston's expression shifted…faintly, almost imperceptibly. Not approval. But not disdain either. A recalibration.

He placed a hand on Nicholas's shoulder, a subtle assertion of authority. "You're bold," he said quietly. "I like that about you. Just be certain your boldness doesn't outrun your judgment."

Nicholas met his gaze unflinchingly. "On the contrary, Your Grace. I believe my judgment has never been clearer."

Bea's eyes caught his again from across the room, guilt, worry, conflict, all swirling together.

As Nicholas watched her, he was certain. He would face down every man in England if it meant easing that look from her eyes.

Hours later, when the party finally dispersed, Bea stood with her parents near the front door. Nicholas stepped to her side. He offered his arm again.

She hesitated—not from disdain, not from carefully cultivated Winslow nonchalance, but because everything inside her had been rattled loose tonight. Still, she set her hand on his sleeve. Her fingers betrayed her with a tiny tremor. She prayed he didn't feel it.

"I'm riding back with you," he said quietly. "Your father may prefer to pretend I do not exist at present, but I would see you home."

A ridiculous flutter moved through her middle. "You needn't trouble yourself."

"Too late," he murmured. "I've already made it my trouble."

She had no response for that, not one that wouldn't reveal far too much.

When they reached the Winslow carriage, he handed her up with a care that felt…intentional. Protective. Her parents were already seated opposite, her father's attention fixed firmly on the window as Nicholas took his place beside her.

Bea sat, pulse misbehaving. He sat close enough that even the warm summer night air between them seemed charged.

The door closed.

For the first time since dinner, silence wrapped around them, thick, humming, intimate. She should have been more worried about her father. About the inevitable disdainful lecture she would receive once they were privately behind closed doors at home. And yet, all Bea could think of was Nicholas. *He defended me. Twice. He defended me against my father.*

Every moment from the last several days flashed through her in a dizzying cascade. Him listening, really listening; him watching her with that frustratingly perceptive gaze; him coaxing her opinions forward instead of dismissing them; him teasing her out of moods she didn't even realize she was in; him bringing her to Parliament; and then…defending her as though he'd been *waiting* for the chance.

Piece by piece, an unavoidable truth settled, heavy and hot, low in her chest.

She didn't just want him. She *liked* him. Admired him. Looked forward to him. Missed him. And that—dear God— that meant…*she was falling for him.*

The realization struck like a physical blow. Her breath faltered. Her pulse stumbled.

But beneath that heady rush, guilt twisted sharp as a blade.

Her drawings. Her mistake. The Bow Street Runner. She was falling for the very man she had mocked and maligned in print for months. He saw the guilt in her eyes. He had to.

Nicholas shifted beside her. "Bea," he said softly.

Her name in his voice sent a quiet, unwelcome tremor through her, and she hated that it did. She kept her gaze fixed ahead, acutely aware of the carriage's close quarters—and of her parents seated opposite them.

Still, she looked at him. Just briefly. The open sincerity in his eyes caught her off guard, made her pulse stumble.

The carriage jolted over a rut. She tipped toward him, and his hand came out at once, steadying her elbow.

She stilled, and so did he.

For a suspended moment, neither of them moved, as though the smallest shift might draw notice. His hand remained where it was—correct, careful, unmistakably restrained—yet the contact was impossible to ignore.

Her breath caught. She willed herself to steady it.

Nicholas withdrew his hand at last, slowly, deliberately, as though to prove—to himself as much as to her—that he could.

Their eyes met again. Something unspoken passed between them, taut and unresolved.

The carriage wheels slowed.

They were home. The familiar outline of her parents' town house came into view through the window, a reminder —solid and immovable—of where she stood and what she could not afford to risk. If Nicholas discovered that she was B. Adroit and told her father...he would disown her. Or worse.

The carriage rolled to a stop. The footman opened the door, and warm lamplight spilled inside.

Bea drew a careful breath and straightened, schooling her features, even as her pulse refused to settle.

Nicholas deserved the truth. Not an explanation. Not a clever evasion. The truth.

The certainty of it sat heavy in her chest, for she had no

notion of how one confessed something like that to a man who had just defended her honor as though it were his own.

She knew one thing for certain. Not here. Not tonight.

But as she prepared to step down into the lamplit street, an awful thought occurred to her.

Soon, she might have to choose between her secret... and him.

CHAPTER TWENTY-SEVEN

The moment Father stepped down from the carriage, every nerve in Bea's body coiled tight. Mama followed, murmuring something about the lateness of the hour, but Bea barely heard her. All she knew, all she *felt*, was Nicholas at her side.

"We'll just let you two say goodnight," her father said blandly, already crossing the walk. It was shocking, really. An impropriety. It just proved how much her father trusted Nicholas to allow them a moment alone together.

But the instant the duke and duchess disappeared up the steps, the night took on a different weight. Quiet. Breathless. Charged.

Nicholas quickly pulled the door closed and turned to Bea.

She opened her mouth—she thought to thank him, or perhaps to apologize, or to demand why he had to look at her like that at the dinner table—but Nicholas moved closer.

And the world tilted.

He kissed her first.

Not politely. Not cautiously. Not like a man feeling out the edges of propriety.

He kissed her like a man who'd been holding himself back all night and had finally decided he'd had quite enough of it.

Heat flashed through her so fast her breath tangled in her throat. His hands framed her face, and her fingers clutched his lapels on instinct, pulling him closer, anchoring herself to the only steady thing in a world that suddenly felt as though it were pitching beneath her.

A sound escaped her, helpless, hungry, horribly honest.

And God help her, she kissed him back with everything she had been trying not to feel.

The taste of him—warm, intoxicating—hit her harder than the wine she'd drunk at dinner. Her pulse stuttered wildly, her balance wavering despite the seat beneath her, as though will alone kept her composed. Nicholas made a low, rough sound in response, a vibration she felt everywhere, and his hands slid from her cheeks down to her waist, pulling her sharp against him with a decisiveness that unraveled her.

She leaned into him without thinking, pressing so close she could feel the rise and fall of his chest, the heat of him searing through every fine layer of her gown. His scent— clean soap, warm skin, the faintest trace of brandy—wrapped around her like a spell.

He angled the kiss deeper, and her world tilted further.

Her hands went from his lapels to his shoulders, then higher, threading into the hair at his nape, knocking off his hat, fingertips sinking into soft, dark waves. He shuddered at her touch. Actually shuddered. The realization sent a bolt of power through her she hadn't been prepared for.

"Bea," he whispered against her mouth, half groan, half prayer.

Her name had never sounded like that before.

She felt the seat beneath her a second before she realized he'd pushed her backward, guiding her until she was pressed against the squabs and he was pressing her gently—but unmistakably—into the cushions.

Heat roared through her. Her body arched into his without deliberate will. The kiss deepened again, dizzying, desperate.

When she gasped for breath, he pulled back slightly, his forehead brushing hers, his lips grazing her cheek, her jaw, the vulnerable space beneath her ear. Her eyes fluttered shut, knees weakening. His mouth found a spot on her neck that made her clutch at him, a soft gasp tearing free before she could swallow it down.

"This is your fault," she whispered, breathless, mortified by how undone she felt and how badly she wanted more. "You were absolutely irresistible tonight."

He laughed, voice shaking. "I accept full responsibility."

She tugged him back to her mouth with entirely too much confidence for someone trembling as violently as she was.

The kiss turned fervent again. Hotter. Hungrier. His hands splayed across her hips and guided her closer, so close she could feel the unmistakable evidence of how deeply this affected him.

A shock ran through her, lightning-quick and devastating. Her breath shuddered out of her. Her fingers tightened in his hair. Everything inside her spiraled.

And then—then—he shifted, pulling her up in one fluid movement until she found herself, skirts pushed up above her knees, straddling his waist.

The carriage swayed.

So did she.

He pulled her tight against his hips, and her head fell back. Heat flooded her, up her spine, across her chest, blooming in low, overwhelming places she did *not* dare acknowledge. Her heart thundered wildly. Her breath stuttered in her throat. She felt—

She felt *everything.*

"Nicholas," she managed, though it emerged as a gasp, not a warning.

He froze immediately. Not pushing her away, but holding perfectly still, like a man poised on a precipice.

He tipped her head toward his, his forehead resting lightly against hers, their breaths mingling, both of them shaking.

"I'll stop," he murmured, voice hoarse, "if you ask me to."

He meant it.

She could feel that truth vibrating beneath his skin, see it in the strain tightening his jaw, the fear and desire warring in his eyes.

She should stop this. She should climb off his lap and move away before her body gave away every last secret she possessed. He did not yet know her secret. And when he found out, he might well hate it. It was unfair of her to continue this.

But when his hand slid, slowly, reverently, along the curve of her waist, when his thumb brushed the narrowest part of her stays with breathtaking tenderness…

Something inside her simply gave way.

Her fingers skimmed his rough cheek, then curved around the back of his neck. She drew him closer until his breath ghosted across her parted lips.

"Don't stop," she whispered.

He stilled. Completely.

Then—very slowly—his hands moved again, tracing the line of her waist, her back, her hips with a kind of worship that made her body tremble against his. He kissed her again.

God, he *kissed* her—slow and deep, as though savoring every moment.

Sensation built—too much, too fast, too startling—and the carriage seemed to shrink with every breath they shared. The night outside disappeared. The house. The city. The world.

There was only this.

Only him.

Only the dangerous, impossible, world-altering truth that she wanted him with a ferocity she had never known.

He broke the kiss first—barely—pressing his forehead to hers again, both of them gasping.

"If you'll regret this tomorrow," he said quietly, "tell me now."

She stared at him, chest heaving, lips swollen, pulse racing, every nerve alight.

Regret?

Tomorrow?

No. God, no.

But she had done something unforgivable. Something that would come crashing down the moment his Bow Street Runner discovered the truth, *if* he discovered the truth. Guilt flickered up, sharp and panicked. She had to say something, tell him some truth, even if it wasn't everything.

"For so long… I thought…" She swallowed, unable to look away from him. "I thought you only wanted to win."

His jaw tightened. "Win what?"

"Me. My father's approval. Your political future." She tried to laugh. "All of it."

The pain that crossed his face was brief but unmistakable.

"You are not an obstacle," he said softly, squeezing her hips. "You are the only part of all this that feels real."

Her breath hitched, and something molten and terrifying and wonderful unfurled inside her.

The truth—her truth—landed with the force of a blow.

All evening—no, for days now—touchstones kept clicking into place. Him listening, really listening. Him noticing her thoughts, her moods, her passions with unnerving accuracy. Him taking her to Parliament. Him defending her with the sort of boldness she had never expected from a man who spent half his time charming political opponents.

Piece by piece, all of it slammed into her at once. She wanted him. She'd known that for days. Not because he was handsome or charming or wicked or persistent. But because he had seen her. Defended her. Asked her what she thought. Asked her what she believed. Treated her mind like a marvel instead of a nuisance.

A fierce ache bloomed low in her chest, a mix of wanting and wonder and dread. Because beneath all of this heady, impossible feeling, there pulsed the sharp thorn of her secret.

Her caricatures. Her mistake. The Bow Street Runner he'd hired. The reckoning barreling toward her with every passing hour.

She swallowed hard.

Her lips brushed his again, soft, aching. A whisper of a kiss that felt far more intimate than all the breathless, hungry ones before.

"Nicholas," she whispered again.

His hand slid up to cup her cheek, thumb stroking just beneath her eye. "Beatrix," he murmured. The name was like a caress across her skin.

That was when she knew they were seconds—seconds—from crossing a line they could never uncross. And she couldn't let that happen until he knew the truth.

The knowledge hit her like cold water.

She tore her mouth from his, chest heaving, her fingers gripping his coat as if she needed it to keep from completely collapsing.

"I want to, but… We—we can't—" she managed, voice cracking with conflict. "Not tonight. Not yet."

He stiffened instantly. "Jesus, Bea. I'm not planning to *take you* in the back of your father's coach. I just want to touch you."

She closed her eyes. Oh, God. She wanted that too, so much.

His deep voice rumbled against her throat. "Just let me touch you a little longer. Lie back for me. Let me kiss you until you're trembling and wet and begging for more."

The way he said it—low, rough, threaded with restraint that was rapidly fraying—should have terrified her. Instead, it sent heat flooding through her, pooling low and deep until she could hardly breathe.

"Nicholas…" His name crumbled into a sigh as he moved her gently off his lap and onto the soft carriage seat, where he knelt before her, not with reverence, but with a hunger so raw it made her stomach swoop.

His hands slid along her bare calves first, slow enough to make her tremble, sure enough to undo every sensible thought she had left. He pushed up her skirts, and they fell around his shoulders like a tent of secrecy, shutting out the world until there was only the warm dark, her racing pulse, and Nicholas—Nicholas—moving closer.

Too close.

Not close enough.

She sucked in a breath as he pressed his palms along the insides of her thighs, urging them open. The carriage rocked slightly with the shift of her weight, her heart slamming against her ribs as he eased her farther back into the cushions.

"Tell me you want this," he demanded.

A soft sound escaped her, barely a whisper, barely even a word. "Yes. Please."

His breath caught. And then—

Heat. A single, devastating stroke of his mouth through the fine, damp-softened layers between them.

Her entire body jolted.

He didn't rush. He didn't tease. He didn't give her time to overthink or panic or pull away. Nicholas touched her with his mouth the way he argued…focused, deliberate, absolutely certain of the effect he meant to have. Each slow, seeking caress sent a ripple of pleasure through her, tightening her grip on the squabs until her knuckles whitened.

"Nicholas—oh—" Her voice broke as he found the place she was already aching for him to find. His rhythm was careful at first, then firmer when her hips betrayed her, lifting into his touch.

He made a low, satisfied sound. "There," he breathed against her. "Just like that."

Her head fell back. Every inhale was a fluttering gasp. Every exhale a plea she couldn't quite form. The world dissolved around her…no carriage, no street, no parents in the house. Only darkness. Only his mouth. Only the unbearable, exquisite pull building tighter and tighter inside her.

He guided her with his hands, keeping her open, steadying her when her thighs trembled. When she tried to muffle a moan, he coaxed it back out of her with a slow, sinful sweep of his tongue that made her entire body arc.

"I can't—" she whispered.

"Yes," he murmured against her thigh. "You can."

His hand slid up to brace her hip. "Hold still," he murmured. "Let me do this. I want to feel you come on my tongue."

"Oh—" She gasped, the sound rough and unguarded. She clutched at his shoulder with one hand.

And then with one last devastating swipe of his tongue, he gave her exactly what her body had been begging for.

Pleasure ripped through her so fast she cried out, quietly, but she couldn't stop it. The sound spilled out of her like something pent up for years. Her fingers flew to her mouth, then to his head, then gripped helplessly at her skirts as her body tightened, tightened—

And shattered.

Her breath stuttered on the release, heat unfurling inside her in a rush that made her thighs quake around his shoulders. He didn't move away, not until the last tremor faded, not until she was boneless against the cushions and barely remembered her own name.

Only then did he lift his head and push the skirts away.

Her vision blurred at the edges as she stared down at him —the disheveled hair, the flushed cheeks, the glistening lips, the wicked satisfaction written all over his face.

She had never felt anything like it.

She would never be the same again…

For a long, taut moment, neither of them moved.

Then Nicholas nodded—once, sharply—pulling back just enough that the air cooled between them.

His hands stayed on her knees, steadying her as she tried to breathe again.

The loss of his warmth was agony.

They sat like that for a long, trembling breath before he spoke.

"This," he said softly, moving to sit next to her once again, "changes everything."

She swallowed hard. "I know."

"Come to me," he pleaded. "Tomorrow. Steal away. Let me make you mine."

"I want to," she said, but every thought in her head was reminding her of what she'd done.

Nicholas helped her straighten her gown and moved back against the seat, though her body ached at the sudden distance. His cravat was rumpled. Her hair was a disaster. Their lips were unmistakably swollen.

He lifted one hand—hesitated—and brushed a loose lock of hair behind her ear.

She almost leaned into the touch.

Almost.

"You should go in now," he said.

"Yes," she whispered.

He knocked on the top of the carriage to alert the driver, while Bea gathered her skirts. When the carriage door opened, she stepped out into the night on unsteady legs.

The driver escorted her.

At the top of the steps to the house, she looked back.

Nicholas sat in shadow, watching her as though she had just undone him completely. He'd sent his own coach home earlier. Father's coachman would drop him at his house and return.

Her heart clenched.

She turned away quickly and slipped inside before she could do something foolish.

Like run back to him and confess everything.

Or kiss him again. And she *would* kiss him again. Hopefully. Only…first, she had to find a way to tell him the truth.

CHAPTER TWENTY-EIGHT

Bea had not slept. She had tried. She had extinguished her candle, pulled her counterpane up to her chin, closed her eyes, and willed her mind to calm, but her body—traitorous, disloyal, maddening—still hummed with sensation. Her skin remembered the feel of Nicholas's hands. Her throat remembered the drag of his breath. Her legs…well. Her legs had memories of their own, and all of them were entirely unsuitable for a wallflower with any interest in maintaining her virtue.

And she was not even certain she *did* wish to maintain it anymore.

That was the most unsettling part.

Nicholas's offer was nearly irresistible. And she was seriously considering making that choice. To go to him. To let him make her his.

By the time dawn light crept through her curtains, Bea had abandoned sleep entirely. She wrapped herself in a thick dressing gown, tied the belt too tightly, then paced her sitting room in increasingly agitated lines.

A footman delivered breakfast. She ignored it.

Her mother sent a note urging her to take a morning ride with her. Bea crumpled it.

Her father shouted something down the corridor about her being "ready for callers after luncheon." Bea pretended not to hear.

She could not think of callers. She could barely think at all. She could only replay the night before, the flush of heat in the dark carriage, her own reckless hands, the hunger in Nicholas's eyes when she pulled back, breathless, wanting him in a way she had never wanted anything.

And now?

Now she had precisely one option. *Tell him.*

Tell him she had caricatured him more savagely than any other MP, Whigs and Tories combined. Tell him she had mocked his speeches, lampooned his alliances, turned him into both a preening, corrupt peacock...and a sly fox.

Tell him she was *B. Adroit.*

Bea pressed her palms over her face and groaned into them.

There was a soft knock at the door to her sitting room. She could not take a lecture from her parents. Not today. Not now.

She almost shouted, "Go away," until she recognized the cadence—one rap, two quick taps.

Poppy.

"Oh, thank God," Bea murmured. "Enter before I combust."

Poppy flung open the door with all the subtlety she had never once possessed. She wore a morning gown—a buttery yellow muslin with her bright hair hastily pinned and likely to fall at any moment—and she marched across the room and came to stand directly in front of Bea.

"I saw the story in the paper this morning. I came as soon as I could," Poppy declared, hands on hips.

Bea's head snapped up. "What story?"

"The one about—"

Another knock cut her off.

"That will be Georgie," Poppy said with a definitive nod.

"Yes, it's Georgie," came a muffled voice through the door. "May I come in before someone sees me loitering like a woman whose reputation for trouble is entirely *earned*?"

"Enter." Bea sighed.

Georgie slipped inside, cheeks flushed, dark hair rebelliously swirling around her face. Her pink muslin gown was wrinkled from haste, as though she'd barely paused to breathe. She shut the door carefully behind her, crossed the room, and dropped onto Bea's settee.

"All right," Georgie said, rubbing her hands together. "Poppy is here, I am here, and you apparently had quite a night last night. Tell us everything."

Bea blinked at them. "How did you—?"

"The paper reported that Lord Vanover publicly contradicted Lord Hargraves. Twice," Poppy informed her.

Bea sank onto the chair opposite her friends, feeling suddenly small beneath their scrutiny. "Oh…it's true." The gossip about the incident at Lord Hillary's house had been spread solely through word of mouth. Apparently, last night's incident had made the actual paper. Unfortunate, that. Her father would be even more furious.

"And is it also true that Lord Vanover contradicted Lord Hargrave while defending *you*?" Georgie asked next.

Bea nodded slowly. "Yes. Also true."

"How terribly romantic," Poppy said, clasping her hands together near her ear and smiling dreamily.

"That's not all," Bea added, biting her lip.

"Do tell," Georgie said.

"I kissed him again," Bea blurted. "And…more."

Two identical gasps filled the room.

"You kissed Lord Vanover again?" Georgie exclaimed. "In public?"

"Yes," Bea said. "Well…in a carriage."

Poppy looked positively scandalized. "His carriage?"

"No," Bea groaned. "My father's carriage."

There was a beat of stunned silence.

Then Georgie collapsed sideways onto the cushions. "Oh, well. That's something."

Poppy sat down hard on the settee. "Your *father's* carriage?"

Bea covered her face again. "I have no excuse. Well, I do actually, but it's quite a long story."

Georgie recovered first, propping herself up on one elbow as she regarded Bea with barely contained alarm. "It's ever so convenient that we enjoy long stories then. Isn't it, Poppy?'"

"Oh, indeed we do," Poppy agreed, rubbing her hands together in gleeful anticipation.

Bea had always considered herself immune to such girlish nonsense as blushing, but an unmistakable flush stole up her throat. She forced herself to straighten her shoulders and plow through a general rendition of the last few days between herself and Nicholas, including the part where she'd learned that he hadn't voted the way she assumed he had.

"What exactly happened in the carriage?" Georgie, ever the pragmatist, wanted to know.

"We kissed a lot and then…"

"Then?" Georgie prodded.

"Then…well." Bea gestured vaguely in the direction of her thighs, cheeks burning.

Poppy straightened her back. "Oh, my God."

Georgie slapped both hands over her mouth. "You saucy baggage. Excellent initiative."

"Not excellent," Bea snapped. "Ridiculous. Irresponsible. Dangerous."

Georgie arched a brow. "How dangerous?"

Bea said nothing.

Poppy's jaw dropped. "Did you lose your virtue?"

"Poppy!" Bea nearly shouted, horrified.

"Well?" Poppy demanded. "Did you?"

Bea wilted. "No. But nearly."

The room exploded into shrill, scandalized joy.

Georgie's jaw nearly hit the floor. "Why, Beatrix Winslow, I am so proud of you."

Bea groaned. "Please stop talking."

Georgie leaned forward. "Be honest—how far *did* it go?"

Bea stared at the carpet. "Far enough."

Georgie's eyes widened. "Did he touch—"

"Georgie!" Bea practically yelped.

Georgie waved a hand. "Fine, fine, never mind. We'll assume 'far enough' means far enough to make a grown man contemplate repentance."

Bea groaned again. "This is a disaster. Didn't you hear me? I've been all wrong about him, and he has no idea it's been me skewering him all this time."

Georgie eyed her shrewdly. "A minor detail."

"It's not minor at all," Bea said reflexively, crossing her ankles. "He's certain to hate me when he finds out. And what if he tells Papa?"

"He's clearly on your side," Georgie pointed out. "He defended you at dinner."

Poppy nodded. "And quite heroically, I might add."

Georgie arched a brow. "Sounds like the type of man one ought to marry if one wasn't committed to being a spinster."

Bea scowled. "Wallflower. And I don't know what I'm committed to any longer. I feel as if everything I believe in is wrong. It's as if I don't know anything anymore."

Georgie folded her arms. "Well, you had better start knowing things, because that man is planning to marry you, is he not?"

Bea stood and paced in front of the fireplace. "Yes. I mean, no. I mean…he was, but I have to tell him the truth before it goes any further. I must tell him I'm B. Adroit. Before he finds out on his own."

"So tell him," Poppy said simply.

"But what if he wants to rescind his offer?" Bea groaned. "What if he hates me?"

Georgie leaned forward. "I doubt he'll want to rescind his offer."

Bea paled. "What if he tells my father?"

"Won't your father forgive you?" Poppy asked.

"For making him a laughingstock among his peers for years? Have you met my father?"

"Honestly, no," Poppy replied with a shrug.

"Suffice it to say, I'll be lucky if all he does is cut me off and toss me onto the street."

Georgie nodded gravely. "Bea has a point. Satire against the government is one thing. Satire against your own father? Satire that has already stirred political unrest? Bea, B. Adroit has become notorious."

"Exactly," Bea whispered.

Bea's stomach dropped. There wasn't a world in which she could keep this secret from Nicholas. She'd thought about it endlessly. But telling him meant trusting him completely. With her safety. Her reputation. Her future.

"Oh, God." She covered her face again and collapsed back into her chair, staring at the ceiling. "I'm doomed."

"You're not doomed," Georgie said. "Not yet."

"Yes, I am," Bea insisted. "Nicholas is certain to be furious. He'll feel tricked. Betrayed. Humiliated."

"Well," Georgie said slowly, "yes."

Bea shot upright. "Georgie!"

"I'm *agreeing* with you," Georgie said. "That's what you want, isn't it?"

"No," Bea said miserably. "Tell me not to tell him."

Poppy exchanged a knowing glance with Georgie.

Then Poppy asked softly, "Do you wish to not tell him?"

Bea opened her mouth. Then she closed it. Then she tried again.

"No," she finally whispered.

Georgie softened. "Bea…"

"I *want* to tell him," Bea said, voice cracking. "I want him to know me. The real me. The part of me that doesn't bow and curtsy and allow men like Hargrave to define my worth. The part that fights. The part that doesn't belong anywhere except behind a quill and a locked door." Her throat tightened. "I want him to know her."

Poppy's face softened. "Because you want to marry him."

"Because I—" Bea stopped, choking on the word. "Because I *feel* something. And I don't want whatever it is to be built on a lie."

Georgie curled her legs beneath her. "Then we've circled back to the start. You have two choices." She held up one finger. "One, trust him."

Poppy held up a second. "Two, never see him again."

Bea's breath hitched.

Never see him again.

Never hear his laugh. Never argue with him about policy. Never see his eyes soften the way they had last night. Never feel his breath on her throat or the way his hand slid up her thigh in the dark—

She pressed a trembling hand to her mouth.

"I don't think I can stop seeing him," she admitted. "And what would I tell Father?"

Poppy's brows rose. "Well, then."

"But I don't know if I can *trust* him," Bea whispered.

Georgie leaned forward. "That's the problem, isn't it? Loving anyone—"

Bea inhaled sharply. *Loving.* She said nothing.

Georgie went on, untroubled by the silence. "Trusting anyone means handing them a knife and hoping they decide not to cut you with it."

Bea stared at her.

"And it sounds as if you've already given him the knife," Georgie said softly. "Whether or not you meant to."

Poppy nodded solemnly. "This is only deciding whether you're brave enough to let him keep it."

The room fell silent.

Bea's heartbeat thudded painfully in her chest.

"I'm frightened," she confessed.

Georgie squeezed her hand. "Good. Only idiots aren't frightened when it matters."

"It matters," Bea whispered.

"Of course it does," Poppy said. "You're not deciding whether to tell him you fibbed about your age or hid a letter from another suitor. You're deciding whether to give him the truth that defines you."

Bea rubbed her hands over her face. "What if he can't accept it?"

"Then he doesn't deserve you," Georgie said instantly.

"What if he thinks I used him? What if he believes I kissed him to manipulate him? What if he—"

"What if he doesn't?" Poppy countered.

Bea froze.

Poppy shrugged. "What if he chooses you? What if he listens? What if he understands?"

"What if he admires you even more?" Georgie added.

"That seems unlikely." Bea blew out a shaking breath.

"It isn't," Georgie insisted. "He defended you last night in front of two dozen powerful men. He risked everything to support you."

Poppy nodded. "He looked at you as if you hung the moon."

Bea frowned. "I didn't say that."

"You didn't have to," Poppy replied, looking dreamy again. "I can just imagine it. Admit it, he's smitten with you."

"Him being smitten isn't the issue," Bea said, stalking toward her window. "I have a much larger problem."

"You are the problem," Georgie said cheerfully. "And the solution."

Bea thunked her forehead lightly against the glass.

Poppy rose and stood behind her, resting her hand on Bea's shoulder. "Listen. You're allowed to be terrified. But you shouldn't lie to yourself."

Bea closed her eyes. "What am I lying about?"

"That you trust him," Poppy said, then added gently, "at least a little."

Bea's throat tightened until she could barely breathe. "I don't know," she whispered.

"Then," Georgie said, "it is time to find out."

Bea turned to face her friends.

Poppy and Georgie both looked at her with the quiet, fierce solidarity only true friends possessed. "We are the members of The Wallflowers' Revolt, are we not?" Georgie asked.

Bea stared at them, heart pounding. Trust him. Or let him go. Two choices. Both terrifying. Both irreversible.

"I need," Bea said slowly, "to see him."

Georgie brightened instantly. "Excellent. We can fetch him."

"No," Bea said, lifting a hand. "I need to go see him. Alone."

Poppy nodded, approval shining. "Oh, well then, we'll help you dress."

Georgie stood, clapping her hands. "Yes. Something bold. Something honest. Something that says, 'I'm about to destroy or solidify the rest of my life.'"

Poppy snorted. "So…green?"

"Green," Georgie agreed. "Definitely green. Bea looks divine in green."

Bea gave a helpless laugh, the first she'd managed all morning. "All right," she said, feeling the first tremor of something like courage. "Green it is."

Her friends flanked her like battle generals preparing a soldier for war. And somewhere in the back of her mind, beneath the fear and the shame and the longing, was the faintest whisper of hope. She would face Nicholas. She would tell him the truth.

Today would decide her fate.

For better or for worse…

CHAPTER TWENTY-NINE

One hour later, Bea had never been so certain of anything in her life as she was that going to Nicholas's house alone was a terrible idea.

She was equally certain she was still going, regardless.

The hackney jolted over a rut and nearly threw her against the opposite squab. She caught herself with a hand to the cracked leather, muttering something that would have made her mother swoon. She'd chosen a hackney for the anonymity of it. And she was wearing the cape she normally wore to drop off her latest sketch. Its dank brown color covered the bright green day dress she wore underneath.

She should have written a letter.

She should have set the entire stack of B. Adroit sketches on fire and then joined a convent.

Instead, she smoothed her skirts, swallowed hard, and watched Nicholas's town house come into view through the hack's grimy window. Cool, pale stone, black railings, polished knocker. Respectable. Controlled. Like him.

Like the outer shell of him, she corrected.

Because beneath all that control and polish and political

calculation, he was…something else. Something she had felt clearly last night with her body draped over his thighs, skirts hiked, his hands—

Bea pressed her knees together and glared at the window as if it were to blame.

She was not here about last night, she reminded herself. She was here about the truth. Her truth.

The carriage pulled to a halt. The driver hopped down, opened the door, and offered his hand. Bea ignored it and stepped out on her own, every line of her body rigid with resolve. She slipped the hood of the cape over her head. Must be discreet.

Up the steps.

Ring the bell.

Confess.

It should be simple. So why did she feel as if she might cast up her accounts at any moment?

She tugged the bellpull before she could think better of it.

The door opened almost at once, as if someone had been waiting on the other side. Nicholas's butler, of course—tall, calm, entirely unruffled.

"Good afternoon, miss," he said with a bow. He obviously didn't know who she was. *Good.*

Bea stepped inside swiftly. It was egregious enough to be visiting a bachelor's house alone. She didn't want to be visible from the front stoop.

"Is Lord Vanover home?" Her voice came out thinner than she liked. "Please tell him Lady Beatrix— Er, tell him Bea is here to see him." No need to spread her name about. What if Nicholas's servants were gossips?

The butler's face did not hide the confusion he clearly felt over seeing a woman who had initially called herself a lady wearing a simple cloak.

"Very well, er…madam. If you would wait in the cream drawing room, I shall inform him at once."

The cream drawing room. That sounded safe. Mostly. She could sit on an upright chair with her spine straight and her hands folded and announce, like a sensible person, that she was the scandalous cartoonist Nicholas had been plagued by for years, ask him to forgive her and not tell her father, and return home before tea.

If only it could be that simple.

She followed the butler down the hall. He opened the door to a pleasant, tasteful room dressed in shades of vanilla before he bowed and withdrew, closing the door behind her.

Bea paced. She removed her brown cloak and tossed it across the back of a chair.

She crossed to the mantel and stared at the clock. She walked to the window and stared at the street. She ran a fingertip along the spine of a book that had been left on a side table—*Tacitus*, naturally; Nicholas would read political philosophy for pleasure—and told herself she could do this.

If she could sketch her father with a beak and Hargrave with toad eyes, she could tell one man the truth.

The door opened.

She spun.

Nicholas stepped in, closing the door behind him. He was in his shirtsleeves, waistcoat unbuttoned, cravat loosened as if she'd interrupted him working. Dark hair annoyingly perfect. Mouth she'd kissed breathless the night before looking as tempting as ever.

Every thought she'd rehearsed fled her head like frightened birds.

"Bea," he said quietly. "You came."

Her name in his voice did something low and dangerous to her.

"Lord Vanover," she replied, because formality was a shield, and she needed one.

He took a few steps into the room, studying her. "I did wonder when I'd see you again…or if what happened last night would scare you off."

She stiffened. "Last night happened. That is… It was quite —" She cut herself off before she could say things like *good* or *wonderful* or *life-altering*.

One corner of his mouth twitched. "Memorable?"

"Catastrophic," she said.

He narrowed his eyes and frowned. "For whom?"

"For me," she replied. "For my sanity. For my virtue. For —" *For my ability to lie to you,* she thought, and bit the words back.

He came closer. Not too close yet, but closer than was strictly necessary for civil conversation.

"And for me?" he asked softly.

She swallowed. "You seemed rather pleased with yourself last night."

"I was," he admitted. "I still am. But you didn't come here to argue about my level of satisfaction." His gaze sharpened. "Why did you come?"

She clenched her jaw. No doubt he was wondering if she was here to make love to him. He'd suggested as much last night. She needed to make it clear that her purpose was entirely different.

"We must talk," she blurted.

His brows shot up. "Three of the most alarming words in the English language."

"Yes, well," she said. "We must."

He inclined his head. "Very well. Talk."

He stopped a pace or two away, hands loose at his sides, as if he were making a point of not reaching for her. It should have helped. It did not.

Bea drew a breath, willing her heart to stop thumping. "Nicholas, I haven't been honest with you."

His brows lifted. "If this is about B. Adroit, you needn't—"

"I must tell you." She briefly closed her eyes. "This is important."

His expression sobered. "Go on then."

She opened her mouth. *I am B. Adroit,* she tried to say. "I—"

He watched her, waiting.

The words lodged in her throat.

Blast him. Blast his eyes and his patience and the way he stood there, looking at her as if what she said mattered. And a horrifying thought occurred to her. Was she about to break his heart?

Heat crept up her neck. "This is…difficult."

"Then we can make it easier," he said gently.

"How?"

"By sitting down," he suggested. "You look as if you're about to bolt."

"I don't need to sit," she informed him.

He nodded gravely. "Are you certain? You're positively vibrating with nerves."

She swallowed. "Do you wish to hear this or not?" Her voice shook.

"I do," he said. "Very much. But I also wish you to breathe while you say it." He gestured to the settee near the hearth. "Please."

Her spine wanted to remain rigid. Her knees, unfortunately, felt oddly unreliable. After a moment of trying to catch her breath, she relented and crossed to the settee, sitting on the edge as if she might spring up again at any moment.

Nicholas followed and took the other end, leaving a

respectable space between them. *Too much space*, part of her thought. *Not nearly enough*, another part countered.

She folded her gloved hands tightly in her lap and fixed her gaze on the mantel. "I need you to know that if I don't say this now, I may never say it."

"All right," he said calmly. "Say it now."

"I'm trying," she insisted, but she still couldn't catch her breath.

He said nothing. Just waited.

The silence roared in her ears.

"Nicholas," she started again, "there are things about me you don't know. Things that would change how you see me. I am not just Winston's daughter, or your prospective bride, or—"

He exhaled a soft laugh. "I should hope not."

"I am serious," she said.

"So am I," he replied. "I have never once looked at you and seen 'just' anything."

Her throat tightened. "I am not fishing for compliments. This is—"

"A matter of trust," he said quietly.

She looked at him then. A lump the size of a goose egg lodged in her throat.

His gaze was steady, dark, and disconcertingly unguarded.

Her heart stumbled. "Yes," she whispered.

"And you're afraid I haven't earned it," he said.

"I'm afraid," she said, "that if I give it to you, you'll cut my head off with it."

"Bea." His voice gentled.

The way he said her name—soft, not teasing—pulled at something inside her. He shifted, angling his body toward hers, closing a fraction of the distance between them.

"You are shaking," he observed.

She looked down. He was right. Her hands trembled against the fabric of her gown.

He reached, slowly enough that she could have pulled away, and covered her clenched hands with one of his own.

Warm. Steady. Very real.

Her breath caught.

"Whatever it is," he said, "you can tell me."

He meant it. She heard it in his voice. Not as a tactic. Not as a politician. As a man. As a *friend*.

It should have made it easier.

Instead, it broke something loose in her chest.

"I can't," she blurted.

His brows drew together. "You can't tell me, or you don't want to?"

"Both," she said desperately. "If I tell you, I'm afraid you'll hate me. You'll tell my father. You'll never speak to me again."

His thumb brushed absently over the back of her hand. "Those are very confident predictions for someone who I hope has come to know me better over the past several days."

She jerked her hand back as if burned, shot to her feet, and stalked toward the fireplace. Her reflection flickered faintly in the glass, hair pinned perfectly, cheeks flushed, eyes too bright.

"I came here to be honest," she said, pressing a hand to the mantel. "I rehearsed it. I was going to tell you everything. I was."

"What changed?" he asked behind her.

"You," she said.

Silence.

Then quietly, "What did I do?"

She laughed, harsh and thin. "First, you upended your reputation. Then you defended me. You looked at me as if I were worth defending. You told a room full of men whose opinions mean something in Parliament that my thoughts mattered more than their comfort." Her fingers dug into the wood. "It was intolerable."

"I suppose that's one way to describe gratitude," he said dryly.

She spun. "Don't you see? I have done nothing but mock you for years. I have turned my words into weapons against everything you stand for. I have done things that would make you want to never speak to me again, and yet you—"

Her voice broke. She swallowed.

"You've made me feel," she whispered, "like I am not wrong for being who I am."

His face changed.

The control didn't vanish; Nicholas never lost it entirely. But something in his expression warmed and darkened and sharpened at once, as if she'd reached past his armor without meaning to.

He stood.

"Bea," he said softly.

She backed up a step. "Don't."

"Don't what?"

"Don't come over here and say something kind to me," she said a little desperately. "I don't deserve it."

He crossed the room.

She retreated until her back hit the wall beside the mantel.

He stopped a breath away, not touching her.

"Why not?" he asked.

"Because I am trying to think," she said, hating the tremor in her voice. "And I cannot think when you…when you look at me like that."

"Like what?" he murmured.

"Like you've already decided," she said. "About me. About us. About…everything."

His gaze dropped briefly to her mouth, then returned to her eyes.

"No," he said quietly, "I haven't decided anything." His voice roughened. "Except that I want you."

Heat surged through her so abruptly she nearly swayed.

"This is exactly what I mean," she said weakly.

"Do you want me?" he asked.

"Yes," she said before she could stop herself.

His breath caught. "Say it again."

"I—" She clamped her lips together.

His mouth curved, slow and wicked. "You want me," he said softly, as if testing the words. "You, Lady Beatrix Winslow, terror of Tory salons, scourge of suitors, voluntary wallflower. You want me."

"Don't be smug," she said, but it came out more like a plea than a rebuke.

He lifted one hand. She felt it coming before he did it. The anticipation crawled over her skin.

His knuckles brushed her cheek.

Barely.

She shivered.

"I won't touch you," he said, "unless you ask me to."

Liar, she almost said, because he was already touching her, his fingers tracing a featherlight path along her jaw. But she knew what he meant. He would not kiss her, would not close that last charged space, unless she closed it first.

It should have been a mercy.

It was torture.

"Why do you make everything so difficult?" she whispered.

"I don't," he said. "You do. You came here determined to bare your soul, and now you're hiding from it." His thumb stroked the edge of her lower lip. "You're shaking, and you're furious, and you want me regardless. That is not my fault, sweetheart."

The endearment undid something in her.

"I am *trying* to tell you the truth," she said. "I am trying. But all I can think about is—"

She broke off.

His eyes burned. "All you can think about is what it felt like last night," he said roughly. "In that carriage. With my mouth on your—"

"Stop," she gasped.

He stopped.

But his hand stayed on her face.

"Bea," he said, voice low and strained, "if you want a saint, you have chosen poorly."

"I don't want a saint," she blurted.

"Oh?" His mouth tilted. "What do you want?"

"You," she said. The word came from somewhere low and unguarded inside her. "Just you. The infuriating, arrogant, overconfident man who drove me mad and then somehow —" She swallowed. "Somehow made me feel safe."

His hand trembled against her skin.

"Say it again," he whispered.

She met his eyes, heart pounding so hard she felt it in her throat.

"I feel safe with you," she said.

That did it.

Whatever thin tether of restraint he'd been clinging to snapped. He closed the remaining distance and claimed her lips.

It was not a gentle, grateful little brush of mouths. It was deep and immediate and hungry, as if he'd been waiting for her permission for far too long.

Her back hit the wall harder as his body pressed against

hers, solid and hot and entirely too welcome. Her hands found his shoulders, fingers clutching at the fine weave of his shirt as his mouth moved over hers in slow, devastating strokes.

This was a mistake. She knew it. Somewhere in the fogged corners of her mind, reason waved a frantic little flag and whispered, *Tell him. Tell him now. Before it's too late.*

She opened her mouth to speak.

He took the movement as an invitation and deepened the kiss.

Words disappeared under the onslaught of sensation. His tongue stroked against hers, coaxing, teasing, turning her bones to liquid. The hand cupping her cheek slid back into her hair, gentle but insistent, angling her head, holding her as if he'd never let her go.

She made a small sound against his mouth. He swallowed it with a soft groan of his own.

"Wait," she managed between kisses. "Nicholas, I have to—"

"Later," he breathed, mouth against the corner of hers. "You can tell me everything later."

"I meant to tell you now." She gasped as he trailed kisses along her jaw.

"Yes," he said. "You also meant to not kiss me. We are both failing miserably."

His teeth grazed the base of her throat where her pulse hammered, and her protest melted into a helpless shudder. His hands slid down from her face to her shoulders, then lower, palms spanning her ribs through the layers of her bodice.

"If you truly don't want this, tell me now," he said against her skin. "Say it now."

She squeezed her eyes shut. "I…can't."

"Good," he said, voice rough.

He kissed her again, and that was the end of coherent intention.

He did not pounce or drag or manhandle. He kissed her until her knees weakened and her hands slid from his shoulders to his chest to keep herself upright; he kissed her until the world narrowed to the heat of his mouth, the scent of him, the delicious friction of his body against hers.

At some point, her fingers found the knot of his cravat. It was already loosening, but she still tugged at it, desperate for more skin. The knot gave under her fingers; the linen slithered away. She slipped her hand beneath, palm flattening against his throat.

He sucked in a breath.

"Bea," he rasped. "If you touch me like that, I'm going to forget every single noble impulse I've ever had."

"You're suggesting you've had any," she whispered.

His laugh was strangled. "Fair point."

She dragged her hand down over the hard curve of his collarbone, the smooth line of his chest under his shirt. He felt like heat and strength and recklessness.

His own hands found her waist, fingers splaying, thumbs sweeping over the curve of her stays. He pressed closer, guiding her away from the wall, across the room with unsteady steps. She didn't know where they were going until the back of her calves hit something padded.

The settee.

He broke the kiss long enough to look into her eyes.

"Last chance," he said roughly. "To tell me to stop."

Her lungs dragged in air. Her heart hammered. Her body ached.

"Nicholas," she whispered.

"Yes."

"Please," she said.

He made a sound that was half curse, half prayer, and lowered her onto the settee.

The room blurred.

His mouth was on hers again, then on her throat, then lower, the edge of her bodice suddenly far too high and far too tight. His hands explored the nipped-in line of her waist, the flare of her hips. She felt him everywhere, the heat of him imprinting her through every layer of fabric.

She tried again, once, to remember the speech she'd rehearsed. *I'm B. Adroit, and I—*

But his palm slid, bold and sure, over the top of her thigh, fingers curving around to the back of her leg, catching up a handful of muslin. The whisper of her skirts rising swallowed the thought whole.

"Nicholas," she gasped, hips jerking.

"Come upstairs," he whispered against her throat.

Her eyes flew open. "Upstairs?"

"Yes." His gaze burned into hers. "Because if I keep you in this drawing room, I'm going to do something unforgivable on this very respectable furniture."

Her heart thudded. "Upstairs is your bedchamber."

"Quite astute," he said.

"My reputation—"

"Already in tatters the moment you stepped into my house alone," he said quietly. "I am not pretending coming to my bedchamber will make it worse."

She sucked in her breath, trembling—not only with want, but with the sharp edge of why she'd come here in the first place.

To tell him. To be honest, as she'd promised herself she would be.

And if she went upstairs…if she crossed that threshold… she would be choosing something else first. Something that could not be unsaid. Something she could never pretend had been an accident.

Her conscience clawed at her. *Tell him now.* Tell him before you let him touch you again. Before you make this—make *him*—a refuge.

But another voice, stubborn and very much her own, rose up beneath the fear.

This is my life, it said. *My choice.*

Her father had been choosing for her for years. Society had been choosing for her. Even B. Adroit—brave as that secret life was—had been a version of herself she could only inhabit in shadows.

Tonight, for once, she wanted to choose something in the light.

Not because she was weak.

Not because Nicholas was irresistible—though he was.

But because she was tired of living like every decision must be a sacrifice offered to other people's expectations.

And because—damn him—Nicholas always looked at her as if she mattered.

If she confessed now, she risked losing that in an instant. Losing *him*—his respect, his protection, his regard—before she even knew what it felt like to have it.

And if she was going to blow up her life, she wanted it to be on her terms.

Nicholas didn't move. Didn't press. He simply waited, breath hot at her throat, his hands stilling as though he was holding himself back by sheer will.

"Bea," he said, almost smiling, though his eyes were still dark and serious. "I will walk you out that door right now if you want me to. We can pretend we had tea in this drawing room and try to mitigate the damage. Or…"

"Or?" she whispered.

He held out his hand. "Or you can come upstairs," he said. "And tell me whatever it is that is gnawing at you…after."

After.

After she'd let herself want him without apology. After she'd taken one selfish thing for herself. After she'd proven—to him and to herself—that she wasn't being cornered into this.

She stared at his hand.

The fork in the road jabbed her beneath her ribs. The safe path, where she clung to principle like armor…or the dangerous one, where she admitted that desire could be a choice too.

Her mother would call it a scandal.

Her father would call it unforgivable.

Society would call it ruin.

Bea called it something else entirely.

Revolt.

She lifted her chin, steadying her breath, and made herself look at Nicholas—really look—so he would know she understood exactly what she was doing.

So he would know she was not being carried, not being convinced.

She'd made her decision, and she was walking.

She placed her hand in his. "Upstairs."

CHAPTER THIRTY

Nicholas closed his fingers around hers as if she were something precious and pulled her gently to her feet.

The walk up the stairs felt not like walking into battle, but toward surrender. The hallway was empty, the house muffled around them. A maid passed at the far end of the corridor, eyes downcast, veering away. Bea's cheeks burned. Nicholas's grip on her hand tightened, reassuring.

At the top of the second flight, he led her to a door at the end of the corridor. He opened it and stepped back, letting her enter first.

His bedchamber was large and masculine, all deep blues and rich woods. The bed dominated the space—wide, high, curtained in dark fabric drawn back to show linen sheets. A fire burned low in the grate, filling the room with a soft glow.

Bea hovered just past the threshold, heart pounding.

Nicholas closed the door behind them and locked it with a quiet click.

"No one will disturb us," he said.

"How comforting," she murmured faintly.

He came around to face her.

"I know what this looks like," he said. "I know what it is. I will not pretend this is honorable. But I also know that nothing in my life has ever felt as right as you walking into this room."

Her throat worked. "I chose to come up here."

"Yes," he said. "And I'm infinitely glad you did. Come here."

She did.

The moment she was within reach, his arms went around her, drawing her against his body with a hunger that stole her breath. His mouth found hers again, and she stopped thinking.

The kiss turned fierce, almost frantic, as if some shared instinct told them this was the last moment they might pause, question, retreat. His hands slid down her back, over the curve of her hips, to the small of her spine. He pressed her closer, and she recognized the hard, unambiguous evidence of his desire against her belly.

She gasped. His mouth swallowed the sound.

Her fingers fumbled at his waistcoat, pushing it back off his shoulders. It landed somewhere behind him with a soft thud. His shirt was next. She slid her hands beneath the fine linen, palms skimming over hot skin, muscles jumping under her touch.

He groaned into her mouth, a low, rough sound that made her toes curl.

Her hands found his muscled abdomen, and she pressed her palms flat against him.

"Bea," he said against her lips, "if you keep doing that, I'm going to forget my own name."

She smiled shakily. "Then I shall call you Nicholas, and you won't need to remember."

His answering laugh broke on a breath as she traced the line of his spine, feeling every inch of him. He pulled back just enough to look at her, breathing hard.

"You are going to be the end of me," he said.

She thought wildly that she wouldn't mind being the end of him if it meant she could also be everything in between.

Instead of saying any of that, she reached for the fastenings of her gown.

His hand caught hers.

"Let me," he said.

The words sent a shiver through her.

She nodded, suddenly shy in a way she hadn't anticipated. He turned her gently, so her back faced him, and his fingers went to the row of small buttons that marched down her spine.

He didn't rush.

She felt each one, a tiny loosening, a gradual surrender. With every bit the gown gave, more of her skin met the air, and more of her reason fled.

His knuckles brushed her bare back. She shivered. He bent, pressed a slow, open-mouthed kiss between her shoulder blades. Her knees nearly gave out.

Nicholas didn't undress her all at once. No, he took his time, kneeling beside the bed and sliding off one glove, then the other, with slow precision. "I want to unwrap you like a forbidden gift," he murmured, "and savor every part of you."

He slid a hand under her skirts again, not to tease this time, but to remove them. His fingers worked at the ties, the fabric falling away piece by piece. The buttons at the back of her gown. Her stays. Her shift. Her stockings. His hands reverent, his mouth trailing kisses along her ribs, the underside of her breasts, her belly.

"You're exquisite," he whispered, brushing his lips over the curve of her hip. "A goddess hiding in plain sight."

She made a helpless noise and reached back to clutch at the bedpost for balance. At last, the gown slid from her shoulders and pooled around her feet in a whisper of silk. She stepped out of it, feeling more exposed than she ever had in her life, even though her chemise and stays still covered her.

"Turn around," he said softly.

She did.

The way he looked at her then unraveled the last of her composure. No mockery. No smugness. Just heat and awe and a tenderness she had not been prepared for.

"Bea," he whispered.

She turned, crossed the last step between them and kissed him, and the rest blurred, the tug of laces, the rustle of linen, the shock of his skin against hers, the way he groaned when she pressed herself full-length along the hard lines of his body.

She didn't know exactly how they reached the bed. Only that his hands were on her, reverent and greedy; that his mouth traced a path down her throat, across her shoulders; that his breath grew ragged as he whispered her name.

NICHOLAS HAD her back pressed to the mattress in mere seconds. His jaw was at her neck, and she shuddered as he whispered in her ear, "Shall I touch you?"

Her answer was a glare, but her chin tipped up…defiant, aroused, glorious.

He took it as permission.

His fingers on her thighs slowly moved toward her center, and she gasped.

"I only need one word from you," he rasped, the rough skin of his jaw sliding against her soft neck.

The only sound was her panting.

"Say yes, Bea. And I'll give you pleasure you've never known."

"Yes," came the one word, unmistakable.

Nicholas let his finger find her then. Slide to the spot she most needed him. This woman was far too fiery and proud and beautiful to have never been given an orgasm until recently. She deserved another one. Immediately.

The moment his finger found the soft little nub of flesh, her head fell back to mattress, and she whimpered. His finger found the aching nub nestled in her folds and stroked...softly at first, featherlight, the barest brush of sensation that made her eyes flutter closed and her mouth part on a sigh.

Her panting increased, her gorgeous breasts rising and falling. He moved his head down to suck one succulent nipple into his mouth. But first, he was going to watch her face as she came on his finger. With nothing more than his touch guiding her to ecstasy.

He increased the tempo, watching as pleasure-pain streaked across her perfect features. Her brow knitted. She bit her lip.

"Do you like that?" he growled in her ear. "You want more, don't you?"

All she could do was whimper in response. And when her hand moved down to grab his arm, at first, Nicholas worried she would push him away. But her hand clamped over his wrist. By God, she was holding him to her, making sure he *didn't* stop.

She gasped again—part moan, part breathless anticipation—and that's when he found her. Slick and warm and already trembling for him.

He slid one finger inside her deep heat.

"You feel that?" he growled. "How wet you are for me? Christ, Bea. You're soaking. You want this. You want me."

She couldn't speak, only nodded, her body taut like a bowstring.

"I could make you come right here," he murmured, circling that sensitive bud with maddening precision. "Right now. With nothing but my fingers."

Her head thumped back against the mattress with a soft thud. "Nicholas…"

"That's it," he breathed, picking up the pace. "Let me hear it. Let go for me, darling. Let me ruin you."

His free hand caught both of hers and pinned them above her head. Her body writhed against his, and he pressed closer, pinning her completely, his rough thigh between her smooth ones, his mouth at her jaw, her throat, her ear… everywhere.

"Tell me what you want me to do to you," he whispered, his breath hot against her skin. "Say it."

"I want…" Her voice cracked.

He nipped her earlobe. "Say it."

"I want you to make me feel like you did last night."

"You want me to make you *come*."

"Yes, make me come," she repeated breathlessly.

He groaned. "You do not know what those words do to me."

He stroked faster, firmer, watching her face as he worked her toward the edge. Her brows knit. Her lips parted. She whimpered, then moaned, then bit his shoulder.

"Do you like that?" he rasped. "You want my mouth on you next? My tongue in place of my fingers? Like last night? You taste so good, my sweet Bea."

She whimpered again. Her wrists strained against his hold.

"No," he said. "I can't let you touch me. If you touch me right now, I can't be held responsible for what I'll do next."

She frowned, but stopped trying to pull her wrists away.

"Good girl," he growled, a feral grin spreading across his face. "You want it rough or gentle? Fast or slow? Shall I make you scream, or will you be quiet like a proper lady while I make you come again and again?"

She was shaking now, her entire body shivering with tension, her hips bucking against his hand.

"Look at you," he said, utterly wrecked by the sight of her. "All undone. And I've barely begun."

He leaned in close, teeth grazing her jaw. "After this, I'm going to spread you out and savor all of you. I'll have your thighs over my shoulders, your hands in my hair, and my name on your lips until you forget your own."

She let out a strangled cry, half shock, half desperate need.

"Oh, yes," he growled. "I know. First, I'll take you from the front. Smooth and easy and slow. And then I'll take you from behind. Have you bent over the bed, over my desk—hell, over the pianoforte if you like. Anywhere. Every way. As many times as it takes until you forget every other man who's ever looked at you."

Her body tensed—tighter, tighter—and then shattered. She gasped, her mouth falling open, eyes squeezed shut, and Nicholas kept his fingers moving until she was wrung out, spent, panting.

He finally slowed, then withdrew his hand and brought his fingers to his lips with a wicked glint in his eye. He sucked one clean, never breaking eye contact.

"You taste like sin," he murmured. "And I am a man utterly devoted to damnation."

Bea arched her back, dazed and flushed and trembling.

But he wasn't done.

He was touching her so gently, but there was nothing gentle about the way he looked at her—as if he'd crossed a desert just to fall at her feet. His eyes were nearly black, ravenous. She'd never been looked at like that. As though he were starved for her. As though she were the only thing on earth that might satisfy the ache inside him.

He rose above her at last. Broad shoulders. Strong chest. Muscles roped and flexed with control—barely. Then lowered himself once more to cover her completely. Skin on skin. Heat on heat. His weight pinning her deliciously, his hand cupping her jaw as he stared down at her.

"I want to hear you again," he said, voice dark and aching. "The sounds you make when I touch you, kiss you, take you. I want to hear what I do to you."

She whimpered when he rocked his hips against hers, the hard ridge of him sliding perfectly against her slick center. Her fingers clutched the sheets.

"Look at you," he rasped. "Squirming. Wanton. Writhing for it. You're giving yourself to me right here, right now, aren't you?"

"Yes," she gasped, shame and decorum burned to ash by the fire in her blood.

"You'll let me put you on your hands and knees, face down on this bed, and drive into you until you scream my name?"

Her eyes fluttered shut. "Nicholas…"

He nipped her throat. "Say it."

"Yes."

He grinned against her neck. "Good."

Then he kissed her, deep and thorough, as if he meant to consume her whole. And he *did*, devouring her moans, her sighs, her whispered pleas as he slid lower, trailing kisses down her body.

When his mouth reached her core, he spread her thighs with broad palms and looked up at her from between them, eyes gleaming.

"Watch me," he said. "I want you to see how much I love tasting you."

And then he did.

With slow, deliberate strokes of his tongue, he licked her as if it were the only thing he'd ever wanted. Bea cried out, her hips arching off the bed, and he growled in approval.

"So sweet," he murmured, licking again, circling that perfect spot with unholy precision. "So wet for me. So perfect."

She was half mad with pleasure, gasping, twisting, trembling. When he added a finger—then two—thrusting in time with the rhythm of his mouth, she nearly came undone.

"Don't stop," she begged. "Oh God, please—"

"I won't stop. Not until you come on my tongue," he growled, and seconds later, she did—shattered and glorious, back arched, a strangled cry torn from her throat.

Nicholas didn't let up until her body stilled beneath him, her chest rising and falling in erratic gasps.

Then he crawled back up her body, kissed her slowly and deliberately, letting her taste herself on his lips.

"Still with me, darling?"

She nodded, dazed and flushed, lips parted.

"Good," he said, positioning himself between her legs. "Because there's much more."

He reached between them, stroking himself once, twice, before teasing her with his tip.

"I should be gentle," he said. "It's your first time. I should go slowly."

He pressed forward, just a little, watching her face.

"But I'm not going to. Because you don't want that, do you?"

She shook her head, her legs wrapping around his waist.

"You want it hard. Deep. A little rough."

"Yes," she breathed. "Please."

And then he thrust.

She gasped—half pain, half pleasure—as he filled her in one smooth stroke. Nicholas stilled, grinding his teeth, every muscle in his body taut with restraint.

"Jesus, Bea," he rasped. "You're so damn tight."

He buried his face in her neck as he moved, slowly at first, then faster, harder, hips pumping, one hand still gripping hers above her head.

"I've thought about this," he groaned. "Every night. Every damn night. What it would feel like to be inside you. To hear the sounds you make when I fuck you. And now—hell—I'm never going to stop."

She met him thrust for thrust, her fingers digging into her own palms, her cries growing louder, more desperate.

"I want you to come again," he panted. "On my cock this time. Squeeze me. Milk me. *Take it.*"

She cried out, her whole body tightening around him, shuddering again as another orgasm crashed through her.

Nicholas followed with a roar, burying himself to the hilt as he spilled inside her, clutching her to him like a lifeline.

For a long moment, they stayed like that. Tangled. Breathless. Utterly wrecked.

Then he rolled to his side, keeping her in his arms, pressing a kiss to her temple.

"You," he murmured, voice rough, "are going to be the death of me."

She smiled against his chest. "You started it."

He laughed, deep and low. "And I'll be starting it again. Very soon."

CHAPTER THIRTY-ONE

Bea woke slowly.

For a long moment, she didn't know where she was, only that she was warm, cocooned in linen, surrounded by heat not entirely her own, and her body felt… different. Languid. Satisfied. Intertwined with something that hummed beneath her skin like an echo of thunder.

Her eyes opened.

She was in Nicholas's bedchamber.

She had no idea how long she'd been asleep, but she needed to get home before her parents began to worry.

The curtains were drawn, but light slipped between them to strike the foot of the bed. Thank God. It was still daylight. Afternoon. The fire in the grate had burned low, embers glowing faintly.

And on the pillow beside her—

Him.

Nicholas lay on his side, propped on one elbow, bare-chested, watching her with a look that made her breath catch.

He'd done it again. Twice more. Taken her in ways that made her gasp his name and wonder how she'd ever lived without him. But the look he gave her now wasn't hungry, not anymore.

Something worse.

Something better.

Something that terrified her to the bone.

"You're awake," he murmured.

Her face flushed so hot she was surprised the sheets didn't smolder.

She pulled the blanket higher, not because it covered anything he hadn't already seen, but because she needed something between herself and the intensity of his gaze.

"Yes," she whispered.

He reached out and brushed a strand of mussed hair from her cheek. "How do you feel?"

How did she feel?

Ruined. Melted. Reassembled. Terrified. Weightless. Anchored. Adored. Seen. Worshipped.

"Fine," she said, which was possibly the most ridiculous understatement ever spoken.

His mouth quirked. "You look…better than fine."

Heat spread down her throat. "How do you feel?" she countered.

"Wonderful," he murmured, leaning closer, kissing her shoulder. Making her want him all over again.

"Nicholas," she said, half-smothering a smile that shouldn't have been there, because reality was waiting, heavy, sharp, and unavoidable.

He kissed her shoulder, slow and devastating.

A tremor went through her.

Focus, Beatrix.

Today's pleasure flickered in the back of her mind like a candle, and with it came a jolt of guilt so abrupt she sucked in a breath. She'd allowed him to make love to her, begged him for it even, without telling him the truth. She was lower than low.

Nicholas's eyes narrowed slightly. "What is it?"

"I…" She pulled the sheet up again, clutching it like armor. "We must talk."

He gave a soft huff of amusement. "We've already established that that's the most alarming phrase in the English language."

"This is serious," she said.

"I gathered." He slid his hand under her hair, rubbing his thumb behind her ear in a way that made her stomach flip. "But must we have it now? This conversation? Can't I have five more minutes of relishing your absolutely perfect body?"

His voice was so low, so gentle, so unbearably tender, that she almost broke.

Almost.

"No," she whispered.

"Are you certain?" he asked, brushing her collarbone with the backs of his fingers and moving closer to nuzzle her neck.

"Nicholas."

He stilled.

She pushed herself upright, gathering the sheet around her. "We have to talk about what this means. About us."

He sat up beside her, the mattress shifting. His expression was suddenly sober, all humor gone. "I think it's obvious. Because of what we just did…we have no choice. We must marry."

He watched her, expression unreadable.

She took a deep breath. "I know I should have been more cautious. I should have thought…should have stopped, but I didn't. I…"

She broke off.

A muscle moved in his jaw. "Bea," he said softly, "did you think I would seduce you and then leave you to bear the consequences alone? Of course I will marry you."

She swallowed hard and nodded. "That's not what I meant."

"Then what did you mean?" he asked, voice quiet but edged.

"I don't want to trap you."

His eyes flared. "Trap me?"

She nodded, throat tight. "My father will demand it. Society will demand it. But I don't want... I don't want you forced. If you don't want me after what I tell you—"

"Beatrix," he said, and the way he said her full name turned her bones to water, "I would marry you if no one in the world demanded it. Including you."

Her breath hitched.

He took her hand gently, thumb tracing her knuckles. "I should have asked before I took you to bed. I should have said the words first."

"You didn't take me to bed," she whispered. "I walked."

He gave a faint, pained smile. "Then we both should have said the words."

She stared at him, chest aching.

"Do you want to marry me?" he asked quietly.

Yes. No. Yes. Perhaps. Too late.

"I don't know," she said honestly. "I don't know anything right now."

"You..." His brow furrowed. "You aren't serious." His thumb kept stroking her hand. Comforting. Steadying. Making it harder and harder to do what she must.

"There is something else," she said.

He went still. "Yes?"

"I was trying to tell you earlier," she said, voice trembling. "I was trying before we... Before all this. I needed to tell you something important. Something that may change everything."

His hand tightened around hers. "I can confidently say there is nothing you can tell me that would change my—"

She pressed her fingers to his lips to stop him from saying more. "No. You don't know that. Let me say it."

"Fine. Then tell me now."

She opened her mouth.

And the words stuck in her throat, because desire, honesty, fear, guilt—all of them were crashing together inside her in a way she couldn't untangle.

Nicholas's brows knit. "Bea, what is it?"

"I—"

A knock shattered the moment.

Sharp. Sudden. Too loud.

She jolted. Nicholas cursed softly under his breath.

"That will be Godwin," he said, already swinging his legs off the bed. "The butler. No one else would dare knock at a time like this."

"Don't let him in," Bea pleaded.

"I won't invite him for tea. But I do need to answer. I won't let him see you, I promise." Nicholas had already crossed to the wardrobe, pulled a dressing robe from a hook, and shrugged it over his shoulders. He tied the belt tightly, though it covered almost none of the evidence that he had just spent hours behaving in ways decidedly not appropriate for a gentleman.

She scrambled, clutching the sheet to her chest. "No, Nicholas, wait!"

Another knock.

"My lord?" the butler's voice came, muffled.

Nicholas raked a hand through his hair and looked back at Bea.

"Stay there," he said gently. "You're safe."

She pressed herself deeper into the covers, heart roaring in her ears. "Nicholas—"

He cracked the door just enough to slip through, leaving only the faintest sliver of hallway visible.

The conversation was murmured, impossible to hear. Bea clutched the sheet tighter around herself, cold despite the residual warmth of the bed. Her stomach twisted with dread.

A moment later, the door shut again. Nicholas leaned his back against it, eyes closed briefly.

Her breath stopped. "What is it?"

He opened his eyes.

Regret. Resolve. A shadow she couldn't name.

"I'm afraid," he said quietly, "I need to get dressed."

Her heart plunged. "Why?"

He crossed to the bed, cupped her face gently in his hands, and kissed her forehead.

Not hungry this time. Not seductive. Something far worse.

"Nicholas," she whispered, throat closing, "what's happened?"

He exhaled slowly, thumb brushing her cheek. "The Bow Street Runner I hired," he said.

Every drop of blood drained from her face.

Nicholas held her gaze. "He's downstairs," he said quietly, "and he claims to have the identity of B. Adroit."

The world dropped out from beneath her.

She stared at him, unable to breathe, speak, move. *It's me. It's me.* Two words that should be so easy to say, and yet she could not force them past her trembling lips.

He pressed one last kiss to her brow. "Wait here," he said softly. "I'll be back soon."

He straightened, tossed off his dressing robe, and pulled on his breeches, shirt, and waistcoat before moving toward the door.

He looked back at her once more. "I promise," he said.

Then he was gone.

Bea was left staring at the closed door, heart pounding in terror, fearing that the truth she had failed to tell him…was about to be revealed in his study, on someone else's tongue.

CHAPTER THIRTY-TWO

Nicholas took the stairs like a man walking on clouds. He had meant what he said to Bea. He needed to hear what Fletcher had to say, but the truth was his mind was only half on the man waiting below.

The other half was still in his bed.

He could feel her in the warm indentation on the mattress, in the faint scent of her on his skin, in the memory of the scrape of her nails along his shoulders. Every step he took away from that room felt simultaneously like sacrilege and triumph.

She was in his house.

She was in his bed.

She was, in every important sense, his.

He smiled to himself as he tugged on the ends of his waistcoat and started down the curving staircase, his boots silent on the runner.

Marriage.

He rolled the word around in his head like a fine brandy on his tongue.

He had always expected marriage to be a transaction. An

alliance. A line on some invisible tally sheet his father and Winston kept in their pockets. House A joins House B to strengthen Position C.

Useful. Predictable. Necessary.

And while he'd wanted Bea for years, he had never, until now, really allowed himself to imagine that it might also be… this.

Madness, certainly. Daily chaos, perhaps. But also something bright and crackling and alive. Like standing in the middle of a summer storm with his arms outstretched, daring the lightning to find him.

Beatrix Winslow.

Beatrix Archer, Lady Vanover.

The thought made his chest feel too full.

Of course, if word got out about Bea's arrival at his town house today, both his father and Winston wouldn't like it. But let them sputter and preen. Let them mutter about propriety. Nicholas would gladly endure a dozen lectures if it meant waking up every morning with Bea in his arms.

He could see it already—her in his breakfast room, hair loosely pinned, eyes flashing over the morning papers as she eviscerated every poorly argued editorial; her in his carriage, arguing with him all the way to a dinner party; her at his side in the gallery at Parliament, lips twitching around remarks she'd never before been allowed to say aloud.

He'd happily defend her against God and country for the rest of his life…*not* that she needed defending. The woman was fully capable of handling herself and anyone who dared cross her path, and as the Marchioness of Vanover she'd be much more powerful. That should please her.

Then there was the little matter of what they were like in bed together.

His lips curved into a smile. He'd never imagined anything like it. Pleasure, yes. But the combustion that had been their making love. He hadn't dared to hope it would be that good.

He reached the bottom of the stairs, the smile still tugging at his mouth. The door to his study stood open; beyond it, the figure of a man waited near the hearth, hat in hand.

Nicholas drew in a steadying breath, schooling his expression into something less like besotted satisfaction and more like professional courtesy.

No one needed to know he had just ruined the Duke of Winston's daughter.

Well.

Not yet. And then, only if it was necessary for her father to see reason and ensure the marriage took place. After the duke's thinly veiled threats last night, their afternoon together was a bit of insurance for Nicholas.

As for what she'd been struggling to tell him since she arrived…he suspected he already knew what it was. And he'd had good reason to attempt to delay her words. He'd hoped for exactly what was happening right now…a visit from Fletcher. Fletcher was about to reveal the identity of B. Adroit, which made Bea's confession unnecessary. She didn't have to torture herself with a betrayal. He was about to learn the name from a source of his own.

Her extreme worry did, however, give him pause. For months, he'd been convinced that the cartoonist was a stranger. Now, he was fairly certain it was someone he knew. It was obviously someone Bea knew. A footman in Winston's house, perhaps?

It was time to find out.

Nicholas stepped into the study.

"Lord Vanover," Fletcher said, straightening. The Bow Street Runner was in his late thirties, wiry, with a sharp, clever face and eyes that missed very little. "My apologies for the unexpected visit, my lord."

"Not to worry, Fletcher." Nicholas glanced at the clock on the mantel: half past four. He'd spent most of the afternoon in bed with Bea. But even if her father was waiting to call him out, he couldn't regret a moment of it.

"I have the information you requested," the man supplied with a deferential bob of his head.

"Excellent." Nicholas moved behind his desk, more to give his hands something to do than from any particular need to sit.

Fletcher reached into his coat pocket and withdrew a small, folded square of vellum, sealed with a dab of wax.

Nicholas's heart gave one hard thump. He was about to discover the identity of the man who had been making his life a particular form of hell for over two years now.

He'd told himself it was about political strategy. About understanding his adversary. About anticipating attacks and parrying them before they landed. About setting the record straight.

But now he had to admit to himself that he wanted to know because he simply couldn't bear not knowing. Because he hated that someone had been moving pieces on the board behind his back.

A thought he rarely let himself consider flashed through his brain. Was it someone he trusted?

He reached for the vellum, his hand suddenly not as steady as he liked.

"Before I open this," he said lightly, "assure me I haven't agreed to pay you a small fortune to be told B. Adroit is, in fact, a figment of my imagination."

Fletcher gave a curt shake of the head. "I assure you, my lord. B. Adroit is quite real."

Nicholas broke the seal with his thumb and looked down at the vellum.

One name. Three words.

Three incomprehensible words.

Lady Beatrix Winslow.

For a heartbeat, his brain refused to process the letters.

He blinked, then read them again.

Beatrix.

No.

That was impossible.

He stared at the vellum, waiting for the letters to rearrange themselves into something sensible. His most formidable opponents in Parliament. Some obscure pamphleteer. Hargrave, even. Winston's footman. Anyone but—

His brows snapped together. "Is this meant to be a jest?" His voice simmered.

Fletcher actually blinked—once, sharply—as if the very idea had knocked his well-ordered thoughts askew. "A jest, my lord?"

Nicholas lifted his gaze, the smile gone from his mouth, the warmth gone from his chest, leaving something cold and sharp in its place.

"You've given me the name of the Duke of Winston's daughter," he said. "The same Lady Beatrix whom I am currently courting. The same Lady Beatrix whose father would have your head on a spike if this were some mistake. So, I will ask you again. Is this supposed to be amusing?"

Fletcher swallowed, then shook his head. "No, my lord. No jest."

Nicholas's jaw clenched. "Explain."

Fletcher shifted his weight, the faintest hint of discomfort crossing his features. "I followed the trail as we discussed, my lord. Talked to the printers' lads. Most had no idea of the person behind the sketches, but one—" He smiled faintly. "One boy likes to talk when he's had a bit of gin."

Nicholas said nothing. His pulse pounded in his ears.

"He said the servant was careful," Fletcher continued. "Always used the slot. Always kept their face in shadow. But came regular as clockwork."

Fletcher continued, "Appeared to be a lady's maid. As I told you before, I followed her home. To a ducal household in London. But I had to be certain of the *artist*'s identity."

"You're certain it wasn't a footman?" Nicholas prodded.

"After I followed the maid the first time," Fletcher said simply. "I kept watch." He met Nicholas's gaze. "And I saw the same woman. Saw her with my own eyes. Turns out she wasn't a maid at all, but a lady. Tall, blond hair, eyes the color of the sea on a cloudy day, and—"

"Enough!" Nicholas's fingers tightened around the vellum. A sick feeling began to coil in his stomach.

But Fletcher didn't stop. "I have served Bow Street ten years. I do not bring a name to a gentleman of your position unless I'm certain of it, my lord."

A strange roaring filled Nicholas's head. His mind flashed back—unbidden—to Bea in his drawing room earlier, standing by the hearth with her hands clenched, saying, *There are things about me you don't know.* To her muttered, *I came here to tell you the truth. I meant to.*

He had kissed her instead.

He felt suddenly, violently tired.

Nicholas folded the vellum slowly, his jaw tight enough to ache.

Bea.

A laugh rose in his throat and died there. Of course. Of course it was her. The sharpness of the lines, the way the humor cut clean, the occasional surprising kindness tucked amid the scathing accusations—it was all her.

She'd been skewering him with her drawings while he'd been searching for a man. Merely assuming she might be feeding information to the real culprit. No wonder she'd been so anxious.

He'd been a fool.

She'd even named herself…B. And Adroit was obvious enough. A cunning nod to her cleverness.

And yet.

He had been paying a man to discover the truth while she had been gathering the shredded pieces of her courage to offer it herself.

Now the truth sat in his hand, written in another man's ink.

"Thank you, Mr. Fletcher," he said, voice clipped.

Fletcher relaxed as if a tension had eased. "You're satisfied then, my lord?"

Satisfied.

The word tasted like ash.

"I am satisfied that you have done the job I asked of you," Nicholas said. "Payment as agreed."

He opened the top drawer of his desk, withdrew a small, heavy purse, and set it atop the polished wood. Fletcher stepped forward eagerly.

"Take it," Nicholas said shortly.

Fletcher did, the purse disappearing into his coat with practiced speed.

"One more thing." Nicholas hoisted a second heavy purse from the drawer.

"Yes, my lord?"

"This name does not leave this house," Nicholas said quietly, waving the vellum between two fingers. "Not to Winston. Not to Hargrave. Not to your superiors. Not to *anyone*." He tossed the second purse at the man.

Fletcher caught it and nodded quickly. "Of course, my lord." His mouth twitched. "I've no wish to cross the Duke of Winston. Or you, for that matter."

"See that you don't," Nicholas said.

Fletcher bowed. "Good day to you, Lord Vanover."

When the door closed behind the Runner, Nicholas remained seated for a long, motionless moment, the folded vellum a small, damning weight in his hand.

Bea.

A hundred images layered themselves in his mind: her in his bed a short while ago, golden hair spread over his pillow, eyes dark and trusting; her at Lord Chelmsford's table, chin lifted, eyes blazing as she refused to be cowed by Hargrave; her in countless ballrooms, cool and aloof, refusing to dance with him.

Her ink, slicing through speeches, exposing hypocrisies, turning his allies and friends into grotesque caricatures, along with himself.

He had known, somewhere deep down where instinct lived, that she was formidable.

He had not realized how fully she was loaded and aimed at the world he inhabited.

He set the vellum down on the desk and smoothed a palm over it once.

Then he stood.

There would be time to think later. To interrogate his own reaction…to the lie, to the truth, to the fact that he had just taken to bed the very mind that had mercilessly dissected his public self.

Right now, there was only one thing that mattered.

She was upstairs. In his bed. Waiting.

And she would know he knew the truth.

He left the study without looking back. He took the stairs two at a time.

His body hummed with a fury he didn't quite know where to direct. At her for lying. At himself for not seeing it sooner. At the world for constructing a system in which the only way a woman like Bea could wield a pen like that was from behind a mask.

He remembered her voice in the drawing room: *I wanted you to know me.* And later: *I feel safe with you.*

He reached the landing and turned down the corridor, heart pounding harder with every step. He didn't know precisely what he would say when he saw her, whether the first words out of his mouth would be, *Why didn't you tell me?* or *How in God's name did you think you could keep this from me?* or—fool that he was—*How long have you been this brilliant?*

He only knew he had to see her face.

He reached his bedchamber door. His hand closed on the handle, twisted. The door swung inward.

The bed was empty.

The sheets—still rumpled, still bearing the imprint of their time together—were cooling. The indentation where her body had lain was flattening slowly, inexorably, as if she had never been there at all.

Nicholas stood on the threshold, staring.

His gaze tracked around the room—the chair by the window, empty; the hearth, quiet; no flash of blond hair tucked in a corner; no telltale swirl of skirts.

"Bea?" he called, even though he knew there would be no answer.

He took a few steps into the room, as if she might materialize if he got closer.

On the floor by the bed lay a small ribbon, bright green, torn from her hair at some point. He bent and picked it up, fingers closing around the scrap of silk.

Gone.

She had dressed herself—somehow, quietly—and slipped out while he was downstairs talking to the man who had just sold him her secret.

Nicholas straightened slowly, the ribbon clutched in his fist.

For a moment he felt…nothing.

Then everything hit at once.

Anger. Not the clean, satisfying anger he sometimes felt in debate, but a muddled, painful sort that tangled with something like panic. She'd walked through his house alone, and slipped past his servants, out into the street. Without him. Without the cloak of his protection. With no idea what waited for her at home, having been gone so long…alone.

And fully knowing he knew her secret now.

Hell. He raked a hand through his hair.

Of course she'd run. The second she was left alone with her thoughts, she would have seen what he had stubbornly refused to acknowledge while her skin was still warm under his hands.

She had been trying to tell him. She had almost told him.

He had kissed her instead.

He looked down at the ribbon in his hand.

Bea.

B. Adroit.

His future wife. His most dangerous enemy.

He had been an utter fool.

CHAPTER THIRTY-THREE

Nicholas had been to the Duke of Winston's town house for political salons dozens of times. It always looked the same. White stone gleaming, polished brass knocker, the discreet hum of elite political life moving like a current just beneath the surface.

Tonight, though, as he handed his hat and coat to the butler, the front hall seemed colder. The paintings sharper. The air thinner.

Or perhaps it was simply him.

The weight of the folded vellum sat heavy in his coat pocket, even though he had memorized the letters and had not needed to look again.

He should not have come. That would have been the sensible thing. But Nicholas had never been sensible where she was concerned.

Over the last few hours, he'd had time to think. He'd done nothing but. And one thought continued to haunt him. The drawings. They'd been vicious…personal. And Bea had given herself to him *after* she'd drawn them. It was true that she'd only just recently discovered he wasn't a dyed-in-the-wool Tory, but still. How could she have drawn him as that fox after Hillary's salon...after the time they'd shared in the park?

He closed his eyes and took a deep breath. He didn't know. But he intended to find out.

He entered the grand drawing room to a familiar hum of voices: lords and MPs clustered by the hearth, a scattering of wives and daughters pretending to talk of music while their ears strained toward politics. Winston was in the corner arguing with Chelmsford. Hargrave was pontificating near the pianoforte. It was a typical Winslow salon.

Except for the one thing the entire group had already surely noticed.

Lady Beatrix was nowhere to be seen.

Nicholas scanned the room once. Twice. A third time, more slowly.

An irrational surge of irritation flowed through him. At what, he could not say. Her absence? The secrecy? The fact that she had melted into his bed, left him with nothing but a ribbon in his hand, and vanished? The fox drawing loomed in his mind.

He crossed the room. The Duchess of Winston drifted over to meet him.

"You're looking for her," the duchess said under her breath. It was not a question.

"Yes," he replied.

Her expression softened. "She's...unwell."

He gave her a disbelieving look.

"Fine," the duchess amended. "She's hiding."

"Upstairs?" he asked.

The duchess nodded. "Her suite. She told us she was fatigued and declined to join the guests this evening."

"Does her father know she's hiding?"

"Her father thinks she's sulking about politics," the duchess said. "And frankly, he's too busy bullying half the cabinet to inquire further."

Nicholas nodded once.

The duchess touched his sleeve lightly, uncharacteristically gentle. "I don't know what happened between you, but she's frightened."

That word hit Nicholas like a blow.

"I would never hurt her," he said.

The duchess nodded.

He left then, slipped out of the drawing room, ignoring Winston's booming voice calling, "Vanover, join us!"

Nicholas climbed the staircase quickly. His pulse thudded. With each step upward, his anger weakened, leaving something rawer behind, something he couldn't entirely explain, even to himself.

Her door was closed when he reached the landing. Somehow, he knew it was hers, a pale blue panel with a brass handle, unguarded, unremarkable, but it *felt* like Bea.

Nicholas exhaled once. Then he knocked.

There was no answer.

He knocked again, softer. "Bea."

Silence.

He pressed his palm to the door. "Bea, please."

A soft rustle came from inside.

He pushed the door open.

The sitting room was dim, lit only by a small fire and one candle on a writing desk. The faint scent of her perfume—a hint of lilacs—lingered in the air. And there she was, standing by the window, arms wrapped around her body as if she were bracing herself against a storm.

She didn't turn.

His chest tightened painfully. "Bea."

"Please leave," she whispered.

"No."

She closed her eyes, shoulders trembling.

He entered quietly, shutting the door behind him. "You're hiding from me."

She let out something like a laugh, thin, brittle. "Of course I am."

He moved closer. "Why?"

"Because I don't know what to say." Her voice cracked. "And you have every right to be furious."

"I haven't decided yet," he said honestly.

That made her whirl around.

Her face was pale, eyes rimmed red. She had not cried—Beatrix Winslow did not cry—but she had come perilously close.

He hated that he had caused it.

She swallowed. "You know."

He nodded.

"And you came regardless."

"Yes."

"Why?" Her voice rose in panic. "To condemn me? To tell me how foolish I've been? How arrogant? How wrong? To remind me that my little drawings could ruin my family? That I've mocked everything my father believes in?"

Nicholas exhaled slowly. "No."

She pressed her trembling hands to her mouth, then dropped them. "Then why are you here?" she whispered.

Nicholas stepped closer, until only a few paces remained between them. "Because I needed to see you."

She drew in a sharp breath.

"You hate my politics," he said softly. "Or at least what you believed were my politics."

"I do," she said instantly.

He blinked. Then, very quietly, "But not me?"

Her chin wobbled. She shook her head. "No."

He nodded once. "That is good to know, but those drawings. They were personal. And filled with hate."

She let out a sob and covered her face with both hands. "I'm so sorry, Nicholas."

He stood still, hands by his sides, wanting to hold her and not trusting himself to move. "Don't apologize for thinking. Don't apologize for having convictions. You've never owed anyone that."

She shook her head, dropping her hands. "Not for that. For hurting you. Not that it matters, but I drew them before I knew how you'd voted. I need you to know that my feelings for you no longer match the sketches I drew."

His jaw flexed. He closed his eyes, bracing himself against the pain. A cold weight settled in his gut. His emotions were a swirl of contradictions threatening to overwhelm him, as if he were a ship adrift in a stormy sea.

Bea winced. "I knew you'd feel betrayed, but I...I didn't understand how deeply I'd wounded you until I saw your face just now."

"Bea—"

"No," she said, voice shaking. "Let me speak. Please."

He fell silent and nodded.

She drew a shuddering breath. "I have been cruel. I know that. You were an easy target. Handsome, self-possessed, favored by every political mentor in London. You said it once, and you were right... You were—" She swallowed. "Everything I resented."

He didn't flinch. But he clenched his jaw.

"Then I spent time with you," she whispered. "And you made me feel... There is no other way to describe it other than you made me feel like what I said mattered. Like my opinions were worth something."

He inhaled sharply.

"And then I kissed you," she whispered even softer.

He closed his eyes briefly, pain tightening his mouth.

"And now," she said, "I cannot bear the thought that you feel trapped or deceived or manipulated by someone you trusted enough to—"

"Stop," he said roughly, squeezing his eyes shut.

"No," she insisted, voice breaking. "I release you."

His eyes snapped open. "What?"

"You're free," she said, tears finally spilling. "You don't have to marry me. You don't have to acknowledge anything that happened between us. No one will ever know. Mother suspects something, but Father didn't even realize I'd been gone." She made a strangled, scoffing noise.

Nicholas stared at her, stunned into silence.

She pressed both palms against her chest as if holding herself together. "Please. Please, Nicholas. Don't marry me out of pity. Or obligation. Or because we were foolish. If I'm with child, there are things I can do—"

"Bea—"

"But if—" Her voice cracked. "If you have ever cared for me at all, please don't tell anyone I'm B. Adroit. My father would never forgive me."

The words struck Nicholas like physical blows.

She thought he might expose her. *That* was her concern? She thought he might destroy her.

Nicholas stared at her as if he'd never truly seen her until now. A slow, brutal ache spread through his chest—so deep it felt like the beginning of grief. His hand lifted on instinct, reaching for her, reaching to wipe away the tears—

And then it stopped in the air.

Because he finally understood.

Beneath everything they'd been—every stolen breath, every fierce look, every promise he'd made with his mouth on hers—she still believed he might use her like a weapon.

His fingers curled, empty. He let his hand fall.

He shook his head, disbelieving, but the movement wasn't mild now—it was a man trying to refuse a truth his body had already accepted.

"Bea…" His voice came low and wrecked. "If you thought I would do that to you. If you believed, even for a moment, that I would reveal your secret to cause you harm—"

Something in him went very still.

Then his words shot through clenched teeth. "You never knew me at all."

Her breath caught, a swift, startled intake she could not disguise. Her mouth trembled.

Nicholas looked away for the first time, jaw working, hand gripping the back of a chair as if he needed something to hold on to.

"I would never expose you," he said, each word clipped with unmistakable pain. "Not for ambition. Not for revenge. Not even to save my own name. I would die before I let anyone hurt you."

The truth of it rang through the room.

Her tears fell freely now.

He still didn't touch her.

"Do you understand me?" he asked quietly. "I will take your secret to my grave. Even if it costs me my standing in Parliament."

Her shoulders shook with silent sobs.

He let out a long, ragged breath, then turned and crossed to the door.

Before he opened it, he paused. "I didn't come here to condemn you," he said softly. "I came here to tell you…" His voice faltered. "I love you."

She gasped, unable to speak.

Nicholas's hand lingered on the door handle.

Then he said the last thing he could manage without breaking. "But that was before I knew you don't trust me."

And even though it was one of the hardest things he'd ever done, he turned on his heel…and walked away.

CHAPTER THIRTY-FOUR

Nicholas did not remember the walk home from Winston's town house. He'd sent his carriage on without him. He needed the air...and the space. Some part of him must have navigated the streets, nodded to footmen, mounted his steps, opened the door. But the rest of him—the parts that breathed and felt and thought—had been left behind upstairs in Bea's sitting room.

With her tears. With her apology. With the words that still lodged inside him, painful and immovable.

I release you, she'd said.

As if he were some animal straining at his leash. As if he had ever once needed pressure or obligation to want her. As if she hadn't already carved herself into him so deeply that removing her would require tearing out organs he needed to live.

He slammed the door to his study behind him hard enough to rattle the frame. The decanter on the sideboard glinted in the lamplight. He seized it, sloshed brandy into a glass, and swallowed half in a single, burning gulp.

Normally, he hated drinking alone. Tonight, he couldn't bring himself to care.

He stood by the window, staring at the ink-black street outside.

She thought he'd expose her. She thought he'd destroy her. She thought he'd marry her only out of obligation. But what gutted him most… What hollowed him out until he could feel the emptiness of it rattle in his bones was the simple, devastating truth—she did not want him.

Not really. Not enough.

At first—when their courtship had barely begun, back when she still rejected him on principle, he'd told himself she simply didn't know him. But today… Today she'd looked at him with such fear and guilt and certainty. Certain that he was wrong for her. Certain that an alliance between them would be a mistake. Certain that he couldn't be trusted.

It was no longer about his politics. It was about *him*. And her utter failure to see who he truly was.

He threw back the rest of the brandy.

His vision blurred for a moment, then sharpened—dizzily, painfully—as he recognized footsteps in the hall.

Who could it be at this hour?

His father entered without knocking, as if this were still his house, as if Nicholas were still a boy and not the man who now held in his hands the power to upend two great political dynasties.

Nicholas's body reacted before his mind could—spine locking, jaw setting, breath going shallow with the old, boyhood reflex of obedience. He hated that his father could still do that to him with nothing but an entrance.

"Good God," his father grunted. "You look like hell."

Nicholas didn't bother turning. "Feel free to leave."

VanDeVere snorted. "Not until you tell me what possessed you to damage your own career so spectacularly."

Nicholas's grip tightened on his glass. "I don't know what you mean."

"Spare me." The duke stalked to the newspaper on the desk and slapped it with the back of his hand. "This. This is everywhere. Every gentleman's club, every drawing room. The caricature of you and Winston looking like the foxes who stole the canary. The one signed with that ludicrous pseudonym. I told you to take care of this."

Nicholas said nothing.

His father continued, voice rising. "You are meant to be leading men to vote tomorrow. Instead, you are the punchline of the Season. You should have shut this down weeks ago."

"I hired someone," Nicholas said flatly. "He failed."

"So I gathered," the duke snapped. "And instead of regrouping, instead of preparing for the most crucial vote of your career, you spend the evening looking like you've been trampled by a cart horse. Not to mention the story about some sort of a spat with Hargrave. Don't be a fool. We need his vote."

That. Was. It.

Nicholas felt something inside him—some quiet, obedient, dutiful part—finally crack down the middle. He turned. Slowly. Deliberately. And the thunderous expression on his face made the duke go still.

"You think this is about my *career*?" Nicholas growled.

The duke blinked. "It is always about your career."

"No," he replied. "It isn't."

His father's nostrils flared. "This is not the time for distractions."

Nicholas laughed once, sharp and humorless. "Distractions. Right. That's all you see, isn't it? A son behaving inconveniently. A vote at stake. A headline that might bruise your standing at the club."

VanDeVere stepped closer, voice dropping. "You will maintain composure. You will attend the vote tomorrow. And you will not allow some anonymous scribbler to derail what you have spent your entire life preparing for."

Another fissure opened inside of Nicholas. He stared at his father. Really stared.

The man was imposing. He always had been. Broad-shouldered, silver at the temples, jaw cut like a Roman statue. A lifetime of command radiated from him like a cold, steady wind.

But for the first time in Nicholas's life, the duke looked small. Not physically. Morally. Emotionally.

He was a man so consumed by the machine of politics he could not conceive of anything outside it. Not loyalty. Not passion. Not truth. Certainly not love.

Nicholas set his empty glass on the table with a soft click. "The vote is tomorrow," he said. "And I will be there."

"Good." VanDeVere exhaled, sounding relieved. "Then see to your duties. And stop drinking like a common wastrel."

Nicholas's eyes hardened. "You misunderstand me," he said slowly.

VanDeVere frowned. "What?"

"The vote is tomorrow," Nicholas repeated. "But it is not your definition of duty I intend to follow."

A dangerous quiet settled between them.

VanDeVere's voice dropped to a disbelieving whisper. "You cannot be thinking of voting against the party."

Nicholas stepped closer. "No," he said. "I'm voting for what I actually believe."

The duke's face went red. "You arrogant, idealistic child. You'll throw away everything. Everything. Your alliances, your standing, your future. You'll make a mockery of your own bloodline!"

Nicholas shook his head slowly. "You've already managed that well enough without my help."

His father reeled as if struck.

Nicholas continued, voice low and iron-hard. "How ironic, Father. You wanted a politician. You raised one. You molded me into something sharp and obedient and unbreakable. And the moment I dared to think for myself—really think—you've decided I've become defective."

"You have no idea what you're doing," VanDeVere spat.

Nicholas smiled. It was not warm. It was not forgiving. It was the smile of a man who had been walking in the wrong direction his entire life and had finally—finally—turned toward the sun.

"Oh," he said determinedly, "I know *exactly* what I'm doing."

"And what is that?" the duke demanded, his eyes flashing with anger.

Nicholas turned away from him and walked toward the window again.

He pulled the vellum from his pocket, holding it loosely in his palm.

The name wouldn't let him look away.

Lady Beatrix Winslow. B. Adroit. The woman he wanted. The woman he lost. The woman who had changed him without meaning to. The woman who had believed—incorrectly—that he had no loyalty to anything but ambition.

Nicholas closed his fist around the vellum. "I'm choosing."

"Choosing what?" VanDeVere snapped.

Nicholas turned back, eyes blazing. "Who I am."

His voice shook—not with weakness, but with certainty. "Tomorrow, I will walk into Parliament as myself. Not your son. Not Winston's protégé. Nor his future successor. And not a puppet carved by other men's hands."

"Fool!" VanDeVere thundered.

"Perhaps," Nicholas said. "But I'll be a fool on my own terms."

His father's nostrils flared. "Do you truly think Winston will allow you to marry his daughter if you vote against the party on this bill?"

"Winston does not grant permission over his daughter's heart," Nicholas said evenly. "And I've already lost her."

VanDeVere frowned. "You speak as though that question has been settled."

"It has," Nicholas replied. "Just not in the way you assume."

His father stared at him, thrown off balance. "I don't follow."

Nicholas met his gaze, unflinching. "No," he said quietly. "You wouldn't."

Then, with all the calm certainty of a man whose path had finally come into focus, he added, "I will not take instruction from you or Winston or anyone *ever* again."

VanDeVere stared at him, stunned, furious, speechless.

Nicholas stalked across the room, reached for the study door, and held it open. "Goodnight, Father."

The duke hesitated—rage, disbelief, and a flicker of something akin to fear battling in his dark eyes—before he swept past him and stormed into the hall.

Nicholas shut the door behind him, exhaling a breath that felt like a victory and a wound at the same time.

He leaned his forehead against the wood.

Tomorrow was the vote.

Tomorrow everything he'd been raised for—everything he'd been told mattered—would be tested.

And perhaps, just perhaps, when he stood and spoke with his own voice instead of the one bred into him, he would finally stop hating himself.

He pushed away from the door, squared his shoulders, and looked at himself in the dark window.

Steady. Unbreakable. Clear.

He no longer belonged to his father's world.

From now on, he would belong only to his own convictions.

Bea had never realized how loud her own heartbeat was. It filled her ears as she stood alone in her bedchamber, hands braced on the edge of her writing desk, staring down at a blank sheet of paper.

Her fingers shook. Hours had passed since Nicholas had left her rooms. He had closed the door with agonizing gentleness, as if he feared she might break even further if he let it slam.

She could still hear the faint click of the latch.

She had cried until her throat burned, and her head ached. Quiet tears, furious tears, exhausted tears. But eventually the storm had given out, leaving behind only a hollow, aching quiet.

She had hurt him. Deeply.

Worse, she had believed he would betray her.

That knowledge curled inside her like a stain she couldn't scrub away...ugly and shameful.

She had expected Nicholas to be like every other man of her station, self-interested, calculating, prepared to sacrifice anything and anyone in the name of advancement.

She had assumed he was a perfect expression of the political world she despised.

But he wasn't.

He never had been.

And she had smugly refused to believe—to see—anything different. She'd been blinded by her own assumptions.

She sat down in her chair slowly, bracing herself as though her knees might give out. She opened the box where she kept her drawings, hidden from others' prying eyes. Her gaze drifted to the scattered pamphlets and sketches—old plates she'd carved months ago, earlier drafts, discarded drawings. Her hands brushed over them lightly, almost tenderly.

Every one of them had been a blow. To a cause. To a man. To *him*.

Whenever she had sketched Nicholas as a bumbling aristocrat, she'd told herself she was doing her duty. She was skewering a system, a party, a position.

But she'd also been skewering *him*.

Now she remembered, with startling clarity, the look on his face in her sitting room tonight. It hadn't been anger. Nor outrage.

It had been hurt.

Real, honest hurt.

Not only because she'd lied. But because she'd believed— truly believed—that he might turn on her.

She pressed her hands to her eyes. "You fool," she whispered to herself. "You utter, absolute fool."

Slowly, painfully, the truth formed inside her like dawn breaking over the horizon. She had always prided herself on seeing the world clearly. Seeing hypocrisy, arrogance, cruelty, and cutting it down with a single stroke of her quill.

But when it came to Nicholas…

She had been blind.

Blind to his compassion. Blind to his restraint. Blind to his decency. Blind to the way he looked at her—really looked at her—as if she were something rare and extraordinary.

She had been so busy protecting her heart from men who wouldn't value her that she had locked it against the one man who would.

A sob rose in her throat, but she swallowed it down.

No more tears.

What was needed now—what Nicholas had always been brave enough to show and she had always hidden behind ink —was courage.

Real courage.

The kind that required putting her heart on paper.

Bea sat up straight. She reached for her pencil. Her hand hovered over an empty page. For the first time in her career as B. Adroit, she wasn't drawing from anger. Or indignation. Or scorn. She was drawing from *love*.

It terrified her.

But it steadied her too.

She lowered the pencil. Slowly, strokes formed on the page, light at first, then firmer, then fierce.

Nicholas Archer.

Not the buffoonish caricature she'd drawn dozens of times. Not the elegantly dressed puppet she'd portrayed him as. Not the man bending under the weight of party politics.

But the man he had shown himself to be. The man she knew he was.

Jaw set with purpose. Eyes bright with conviction. Spine straight.

Not Hargrave's co-hort. Not Winston's pawn. Not VanDeVere's shadow.

Just Nicholas.

A man standing alone on the floor of the House, papers in hand, not flinching despite the jeers around him. A man speaking his mind with clarity and fire. A man finally breaking free of every chain that had held him.

A man brave enough to love her, even when she had made that impossible.

Tears fell onto the vellum, but she wiped them away quickly before they could smear the drawing.

By the time she added the final lines—a subtle shading of light behind him, a symbolic burst of illumination—her heart was too big for her chest.

This wasn't satire. It was a tribute. The vulnerability of it nearly sent her to her knees. But the truth if it made her proud. She didn't stop. She added her signature. *B. Adroit.* For the first time, the pseudonym didn't feel like a mask.

It felt like a promise.

The clock on her mantel chimed midnight. Bea startled, looking toward the window. The house was silent. Even the servants had long since retired.

She stared down at the drawing, hands trembling again, but for a different reason now.

This sketch was dangerous. Not because it mocked the powerful, but because it revealed her heart.

If Nicholas saw it, he would know.

Perhaps not immediately. Perhaps not consciously. But some part of him would understand that she believed in him.

Not in his party. Not in his family. Not in his ambitions.

In *him.*

And that was the one truth she had never dared to give him.

Until now.

She moved quickly, gathering her things with a clarity she had not felt in years. She snatched up the drawing and placed it solidly between the pages of a pamphlet.

She changed into the brown cloak, pulled up the hood, and slipped out of her room.

The corridor was dark and still.

Good.

She crept down the servants' staircase, heart pounding wildly. She had done this dozens of times before, but tonight it felt more important than ever. The back door gave a quiet groan as she eased it open. The cool night air slapped her cheeks, but she wrapped the cloak tighter around herself and stepped into the darkness.

Normally, she did this at dawn. The streets were quiet at this hour, but not empty. A carriage or two rumbled far off. A watchman's distant call echoed through the square.

Bea kept to the shadows, moving quickly and determinedly toward Gutter Lane.

Toward the printshop.

Toward the place where she had created half her destruction, and where she would now attempt her redemption.

Her boots struck the cobblestones softly, rhythmically.

Fear gripped her. But beneath it—beneath the terror, beneath the guilt, beneath everything was resolve.

She had hurt him. She had doubted him. She had wounded him in a way she could not undo.

But she had one thing left. One weapon she understood better than anyone. Her art. Her truth. Her heart. Tonight, she would put all three into his hands.

AFTER JUMPING from the hackney near the corner, she reached the printshop, breathless, a thin sheen of sweat cooling on her neck despite the chill. It was dark, of course, but the slot was always left open for deliveries.

Her hands shook as she eased it open and slipped her drawing inside.

The air around the shop smelled of ink, metal, and stale

heat from the press. Familiar, comforting, and terrifying all at once.

"Please let him see this." Her voice cracked. "Please let him understand."

She hesitated one last second, then turned and fled into the night.

WHEN SHE REACHED her house again, Bea's heart was racing. She paused on the steps and looked back. For the first time since her courtship with Nicholas had begun, she knew she'd done the right thing.

She had fought for him. For herself. For both of them. For the truth.

Whatever happened tomorrow—

It would be a beginning.

Or an end.

But not silence.

And Beatrix Winslow, the same young woman who had once hidden behind ink and anonymity, finally understood—

If she wanted something, truly wanted it, she had to be brave enough to put her heart on the line. Even if it shattered.

CHAPTER THIRTY-SIX

T he great hall that housed the House of Lords had never seemed so small. Nicholas stood behind the bench, fingers clenched around the stack of speech notes he'd written many nights ago, notes he now realized he would not be using.

Men filled the chamber in waves, MPs crowding benches, voices echoing off the dark leather, the sound of quills scratching, papers shuffling, murmurs rising like a growing tide.

Hargrave lounged smugly across the aisle. Winston was seated near the front, rigid with expectation, his jaw set in stone.

Nicholas felt all of them watching him, waiting for him to play his part.

His father's voice rose in his mind—*Don't perform, Nicholas. Never give them a spectacle.*

The old reflex tightened, swift and familiar. He inhaled deeply.

Today, he would not obey it. He was done being his father's instrument.

He rose. A hush fell.

He did not read a single word from his notes. Instead, he set them down deliberately and met the gazes of every man in the room.

"Gentlemen," he began, voice steady, echoing through the chamber. "For years I have stood here as a representative of my constituency. A frequent supporter of the Tory party. As a disciple of tradition, expectation, and duty."

A murmur ran through the benches.

"But I realized—belatedly—that I have confused obedience with principles," he continued. "That I have mistaken inherited conviction for personal belief. I have confused loyalty with silence."

Several MPs stiffened. Winston's head tilted sharply. Hargrave's smirk faded. Langford's eyes narrowed.

Nicholas pressed on. "Today's vote has been framed as a question of party. A question of duty. A question of which faction will emerge victorious."

He drew a breath.

"Let me be clear. *I no longer accept that premise.*"

Gasps. A wave of shock rolled across the room.

Nicholas looked up at the gallery—just briefly—and something inside him jolted.

She was there.

Hidden beneath a modest bonnet. Hands clutching the railing. Pale, tense, trembling.

Bea.

His chest tightened.

Was she crying? Or was that only his imagination?

He cleared his throat and forced himself to continue.

"I have spent years believing that the work of this chamber was a game to be maneuvered, moves to be strategized, speeches to be sharpened, alliances to be negotiated."

His voice softened. "And then...someone showed me differently."

The gallery went still.

Bea's fingers froze around the railing.

"She opened my eyes," Nicholas said, his voice quieter now, more vulnerable than he had ever allowed it to be in public. "She showed me the cracks in the foundation I defended. She challenged me. She forced me to think. She made me a better man."

It was unmistakable now. Tears slipped freely down Bea's cheek.

Nicholas saw them.

It nearly undid him.

"In her words, I found a mirror held up to my own weaknesses. And in that mirror, I saw a truth I can no longer ignore."

He swept the chamber with a steady gaze. "I am not a Whig," he said. "But neither am I a Tory."

Chaos erupted.

Men leapt to their feet. Voices rose in outrage. Half the chamber shouted over the other half. The chancellor pounded his gavel. Winston surged up from his seat as if he'd been struck.

Nicholas did not flinch.

"For the first time in my life," he continued over the uproar, "I shall cast a vote today not for ambition."

He paused.

"But for what I truly believe. Unlike the caricatures in the paper would suggest...I am voting *for* the reform bill, and I urge those of you with a conscience to do the same."

He stepped back.

Silence followed, shocked, disbelieving silence.

Nicholas turned once more toward the gallery...just in time to see Bea stand.

Her bonnet trembled slightly as she lifted her chin. Her eyes locked onto his.

Then, before anyone could stop her, she pushed past two startled gentlemen, rushed through the gallery door, down the narrow stairwell, and into the chamber itself.

Gasps filled the air.

A lady—Winston's daughter, no less—had entered the floor of the House.

Several MPs rose in scandalized outrage. The chancellor shouted for order. Nicholas froze.

Bea.

She stood in the open space at the foot of the benches, chest heaving, eyes shining with tears and fierce resolve. She'd ripped off her bonnet. Her cloak billowed behind her, her hair tumbling loose in golden waves.

She looked wild.

And glorious.

And utterly unstoppable.

She was cradling a copy of the morning paper against her chest.

Nicholas's breath caught painfully in his chest. "What are you doing?" he whispered.

Her voice shook, but it carried through the chamber like a bell. "What I should have done long ago."

Winston remained standing, face purple. "Beatrix Winslow, what in God's name!"

She ignored her father. Her eyes remained locked on Nicholas.

"You didn't have to say those things," she said, voice trembling. "Not for me. Not in front of all these men. You didn't have to—"

"Bea," Nicholas replied hoarsely, stepping forward. "I did. You're the one who made me see."

She shook her head, tears falling faster. "Then I must be

honest too." She pushed the paper into his hands. "Look at this."

A murmur ran through the room, anticipation, confusion, dawning realization, while Nicholas studied her newest drawing.

Beatrix lifted her chin. Her voice broke as she turned to face the gallery and announced, "I am B. Adroit!"

Silence.

True, crushing silence fell over the House of Lords.

Then…absolute anarchy.

Shouts erupted from every bench. Men stood, outraged. Some laughed in disbelief. Hargrave sputtered like a kettle ready to boil over. Winston lunged toward his daughter, face redder than Nicholas had ever seen.

"You!" Winston choked. "You—you cannot—!"

Bea whirled away from him, while Nicholas stared at the paper, breathless, unable to move.

"You didn't have to do this," he said, his voice cracking.

"Yes." Her voice wavered. "I did."

"But they'll—"

"I don't care what they do," she whispered. "I only care that you know I'm not hiding from this any longer. I'm not hiding from you. And," she swallowed hard, "I love you."

His throat tightened.

Hargrave jabbed a finger in her direction. "Arrest her! She has libeled half this chamber!"

The chancellor pounded his gavel desperately.

Winston lunged forward again and grabbed Bea's arm, but Nicholas was there in an instant, stepping between them.

"Touch her again," Nicholas said in a low, deadly voice, "and you will regret it."

Bea gasped.

Winston froze. Outrage quickly covered his features, but he let his hand drop to his side.

Nicholas shoved the paper under his arm, then he took Bea's hands gently, as if everything around them wasn't madness. Around them, men bellowed for order, for discipline, for her removal, for the vote to be cast, for someone—anyone—to explain how the country's sharpest satirist had been living in Winston's house under his nose.

And was a woman no less!

But none of it mattered.

Not to Nicholas.

Not to Bea.

In that moment, there was only them.

Nicholas squeezed her hands, voice low and aching. "You've just upended Parliament."

She gave a watery, shaky smile. "I've always wanted to do that."

He laughed softly, astonished, undone. "Beatrix Winslow, I love you."

She stepped closer, voice breaking. "I love you too, and I'm so proud of you."

His chest tightened. Hard. "And I," he whispered, "am absolutely ruined for anyone else."

She gave him a tender smile. "I feel exactly the same."

The mayhem continued. The chancellor bellowed. Winston sputtered. Hargrave looked ready to faint. Sir Edmund looked as if he'd swallowed a bee, while Lord Hillary looked as if he could barely contain his pleasure.

But Nicholas—

Nicholas had never felt so steady in his life.

He wrapped his fingers around Bea's and said, loud enough for the entire chamber to hear, "If she stands accused, then so do I."

Gasps rippled through the air.

Bea looked up at him, tears shining in her eyes.

"Nicholas…"

He turned to the room. "I am culpable. I am complicit. Because I let ambiguity serve me when conviction was required. The caricatures she drew of me were not entirely wrong."

Shouts, outrage, and calls to order echoed across the chamber.

Nicholas ignored them all. He lowered his forehead to hers. "They cannot arrest you simply for drawing things they dislike. Hell. Half the country's artists would be in gaol. But let them rage. You're not alone," he whispered. "And you never will be again."

CHAPTER THIRTY-SEVEN

London had never been so loud. Nicholas could still hear the echoing pandemonium of Parliament behind him, voices shouting, the chancellor pounding his gavel, half the chamber in hysterics and the other half in scandalized outrage. He had barely managed to get Bea out before Winston or Hargrave could drag her into some back room for questioning or threats.

The corridor outside the chamber had been blessedly empty. Nicholas had wrapped her cloak around her trembling shoulders, taken her hand, and ushered her through a side exit where his coach waited.

The chancellor had declared the state of affairs within the chambers far too turbulent to conduct the vote today. They would all have to return in the morning.

Now Nicholas and Bea rode in his carriage, just the two of them, sunlight slipping through the curtains in bright, fluttering ribbons.

Bea was still flushed—cheeks pink, eyes bright. She sat angled toward him, cloak loosened, one glove half-off as if she'd forgotten she was wearing it. Nicholas watched her mouth as her smile faded.

She stared down at her hands. "I didn't plan it. I didn't go there intending to...to make a spectacle of myself. I just wanted to watch the vote. But when I saw you standing there —alone, defending your conscience—after I'd spent so long mocking you and misjudging you and hurting you... I couldn't hide anymore." Her voice trembled.

Nicholas went still. He moved to sit next to her. His hand stayed at her waist—not possessive, but grounding—his thumb brushing once, a silent *I'm here.*

"Bea," he said quietly.

She drew a shaky breath, still looking at her hands as if they were safer than his eyes.

"Nicholas, when you spoke this morning, when you didn't flinch... I knew I couldn't be a coward for one more minute. Even if I made a spectacle of myself."

Nicholas's throat tightened. He lifted his free hand and, with careful tenderness, turned her chin toward him. "You've never been a coward, Bea. You taught me to be brave."

She shook her head, tears filling her eyes.

"Look at me," he murmured, tipping her chin with his thumb.

Bea did—reluctant at first, then fully, as if she'd decided she would not half-step into courage anymore.

Nicholas held her gaze, expression open, voice low. "You weren't a spectacle," he said. "You were...you." A pause. "And I have never—" He stopped, the words catching, then tried again with quieter certainty. "I have never been prouder to stand beside anyone."

Bea's eyes shone again, but this time she didn't look as though she might shatter. She looked as though she might finally stop running.

She clung to him with a desperate little breath. "I had to tell them," she whispered. "All of them. I had to tell *you*."

"You did." His throat tightened painfully. "With this…" He gestured to the paper that laid on the seat next to them.

"Do you like it?" she asked tentatively, biting her lip.

He allowed the hint of a smile to touch his lips. "It's extraordinary."

She glanced down at the drawing.

The caricature was unmistakable…bold lines, fierce motion. A phoenix burst upward from a scatter of inked ashes, wings flared wide, each feather edged with purpose rather than ornament. The fire that surrounded it was not destructive but cleansing, the kind that burned away rot and left something stronger behind.

And there, at the heart of it, was Nicholas.

Not softened. Not idealized. His profile was sharp, intent, eyes fixed forward as though he were already in motion, already answering some call only he could hear. The phoenix wore his face without disguise, without apology, powerful, swift, and unyielding.

Below him, the ashes resolved into figures: bent backs straightening, empty hands lifting, shadows retreating. Coins fell not into the pockets of the powerful, but into the open palms of the poor. Scales tipped. Chains snapped. Justice—clear-eyed and unsentimental—was delivered not with cruelty, but with resolve.

She had drawn him not as a hero crowned by praise, but as a man remade by fire. A man who chose the harder path and rose because of it.

Nicholas stared at the page for a long moment, utterly still.

"This is how you see me," he said quietly. It was not a question.

"This is who you are," Bea replied, her voice trembling.

Something in his expression gave way, not pride, not triumph, but recognition. As though he had been searching for himself and, somehow, she had drawn the answer.

He lifted his gaze to her, eyes bright with something fierce and reverent. "Then," he said softly, "I will spend the rest of my life trying to deserve it."

She smiled through her tears, and this time, when he pulled her into his arms, there was nothing uncertain left between them at all.

"And now everything will fall apart," she said, voice cracking. "Hargrave is furious. Mother shall faint. Father will probably challenge you to a duel. Society will run wild with it. The papers will—"

"Bea." Nicholas squeezed her hands gently. "Look at me."

She did. And the anguish in her eyes nearly brought him to his knees.

"I know what you risked," he said softly. "I know what will come of it. And still—still—you stepped forward. You stood in that chamber. You told the truth."

She closed her eyes as tears slipped down. "I couldn't let you stand alone."

He brushed one tear from her cheek with the lightest touch. "I will never forget what you did today."

She swallowed hard. "And I will never forgive myself for doubting you," she whispered. "For thinking, even for a moment, that you would ever reveal my secret. That you would use it to hurt me. That was cruel of me. It was unfair. You have every right to hate me."

His jaw clenched, not with anger, but with the force of what he felt for her. "Bea, I could never hate you…even if I tried."

She let out a sound between a sob and a laugh.

Nicholas brushed his thumb over her knuckles. "I was hurt," he said, voice quieter now. "That is true. Last night in your sitting room, when you said you didn't want me to marry you, that you were releasing me… That hurt. A great deal."

She flinched. "I know."

"But the hurt came not from rejection," Nicholas continued, "but from the belief that you didn't trust me. That you didn't want to marry me."

Bea blinked up at him. "I thought I was protecting you."

"And I," he murmured, "was hoping you would not let me go."

She sucked in her breath.

He reached up, brushing a strand of hair behind her ear. "I meant every word I said today," he told her. "You changed me. You challenged me. You made me think. And today…you made me braver than I have ever been."

Her eyes shone again.

"Then I'm glad," she whispered. "Even if everything else falls apart."

Nicholas cupped her cheek, gently turning her face toward his. "Everything will fall into place," he said softly. "Not apart."

Her lips trembled.

He rested his forehead against hers. "You are remarkable," he whispered. "You are clever and fierce and honest and brilliant. And I want to be by your side, not because of obligation. Not because of politics or lineage." His voice softened, reverent. "But because you are the woman I choose."

Her breath stopped.

Nicholas drew back just enough to see her face clearly. Then, very slowly, he slid to one knee before her in the rocking carriage and took her hand in his.

Bea gasped softly, free hand flying to her mouth.

Nicholas looked up at her with unguarded devotion. "I don't care what your father says. I don't care what Parliament says. I don't care what the papers scream tomorrow morning. I do not care what the world believes we should be."

He squeezed her hand. "You are B. Adroit. You are Beatrix Winslow. And you are everything I want."

Tears slipped down her cheeks.

Nicholas lifted her hand to his lips, kissed it tenderly. "Marry me."

Her breath shuddered.

"Marry me," he repeated softly, "and let us face whatever comes next together."

Bea looked too full, too fragile, too immense all at once. Her throat worked. She tried to speak and failed, covering her mouth again as tears continued to slide freely down her cheeks.

Nicholas waited, silent, steady, certain.

Finally, with a trembling breath, she lowered her hand. She leaned forward and framed his face in her hands, pressing her forehead to his. "Yes," she whispered, a laugh and a sob tangled together. "Yes, Nicholas."

His exhale was a sound of relief, gratitude, and something else—something that sent warmth through her like sunlight. His hands wrapped around her waist, pulling her into him, holding her tightly as if he finally dared to believe she was his.

EPILOGUE

fortnight later

The morning sunlight streamed through the tall windows of Nicholas and Beatrix Archer's town house, cutting warm, golden paths across the breakfast table where the couple sat far too close for propriety and exactly close enough for happiness.

Bea still wasn't entirely convinced any of it was real.

Married. By special license. In a whirlwind that had shocked half of London and delighted the other half.

Her father had refused to allow her home after the scandal. The duke had sputtered so hard Bea sincerely worried for his circulation. So, Nicholas had been forced to wake up his friend, the Archbishop of Canterbury, and procure a special license for them to be married that same night. Then —after the reform bill was passed by a large margin the next morning—Nicholas had swept Bea away to Archer Abbey in Devon, where they'd stayed for a fortnight—long enough for the scandal to cool, and for their marriage to begin in earnest, far from curious eyes.

The rumors were waiting for them when they'd returned

to London this morning, however. In addition to Bea's father refusing to acknowledge their marriage, Nicholas's father had refused to speak to him after the vote.

They were cast out by both important families. But none of it mattered.

Not when Bea woke every morning with Nicholas's arm around her bare waist. Not when she heard him laugh, low and warm, as he watched her sketch. Not when she slipped her feet against his on the chaise, earning a wicked grin.

Nicholas glanced up from his newspaper—*yet another one mentioning them*—and smiled that lazy, devastating smile she was beginning to suspect he reserved only for her.

"You're staring," he murmured.

"I'm admiring," she corrected.

He leaned closer, brushing a kiss against her cheek. "As am I."

She blushed. She, Beatrix "B. Adroit" Winslow—now Archer, blushed.

"You know," she said, tapping the scandal sheet with one finger, "I think this is our fifth mention this week."

Nicholas skimmed the headline with amusement.

LORD VANOVER: THE PEOPLE'S CHAMPION? Wife Once Closeted Satirist—Now London's Favorite Marchioness.

He laughed softly. "I suppose that makes me the 'darling of Parliament.'"

"You've always been a darling," she said sweetly. "You just needed someone to tell you the truth from time to time."

"And sharpen my spine?"

"That too."

He kissed her forehead. "I'm fortunate to have you."

Bea's heart warmed and softened like butter left too close to the stove. She traced a small circle on the back of his hand and sighed. "Only weeks ago, we were at war, you know?"

Nicholas's bit his lip and smiled. "Oh, yes. I remember."

"And now, here we are."

He leaned in, his voice a velvet promise. "Truce?"

She tugged him closer. "A very happy one. Though if you misbehave…I reserve the right to declare war again."

His laugh rumbled against her cheek. "Darling, I pray you do."

A knock sounded at the door then, interrupting their banter, just before Georgie and Poppy swept into the room in a flurry of silk and certainty.

Poppy looked as though she'd dressed for maximum drama—a bright pink day dress with a daring ribbon at the neckline and a little bonnet tipped at a mischievous angle, her gloves half tugged off as if she'd been too impatient to arrive properly.

Georgie, by contrast, was sleek and deliberate in a fashionable violet-colored walking dress, the cut elegant and unfussy, with a perfectly tied hat and crisp gloves that made her look composed enough to manage any scandal in Mayfair—preferably before luncheon.

The moment she entered, Poppy threw her arms wide. "We're here! Tell us everything! Are you blissfully happy? Overwhelmed by scandal? Already exhausted by the *ton*'s fascination with your marriage?"

Nicholas greeted his wife's friends, kissed Bea's cheek, murmured something about "important correspondence," and stepped away to work in his study, though Bea caught the unmistakable sound of him chuckling as he went.

Bea motioned for her friends to sit. "We're happy."

Poppy sighed dramatically. "Ridiculously so, I imagine."

Georgie flopped into a chair. "Honestly, Bea, I didn't think anything could top Jason chasing me down with his horse and scooping me up after I ran away from the altar where I was to marry Lord Henderville."

Bea winced and wrinkled her nose.

Georgie leaned forward. "But you, you have managed to shock the *ton even more* than that. I mean, honestly, Bea. Parliament? Announcing your secret identity in the middle of a vote? Marrying the man you once turned into a peacock-headed caricature? It's—well—it's magnificent."

"I agree," Poppy declared loyally.

Bea tried to look solemn, but her smile broke free. "Well," she said lightly, "I'm just glad the reform bill passed. And I'm just getting started."

Poppy's eyebrows shot up. "Oh, dear God."

Georgie clapped her hands. "Are you going to influence Parliament through Nicholas? Because I *truly* think the nation should prepare itself."

Bea took a sip of tea, eyes sparkling. "Influence? My dears, I intend to heavily direct it."

Both friends gasped in delighted amusement.

"I've little doubt you'll rule the country, Bea," Georgie announced.

"Only a small portion of it," Bea replied, shrugging one shoulder. "Perhaps just…all of Parliament."

Poppy sighed happily. "It's glorious. Terribly scandalous. And perfectly romantic." But then her smile faded suddenly.

Bea's brows knit. "Poppy? What's wrong?"

Poppy slumped back in dramatic despair. "Don't get me wrong. I'm entirely happy for you. It's just that…it's suddenly occurred to me…you two are happily married while *my* life is over."

"Oh, dear." Georgie sat up straighter. "Which catastrophe is this? Your mother? The bohemians? The wine merchants threatening to stop selling to her?"

"No," Poppy moaned. "Worse."

Bea's eyes widened. "What could be worse?"

"My mother's long-time solicitor is retiring."

There was a beat of silence.

Bea blinked. "The one who's been helping you manage her…disarray?"

Poppy nodded gravely. "The same. The only man who has ever understood how to untangle her finances, her invitations, her scandals, and her occasional disappearances to Spain. He is abandoning me."

Bea sucked in her breath. "Did he say why?"

"Something ridiculous about 'old age' and 'peace and quiet,'" Poppy said, waving a hand. "The traitor."

Bea bit back a smile. "What happens now?"

Poppy flung her arms wide. "He's sending a new solicitor."

"And?" Bea prompted.

Georgie frowned. "What? You dislike him?"

Poppy shrugged. "I've yet to meet him. But he doesn't know all the…intricacies of dealing with my mother."

"Seems to me he'll learn soon enough," Georgie pointed out.

"I suppose," Poppy replied, crossing her arms over her chest. Her mouth remained curved in a frown. "My first meeting with him is tomorrow morning. I just hope he doesn't decide to sack us when he learns how difficult it is to keep Mama from scandal."

Bea reached across the table and patted Poppy's hand. "Take heart. If there's anything this Seasons has taught us…" Bea grinned. "It's that sometimes scandal can be the beginning of something quite extraordinary. And I suspect, that when your moment comes, Poppy, yours will be the most extraordinary of them all."

Want to know what happened during Bea and Nicholas's

scandalous honeymoon at Archer Abbey? CLICK HERE to read the bonus epilogue and join my newsletter
or type
https://dl.bookfunnel.com/7op43cu3op
into your browser.

Thank you for reading *The Wallflower's Secret War*. If you enjoyed it, I would truly appreciate your recommendations and reviews.
Want more? Find out what happens when Poppy meets her mother's handsome new solicitor. CLICK HERE for The Wallflower Takes All.

ALSO BY VALERIE BOWMAN

The Wallflowers' Revolt

The Wallflower's Great Escape (Book 1)

The Wallflower's Secret War (Book 2)

The Wallflower Takes All (Book 3)

Love's a Game

The Duchess Hunt (Book 1)

The Duke Dare (Book 2)

The Marquess Match (Book 3)

The Whitmorelands

The Duke Deal (Book 1)

The Marquess Move (Book 2)

The Debutante Dilemma (Book 3)

The Wallflower Win (Book 4)

Lords in Disguise

The Footman is an Earl (Book 1)

Duke Looks Like a Groomsman (Book 2)

The Marquess Who Loved Me (Book 3)

Save a Horse, Ride a Viscount (Book 4)

Earl Lessons (Book 5)

The Duke is Back (Book 6)

Playful Brides

The Unexpected Duchess (Book 1)

The Accidental Countess (Book 2)

The Unlikely Lady (Book 3)

The Irresistible Rogue (Book 4)

The Unforgettable Hero (Book 4.5)

The Untamed Earl (Book 5)

The Legendary Lord (Book 6)

Never Trust a Pirate (Book 7)

The Right Kind of Rogue (Book 8)

A Duke Like No Other (Book 9)

Kiss Me At Christmas (Book 10)

Mr. Hunt, I Presume (Book 10.5)

No Other Duke But You (Book 11)

Secret Brides

Secrets of a Wedding Night (Book 1)

A Secret Proposal (Book 1.5)

Secrets of a Runaway Bride (Book 2)

A Secret Affair (Book 2.5)

Secrets of a Scandalous Marriage (Book 3)

It Happened Under the Mistletoe (Book 3.5)

Thank you for reading *The Wallflower's Secret War*. I hope you enjoyed Bea and Nicholas's story.

I'd love to keep in touch.

- Visit my website for information about upcoming books, excerpts, and to sign up for my email newsletter: www.ValerieBowmanBooks.com or at www.ValerieBowmanBooks.com/subscribe.
- Join me on Instagram: http://Instagram.com/ValerieGBowman
- Join me on Facebook: http://Facebook.com/ValerieBowmanAuthor.
- Reviews help other readers find books. I appreciate all reviews. Thank you so much for considering it!

Want to read the other Wallflowers' Revolt books?

- The Wallflower's Great Escape
- The Wallflower Takes All

ABOUT THE AUTHOR

Valerie Bowman grew up in Illinois with six sisters (she's number seven) and a huge supply of historical romance novels.

After a cold and snowy stint earning a degree in English with a minor in history at Smith College, she moved to Florida the first chance she got.

Valerie now lives in Jacksonville with her family including her two rascally dogs. When she's not writing, she keeps busy reading, traveling, or vacillating between watching crazy reality TV and PBS.

Valerie loves to hear from readers. Find her on the web at www.ValerieBowmanBooks.com.

facebook.com/ValerieBowmanAuthor

instagram.com/valeriegbowman

goodreads.com/Valerie_Bowman

bookbub.com/authors/valerie-bowman

amazon.com/author/valeriebowman